THE PORTRAIT

EMILIA KELLY

For my parents, who all but built the desk.

Behind every exquisite thing that existed,
there was something tragic.

Oscar Wilde, *The Picture of Dorian Gray*

PROLOGUE

$\mathscr{P}$enelope looked perfectly composed: eyes steely with confidence and head held high, proud enough to match the peacock feather adorning her red curls. Her violet gown whispered gently around her with each even step. One would never guess at the storm churning within her. But with every click of Penelope's boots upon the sidewalk her mind cheered, *He's back.* If running would not betray the thrill his return brought and her desperation for him to stay, she would have been to the carriage ten minutes ago.

He's back, he's back. Click-click, click-click.

Instead, she took each step deliberately. Her eagerness had contributed to his leaving in the first place. So today, despite the roiling of her insides and the pounding in her ears, she forced herself to be late, keeping her steps short and slow, her eyes only occasionally glancing toward the carriage parked half a block away, outside the Black Bear Inn.

He had always met her outside the Black Bear.

Her heart quickened at the familiarity of it all. It was as though nothing had ever changed, as though he had never told her goodbye. When she received his invitation to meet him again, she knew that she would throw aside everything if he asked. Of all the men she had met, none could match his ability to make her feel alive.

She approached the carriage and pulled open the door. The blood rushing in her ears, the twisting of her insides, the hammering of her heart . . . they all confirmed the potential of this moment, everything she would gladly abandon if he would only ask her. The door swung open and she caught her first glimpse of him in six months. He leaned back on the bench, his eyes narrowed at the pocket watch in his hand. The other hand held a small flask.

"Hello."

He looked up and said nothing, but the heat of his eyes on her spoke her name. She climbed in and ordered herself to feign indifference, even as the storm whipped faster inside.

It was a storm of potential, she thought as she settled beside him, a premonition of all the things that were about to unfold for her: the life she'd longed for beyond her hometown of Moreton-in-Marsh, and the man she had obsessed over since meeting him. As he opened his mouth to complain of her tardiness, she suppressed a smile and hid the thrill of possibility screaming inside.

It never occurred to Penelope that the storm within her might be a warning.

* * *

Local Woman Missing
Moreton-in-Marsh Bulletin
16 March 1849

NINETEEN-YEAR-OLD PENELOPE BROMLEY went missing on 15 March, according to her father, Mr. Abraham Bromley. Miss

Bromley has pale skin and long red hair. She may be in the company of a male, whom her father could neither identify nor describe. Anyone with knowledge regarding Miss Bromley's whereabouts should contact the Moreton-in-Marsh Police Department immediately.

CHAPTER 1

*N*othing broke my heart like the sound of my sister
in a coughing fit, fighting for breath. That morning,
during a particularly violent spell, she gasped out my name, as if
I had the power to heal her.

"*Iris.*"

"It's all right." I rubbed her back. "Get it all out. You're going
to be fine."

Winston Carmichael had promised me a surprise in the park
in five minutes, but when Hope needed me, nothing in the
world—not even my best friend—could distract me from my
eight-year-old sister.

Between her incessant coughs came the creaking of Papa's
rocking chair in the next room. He had bought the chair for
Mama, and now he forced himself inside its narrow frame
because it reminded him of her. He often rocked in there,
surrounded by his towers of books and so intent on his reading
that he did not hear Hope.

She expelled one last, dry cough and collapsed onto her
violet-embroidered pillowcase.

"Go, Iris." She inhaled, catching her breath. She glanced toward my rose-colored dress draped over a chair in the corner. "Put on your dress. For Winston's surprise. He'll think you're not coming. I'll stay with Papa."

I frowned. If I peeked into Papa's room I knew just what I would find. He would be reading a medical journal or textbook on human anatomy, his blunt home haircut falling into his eyes as he read. He had pestered the local librarian and scoured the science section of secondhand bookshops until the medical volumes filled his room. It was his way of dealing with Hope's illness: well-intentioned, but neither helpful nor effective.

I reached across the bed and squeezed Hope's bony fingers. I remembered her baby hands, padded and plump. Her curls, once as defined as my own, were gone now too.

"Winston can wait," I said. "Besides, Dr. Robbins will be here soon."

I would wait all day for Dr. Robbins, a thick man with straw-colored hair and eyes that disappeared when he smiled. I didn't trust Papa to talk to him. The last time Dr. Robbins had called on us, Papa had been distracted by an article he'd just read about smallpox. It took the doctor and me twenty minutes to steer him back to discussing Hope.

I poured her a glass of water. She drank it slowly, restrained despite her thirst. Her coughing fits always left her thirsty.

When Dr. Robbins arrived on our doorstep I did not point out that he was an hour late. His weekly visits were more than most people with consumption could boast. Help was expensive. If left to our own means, we never could have afforded him either.

"You've just missed a coughing fit." I led him up the stairs to Hope's room. "They're lasting longer. Perhaps it's the heat?"

"It doesn't help, mixed with the terrible air." Dr. Robbins sat at the foot of Hope's bed. I looked past them toward the window. Dirt speckled its pane no matter how often I washed it.

6

London lay beyond it, coated in a thick haze that hovered above Hyde Park, stalked the Thames River, and curled around the Houses of Parliament.

The doctor listened to Hope's heart and lungs. He pressed a palm to her forehead, then took her temperature. "Any changes since last week?"

"The worsening cough," I reminded him. "And she's weaker. She hardly gets out of bed anymore."

Dr. Robbins smiled and patted Hope's shoulder, which meant that she could lean against her pillow again. "May I speak with you a moment, Miss Sheffield?"

He followed me downstairs to our small foyer.

"The heat may seem troublesome now," Dr. Robbins said as he pulled the stethoscope from his neck and wrapped it around his hand. "But when the weather becomes colder, she'll fare even worse. How did she do last winter?"

"It all started then. It was our first winter in London. Before that, we lived in the country." A wave of guilt rose inside of me, as always happened when I thought of our move to London. She never had had any breathing problems before. "But we no longer own the country home."

He clicked open his bag and stuffed the stethoscope inside. "Given her condition, I fear the English countryside would be inadequate anyway. Many Londoners who suffer from consumption are moving to the south of France. The city of Nice, in particular. It has a street named after the English, there are so many who walk down it every day to breathe in the sea air."

I shook my head. "Nice would be wonderful, but it's not possible for us." We could not even afford a doctor on our own. A trip to the continent was out of the question.

"In that case," he said as he snapped his bag shut, "I'm afraid there's not much more I can do."

My stomach plummeted to my feet. "What do you mean?

Surely there must be a medicine, or an exercise, some type of treatment."

"I am happy to continue checking on her," he said gently, his smile gone. "But you must understand. London has the dirtiest air in the world. And it's only going to worsen with all the new factories. Given the circumstances, I have little hope for a reversal."

I tried to swallow the stone in my throat, but I could not get it down. Head to the south of France? Perhaps when Mama was still alive, before everything had changed, we could have managed. But now we couldn't possibly.

"I am suggesting that you prepare yourself, Miss Sheffield. In these conditions, I don't see any way Hope will improve."

What do I do now, Mama? I thought in frustration. When she lay on her deathbed and handed the newborn Hope to me, I had promised to care for my sister, but I quickly learned my willingness to care for Hope was not the problem. The problem was not having the means to give her the care she needed.

"I'll let myself out," he offered when I said nothing. "Until next Tuesday, Miss Sheffield."

I waited until he pulled the front door closed behind him. Then I climbed the stairs and stood silently in the hallway. The creaking of Papa's chair had stopped, a sure sign he was napping. I slipped into Hope's room and watched the subtle rise and fall of her shoulders. Her face was finally peaceful with sleep. I knelt before her and spoke in a whisper only slightly louder than a thought.

"We're going to France, Hope. I promise." I pinched my lips. If I had to sell my body and soul to pay for it, Hope would move to Nice. I could not work out the details now. I was late to meet Winston already. But somehow, I would find a way.

The rose dress was cool and slippery in my hands, its silk finer than anything we could afford. My fingers ran down the length of its sleeve and I thought how incongruous it was with the fraying bedclothes Hope lay upon, the thin rug beneath my feet, the scarred wooden floors. I draped the dress over my arm and left the room quietly. If I hurried, I might make it to the park before Winston assumed I wasn't coming.

CHAPTER 2

I was still pinning back my wild brown curls as I
dashed out the front door and onto Kensington
Road. I spotted an omnibus across from the gardens and only
hesitated a moment before hopping onto it. Many Londoners
thought they were not suitable for women, with the passengers
smashed in like cattle, but a strapped woman must take what
she can.

I disembarked at Hyde Park and hurried to the Serpentine,
where Winston had asked me to meet him. The day felt like
summer, September not yet yielding to the chill of autumn.
Three girls rushed past me with hoops and sticks, their corn-
silk braids flapping. I held my breath as I came around a wide
maple. Once my view cleared its broad leaves I saw him.

Winston, still waiting for me.

I smiled. He was leaning with his forearms against the
railing of the bridge, staring into the water, his fingertips
pressed together in a small triangle. Of course he had not given
up on me. I could always depend upon Winston. It was almost
enough to make me forget my worries about Hope and my frus-
trations with Papa.

Winston did not notice me until I stood right before him. When my shadow fell across his face he looked up and broke into a smile of relief. He took my gloved hand and kissed it.

"I was worried about you." He took my arm and we began to stroll over the bridge. "It's not like you to be late."

"I hope you didn't think I wasn't coming."

He gave me a half smile. "I worried you had met someone intent on stealing your attention."

"No suitor in all of London could prevent me from a walk through the park with my best friend," I assured him. Of course, I had no suitors in London. I had received offers of marriage before, when we lived at Pembrooke, our estate in the country. Now that we were in London, though, offers of marriage had ceased altogether. The city crawled with people, all too busy for one another. But I did not mind. I had Hope and Papa. And I had my best friend. Winston was handsome in his Henry Poole suit and looked as thrilled to see me as if I were Queen Victoria.

"Your hair looks lovely."

I smoothed a hand over my ever-wild curls. "I hardly had time to pull it out of my face. Dr. Robbins was late. I am so sorry to have kept you waiting."

"What did he say? Does he see any improvement in Hope?"

Below our feet, the bridge's wooden planks gave way to a pebbled path.

"Perhaps we should discuss it later." When Winston had asked to me join him for a walk through the park this morning, surely he had not envisioned it clouded with such terrible news. "I know you've had something important to ask me."

"Please. I want to know about Hope."

"You always ask about Hope." My eyes filled. It was one of my favorite things about him.

"Oh dear," Winston murmured. "Is it that bad?"

I blinked through my tears. "Dr. Robbins warned us that the upcoming winter will be bad for Hope. She already sounds worse every day. He told us to give her fresh air, but . . . " I swallowed the familiar wave of guilt. "But there's none to be found in London, as you know."

"What does the doctor suggest?"

I looked down at my skirt, which swayed with the movements of my steps. How I wished this wasn't my reality, that it wasn't Hope's reality. For the millionth time, I wondered if we could have managed to stay at Pembrooke, if I never should have persuaded Papa to sell the estate and move to London. Perhaps it would have made all the difference for Hope.

"Please," Winston urged. "What is it? What did the doctor say?"

"Dr. Robbins said our family must relocate somewhere warmer and less populated."

Winston stopped walking. I turned toward him.

"Dr. Robbins recommended the south of France, particularly Nice. He says it is the only solution for Hope."

But how to make that solution possible? Perhaps we could sell our flat and use the money for the voyage. But that could take months, and by then it would already be too cold.

"Of course a move will be necessary," Winston said quietly.

Winston loved Hope. I had witnessed it before, when he bought her chocolates or surprised her with a new grosgrain hair ribbon. Even when he opened her carriage door, he watched her carefully, drinking in her reactions, afraid to miss the smallest delight that might escape her. "If I had had siblings," he once told me, "I would have wanted a sister. One exactly like Hope."

"Hope has no other option," he continued. "The move should be soon, as Dr. Robbins suggested. Before the weather worsens."

I studied a father and daughter feeding ducklings along the banks of the Serpentine. The mother duck paddled around nervously, craning toward the hands feeding her offspring, unsure whether the giver could be trusted.

It occurred to me for the first time that when we moved to France—however I would make that happen—I would leave Winston behind. The thought bruised me, for I would never find a better friend.

When I looked at Winston again, his eyes were sharp and his thin lips were pulled into a tight line. He reached for my hand.

"Your family will have to move, for Hope's sake. I know how much your happiness is tied in theirs, and my happiness is tied in yours, so don't think me completely unselfish when I say I will support your family's move."

"You would . . . " The lump that had formed in my throat this morning returned. "When you say support—"

"I mean I will fund the move. Completely."

I looked at my hand in his. The soft black leather of his gloves interwove with the white lace of my own. I had never held Winston's hand before, but I did not dwell on that now. Only his generous offer fit in my mind, what it possibly meant for Hope's future.

"You would do that? You would take on that burden for Hope?"

"Yes, for Hope. But mostly for you."

His fingers squeezed mine. I looked up.

"But that would mean that I—"

"I know," he frowned. "And I cannot bear the thought of not seeing you every day. And I've been meaning to ask you . . . the thing is . . . " Winston shook his head. "Let me start over properly."

He took a deep breath, then lowered himself onto one knee in the middle of the gravelly path.

Something tightened in my chest immediately, before my brain grasped the meaning of Winston's knee on the ground.

"Iris Sheffield." His black eyes glistened as he looked up at me. "I love you. I have loved you from the day I met you. I looked into your wide hazel eyes and I knew that I would turn my world upside down if it meant being with you."

I could not look at Winston. My gaze fastened on his fingers, still intertwined with my own. It had never occurred to me to hold hands with Winston. We had touched before. Of course we had touched. He was my best friend. He kissed my hand when we met. I took his arm when we walked. But more than that? I loved Winston, but did I love him in that way? Could I?

"I will love you every day of my life, whether or not you are my wife," Winston continued. "If you were in France, it would not change my love for you, but your absence would drive me mad. So I am asking you to stay with me so that I may be near you every day for the rest of my life."

Say goodbye to Hope and Papa—the family I knew—and begin a new life with Winston? Could I marry him? I had always assumed that falling in love would be forceful and undeniable, like stepping into a fire. But as Winston Carmichael knelt before me with one Henry Poole pant leg soaking up mud, I realized perhaps I had been wrong about love. Perhaps love was not a wall of fire but a small flame of possibility that only needed time and care. I could do that with Winston. If love was warmth, not burning, I could easily achieve that with Winston. I already had.

"Hope must go to France until she gets better, and I will see to it that that happens, but please stay with me. Please marry me, Iris." He swallowed. "I will not stop loving you."

Winston looked confused as I pulled him to his feet and paused before him. But when I threw my arms around him and buried my nose in his neck, he laughed. He lifted me off the ground and spun me around, right there in the middle of the walking path at Hyde Park.

CHAPTER 3

"*S*hall we marry in May?"

Winston placed his hat on the bench between us as the hired carriage began moving. Outside the window, Hyde Park's many shades of green provided a lush backdrop.

"That should give Hope enough time to recover."

I admired Winston's profile. His hair was ebony, save for a small white patch at his temple, which he constantly tried to hide. His eyes were as dark as his hair, his nose sharp and aquiline. The thought of a spring wedding, with my best friend as my husband and my sister home and healthy, made a long-dormant happiness swell inside me. I could not help myself. For the first time since knowing Winston, I leaned my face toward his. He quickly met me halfway, and when our lips met it was brief but sweet, enough to confirm my sense that all was finally turning right in my small world.

Outside the carriage, mud thickened the London roads. Flower peddlers, ratcatchers, and beggars lined the streets, desperate for money any way they could find it. I always pulled the curtain of my window back so I could watch it all unfold.

The curtain seemed cruel to me, a means of blocking out the city's suffering.

Winston found a discarded newspaper at his feet and opened it. I let him read in peace until Hyde Park lay behind us and the trees of Green Park appeared ahead.

"Winston, would you mind?"

Without looking up from his paper, he pulled his curtain back so I could see past it.

"Watch closely," he drawled, not pulling his eyes from the paper.

"I am!" I laughed as I leaned over him. "Can you see it yet?"

"I couldn't if I wanted to, not with you blocking my view. It's too soon, anyway."

"No, it's not. There! Do you see it? There it is!" I pointed as it came into view: Buckingham Palace, a sprawling mass of white stone. We had ridden past it dozens of times, but the new addition to the palace still excited me and I always asked to see it. "What is Queen Victoria doing in there right now?" I wondered aloud.

Winston's eyes flickered toward the new wing of the palace. "I would hope she's finding someone to clean its exterior. That east extension's only three years old and it's blackening already. Why one would use Caen limestone in the world's dirtiest city is beyond my comprehension."

Winston may have feigned a lack of interest in the royal family, but I knew he was fascinated by London's high society. When we had first met, he had frequently asked me about my parents' family lines. He admitted that lineage intrigued him because he had none.

"Of course you have lineage," I had laughed. "Everyone does."

But I knew what he meant. He meant lineage with money or title. His father had created a name for Winston's family out of nothing.

"Perhaps the royal family should have consulted with you

before adding their east extension." I leaned back in my seat. "They could have hired you to build it out of glass instead."

Winston smiled. "Funny you should mention that. Did you hear Paxton's design for the Great Exhibition has been approved?"

Joseph Paxton was a local architect. Winston spoke his name in reverent tones. The windows Winston's father supplied for Mr. Paxton's designs had made Carmichael Glass a respected company.

"I don't suppose his design for the exhibition requires any glass, does it?"

Winston's eyes locked on mine, as if I'd just asked Mr. Dickens for his thoughts on social injustice.

"The entire building will be made of iron and glass," he said, a grin breaking across his face. "Like a mixture of a cathedral and a greenhouse. It will have more glass than any structure in the world."

I raised my brows. "Mr. Paxton will need to acquire a lot of windows."

"Nearly a million square feet of them."

"Winston." I shifted beside him so we faced one another. "This is a remarkable opportunity. Why didn't you mention it earlier?"

He took my hand and studied our intertwined fingers. "I only recently heard the details. You've had a great deal on your mind with Hope. And I have been trying to work up the nerve to propose to you. I suppose I did not want to give you too much to deal with at once."

"It's not," I assured him. "It's wonderful. What an honor that would be."

"Nothing's certain," he admitted, "but if I give it my best effort, I'll have a good chance at the commission. Paxton always thought highly of my father."

Winston spoke the words quietly. I held my breath, hoping

he would say more. All I knew of Mr. Andrew Carmichael was that he had built Carmichael Glass into a lucrative company and died not long before I met Winston.

"I'm sure he would be proud just to know you're pursuing this chance. And I will do all I can to support you," I promised.

He squeezed my hand but said no more about his father. "I fear I will have to travel up north to the factory regularly. We're not used to producing panes the size Paxton will need, and the Birmingham factory is better equipped for the undertaking than the London one. I'll have to spend a great deal of time up there, perfecting a new method."

"Whatever you need to do, you have my support."

He moved his face toward mine until our foreheads touched.

"Thank you, dear Iris. Having you at my side while I gain this commission . . . "

He sighed, a look of contentment settling on his face.

"Nothing could make me happier."

CHAPTER 4

"*I* can always tell when we're nearing your home, even when we come from a new direction," I said.

Winston marked his spot in the newspaper with his thumb and looked up. "And how can you tell when we're near?"

"The streets get wider." I leaned toward the window. "And the homes become ridiculously large."

Winston let out a half laugh. "It's hardly anything to envy. This neighborhood is falling to pieces. The moment I can afford somewhere better, I'll sell the house."

I turned to him. "Your mother wouldn't be sad if you did?"

"On the contrary." He shifted uncomfortably. "The place reminds her too much of my father. She dreads coming back to it. That's why you've only met her once. I always go to her."

"Perhaps she fears the house is haunted," I said, more to myself than to Winston.

He frowned. "Why would she think that?"

I hesitated. "Didn't you say your father passed away in the home?"

As if on cue, the carriage rolled to a stop in front of the Carmichael mansion.

Its exterior was ornately Gothic, with pointed-arch windows and a heavy black door. Its gray stone was the color of London fog and its roof pitched so steeply that I prayed its shingles would never need replacement. Surely one could never find footing on it. Of all its severe traits, the turret along the mansion's west side intrigued me the most. It encompassed Winston's library on the ground level and the guest room above it.

"My mother's here," Winston said as we climbed from the carriage. "She knew I intended to propose today so she came to congratulate us. I hope you don't mind."

"Of course not," I said, despite a whiff of annoyance. I held nothing against Winston's mother—I had only met her once—but I was not yet ready to share our engagement with the outside world. I had hoped to keep our news to just the two of us a bit longer.

When we reached the front door of the house, it opened immediately and Stanley, the butler, greeted us with a bow.

"Welcome, Mr. Carmichael, Miss Sheffield." He smiled at me, his doughy cheeks dimpling below his pale blue eyes.

"Blast, I left my hat in the carriage," Winston muttered. He glanced behind him as the hired cab rolled away.

"Think you'll catch him?"

"We'll find out." He left me standing with Stanley in the foyer. I gave Stanley a smile then allowed my eyes to wander the interior of the home, which was only slightly more inviting than the exterior.

Winston had renovated the house when we first met, so I never saw the original floors, wallpaper, and curtains, which he claimed were worn beyond hope.

Now dark Axminster carpets covered the floors, and deep green damask papered the walls. Heavy green curtains draped the windows, and walnut molding lined every corner of the ceilings and floors. An intricate wrought-iron railing adorned the staircase.

I fiddled with the clasp of my shawl.

"Mrs. Carmichael will join you in a moment," Stanley assured me.

"Thank you." He had always been kind to me, and though I suspected the Carmichaels would not approve of me befriending the servants, I leaned close to him and asked quietly, "How is your wife these days?"

"Agnes is well, Miss Sheffield," he replied in a voice as soft as mine.

"Is her back still giving her trouble?"

"Yes, she is unable to work still, but the Carmichaels are good to me. I can manage for the both of us."

I reached out and patted his frail arm.

"Give her my best."

Something rustled at the top of the stairs. I dropped my hand and Stanley straightened. At the height of the staircase stood Mrs. Carmichael, a vision in gray—or perhaps steel, for she radiated an intensity that made her coldness a bit brilliant. Her silver hair was knotted at the nape of her neck, and her gray dress grazed her chin and skimmed the floor.

In her arms lay Cleo, her Siamese cat, whose sapphire eyes were the single flash of color between the two of them. She and the cat stared at me as they descended the stairs, her steps slow and controlled. When she reached the bottom, she looked me up and down slowly, and I could have sworn the cat did as well.

"Mrs. Carmichael." I nodded, then smiled as widely as I dared. "It is a pleasure to see you again."

"Iris." She lifted her head. "You must be doing well, based on the news I have heard."

"Very well, thank you." I dropped my strained smile as Mrs. Carmichael continued to assess me.

"Winston told me you're to be married in May of next year."

"Yes, Mrs. Carmichael. My sister is unwell and must go abroad first to heal."

I chose my words carefully. Winston, in his generosity to my family, always warned me not to mention it to his mother, lest it affect her opinion of me.

"But she should be well enough to return to London in the spring," I added. "A May wedding will be perfect."

I waited for her sympathies for my sister, or perhaps her wishes for a quick recovery, but before she could speak, a voice spoke behind us.

"Mother."

Winston stood in the doorway, recovered hat in hand. He crossed the foyer and planted a kiss on her cheek, and Mrs. Carmichael's strained features—the squinting eyes, the puckered lips, the furrowed brow—relaxed to the slightest degree.

"I'm sorry for the delay, I had to chase the cab all the way to Briar Street. Glad to see the two of you are catching up. You'll soon be family, after all."

Mrs. Carmichael stroked her cat's head. "And you were worried she would say no."

Winston smiled at me. "One can never be too confident."

"Of course she said yes." Her eyes roamed the foyer. "The house looks good—though the glass in the Hall of Mirrors needs cleaning."

"I'll have it taken care of," Winston promised.

"And things at the factory are going well?"

A smile tugged at Winston's mouth. No doubt he was thinking of Paxton. "Everything is going well and looking more promising than ever."

"Excellent. I knew you'd have everything under control. Now I'll bid you farewell. My carriage should be ready for me."

She was leaving? Already? I caught Winston's eye and frowned, but he only responded with a subtle shake of his head.

I thought of our conversation earlier, that Mrs. Carmichael couldn't stand the house without her husband in it.

"Walk me to my carriage, Winston," she ordered. "And Iris? Your handmaid is in the kitchen."

"My handmaid?" I had never had a handmaid—someone to brush my hair, fasten my buttons, and tie my ribbons—even when we lived at Pembrooke. I had never wished for one. But it seemed impolite to refuse Mrs. Carmichael's offer.

"I didn't know you had hired a new handmaid," Winston said.

"I didn't. It's the new cook. She overheard me telling Stanley you planned to propose, and she volunteered to serve as Iris's handmaid after the marriage. We shall see if she is up to performing both tasks."

As Winston saw Mrs. Carmichael out, I showed myself to the stairwell at the rear of the foyer. It led to a half basement, much brighter than our servants' quarters had been at Pembrooke. Once downstairs I found Stanley in the kitchen, reading an old newspaper. A woman perhaps ten years my senior stood at the table, rocking a knife back and forth over a bouquet of basil.

"Hello, Miss Sheffield," Stanley said, standing at the sight of me.

The woman looked up from her work.

"Are you hungry? Mr. Carmichael requested that I bring you tea in a moment, but if it can't wait—"

"No, Stanley." I shook my head. "It's quite all right."

The woman looked down at the basil and resumed her chopping.

I had only caught glimpses of the cook once or twice in the short time that she had been working for the Carmichaels. Her face was gaunt, her bulging eyes framed by lashes and brows so fair they were nearly transparent. She wore her thin hair pulled back tightly from her face. A shabby gray dress and apron hung loosely on her frame.

"I am not sure we have properly met," I said to the woman, who kept her eyes on the basil.

"I do beg your pardon," Stanley said. "Miss Sheffield, this is Anna, our new cook."

I nodded hello. Anna dipped a quick curtsy.

"How do you enjoy working here?"

"It's fine," Anna said to the table. "Better than what I did before."

"And what was that?"

She remained silent.

"Don't mind Anna," Stanley said gently. "She's had an eventful life and prefers not to excite others with its details. But she is an excellent cook. Mrs. Carmichael hired her on the spot."

"She hardly even looked at me," mumbled Anna. "Just asked me to cook her one meal and that was it."

A soft ringing sounded from the row of bells behind Stanley.

"It's the parlor," he said. "That must be Winston ready for the tea."

"The kettle's nearly boiling," Anna told Stanley. "Let me finish this and then I'll slice the lemons."

I took a step toward the stairwell. "Until next time, Anna."

"Good day, Miss Sheffield." She curtsied again, her eyes still lowered.

I studied her for a moment, but as she never met my gaze, I finally turned and climbed the basement stairs.

CHAPTER 5

Winston was waiting for me in the parlor, absorbed in his copy of the *Times*.

"Did you see your mother off?"

"Yes," he said, eyes still fast on the page. "She asked me to bid you farewell."

"That's surprising," I muttered as I sat beside him. I did not mean for Winston to hear me, but he glanced up from his paper.

"Why would that surprise you?"

I paused, gathering my confession. "I don't believe she cares for me."

"Don't be silly. She approves of you wholeheartedly."

I frowned at Winston. "She spoke those words to you?"

"No. But if she didn't approve of you, she would have told me."

"How can you be sure, when she hardly even speaks to me?"

"Mother never hesitates to share her disapproval. It's a trait she learned from my father. If she is distant and quiet, you can take that as a compliment."

"She certainly left in a hurry." I gazed across the parlor toward the foyer. "Doesn't it take her two hours to get here?"

"Yes."

"And when did she arrive?

"Early this morning."

"Why did she bother to come in the first place, then?"

Winston shrugged and moved to the bottom half of his newspaper. "She wanted to congratulate us. I wrote her a letter last week saying I hoped to propose this morning."

"She at least could have joined us for tea." I knew I sounded cross, but my conversation with Dr. Robbins still gnawed at me, and now Mrs. Carmichael's coldness had cast another cloud over the day.

"Mother lives with her sister in a very small community. She and her neighbors are always comparing their families' accomplishments. I suspect that she is proud I am marrying you and eager to share the news with her friends."

The explanation sounded like flattery, and I did not believe it. "I suspect she simply did not care to be in the same room with me."

"If she did not like you, she would never have approved when I told her I meant to propose to you. This house holds many difficult memories for her, that's all."

Stanley appeared with a tray of teaspoons and overturned teacups.

"Come, Iris," Winston said as he handed Stanley his paper. "There is something I wish to show you."

Winston led me by the hand to the fireplace, which was so large one could step inside it. Above the mantel hung a large portrait of Winston's father, standing stiffly in a black suit.

Andrew Carmichael looked like a weathered Winston. His dull gray hair probably once gleamed as ebony as his son's. His lined face softened the intensity of his beady eyes. A portrait of his wife—seated in profile, in a lacy charcoal gown —hung on one side of Mr. Carmichael. On the other side hung the painting of Winston. He stood with a hand resting on the back of an empty chair. I knew little about the portraits, other than that Winston's was completed not long after I met him.

"The portraits were my father's idea," he said, his voice tinged with sadness. "I think they gave him a sense of validation."

He paused, taking in his father's image, before he continued.

"He washed windows as a child, going door to door in fancy neighborhoods peddling his services. The finest homes he ever worked for all had portraits inside them. Father would stare at them through the windows he cleaned. Once, he stared so long that he only cleaned a single house the entire day. His father was furious that he received so little money for a day's work. But in the end, it was good for him, I suppose. It gave him something to work toward."

I moved closer to the paintings, as if I were being introduced.

"When were the portraits of your parents done?"

"My father's was painted two years ago, and Mother's the year before that."

"And yours was completed not long after we met."

Winston walked toward the set of large windows, which provided a generous view of Kennington Road and the trees across the street hedging the commons. He placed his hand against the damask wallpaper between the two windows.

"And this," he said in a soft voice, "is where your portrait will go."

My heartbeat stuttered.

"I beg your pardon?"

"Your portrait," he repeated. "When it is finished."

I slowly turned my head to one side, then the other.

"Oh. Oh, no. I couldn't," I stammered. "I'd be so embarrassed."

"I am sure it will absolutely mortify you." He grinned. "But I

27

insist, and Mother finds the idea agreeable. I hope you'll take that as a sign that she does not disapprove of you."

I raised a hand to my cheek. First my own handmaid, and now a painting of me in the parlor?

"It won't be too large, will it?"

"As large as the wall permits."

Winston's portrait peered down at me, and I imagined how he must have stood behind that empty chair for hours while the artist scrutinized his every feature.

"Will it take long?"

"My portrait only took a few weeks. The artist was particularly quick. Unfortunately, he has since passed away, so I am still in the process of finding someone suitable to paint yours."

"I assume this will wait until after the wedding, when I am part of the family? As it stands now, we're not even officially engaged."

Winston caught sight of his reflection in the window and rearranged his hair to hide the white tuft. "I am afraid not, my dear. Portraitists are difficult to come by, at least the reputable ones. Once I find one, we'd best start the process immediately. But about that second part."

He led me back to our tea and pulled out my chair. Once seated, he carefully turned over his teacup. He looked at me expectantly. I blinked in return.

"May I pour you some?" he asked as he raised the teapot.

I was in no mood for tea. The thought of my portrait staring down upon this room for generations turned my stomach in uncomfortable directions. But Winston looked so eager to serve me that I slowly picked up my teacup and turned it over for him to fill.

And that's when I saw it, sitting upon my plate.

The gold band was thin, its diamond an emerald cut, large but not gaudy. My fingers trembled as I picked it up, and I was relieved when Winston took it from me before I could drop it.

It fit my finger perfectly. I could not stop staring at the tiny circles of light it sent dancing across the table.

"Do you like it?" he asked.

"Incredible," I whispered. "The moment I think I could not be any more indebted to you, you give me something else for which I could never possibly repay you."

He took my hand with the ring on it and raised it to his lips.

"That's the whole point, my darling," he said with a smile. "I want you to feel so doted upon you will never have any cause to leave."

CHAPTER 6

$\mathcal{T}$wo weeks later—the amount of time it took Winston
to purchase a flat in Nice without his mother's
knowledge—a hired driver drove Papa, Hope, and me to Euston
Station.

The morning sun peeked through the London haze as
dozens of carriages wove in and out of the station's Greek
temple entrance. Our driver passed through the Doric columns
and pulled as close as he could to the ticket counter.

Hope had fallen asleep on Papa's shoulder. I pulled her
from the cab and carried her. Papa emerged with his nose in a
copy of *Bradshaw's Railway Guide*. He had been consulting it
since the driver picked us up, and now he did not pull his eyes
from its pages as his free hand reached for the handle of his
trunk.

"The train is due in twenty minutes," I announced. "We'd
better hurry."

"Listen to this," Papa said as he followed Hope and me
toward the ticket counter, dragging the trunk behind him.
"When we return from France, if we claim to have nothing to
declare at the Customs House, we can pass through without

inspection unless they have reason for suspicion." Papa looked up. "Do Hope and I look suspicious?"

"Hardly. Two second-class tickets for the line to Dover, please," I told the ticket attendant.

"Perhaps I will buy something to declare, lest they suspect we're trying to deceive them. Let's see their list of commonly declared items. Cut tobacco, no . . . cigars, no . . . Ah! Patent medicines! Perfect. There are several mentioned in my medical journals that I have not been able to find in London."

"Platform three, Papa. Would you carry Hope? My arm is falling asleep." In truth, Hope was far too light to put any strain on my body, but I could not stand to hear all of Bradshaw's knowledge on travel, and I needed Papa to pay attention while he and Hope boarded the train.

Papa reluctantly handed me his guidebook so I could pass Hope on to him. I snapped Mr. Bradshaw shut and tucked him under my arm, then grabbed hold of Papa's things.

"What do you have in here?" I grunted as I pulled the trunk.

"I only packed the necessities," Papa insisted. "Clothing, shoes. Hope's doll."

I yanked the trunk forward another foot. "And how many books did you pack?"

"Only my favorites," he answered without looking at me.

Favorites. He had dozens of favorites.

"I'm not sure how you'll manage once you get to Dover," I lectured, following him at a jerking pace. "Somehow you'll have to get your trunk and Hope onto the ship to cross the channel, and then onto another train all the way to Nice. And you only have two hands!"

He turned around and waited for me to catch up to him.

"You worry too much, Iris."

Then, to make a point, he took the trunk handle from me, still holding Hope with his opposite arm, and dragged it easily behind him.

We found the steam locomotive at platform three, stretched down the track like a giant black caterpillar. I had not been near a train since we moved to London. Once beside it, Papa dropped the leather handle of the trunk. It hit the pavement with a boom.

"They will have books in France, you know," I said as I handed him *Bradshaw's Guide*.

"Well," he huffed, shoving it into his breast pocket. "French ones."

"You must promise to write to me."

"I will," Papa said as he studied the train.

"Do you promise?" My throat constricted and I struggled to keep my voice even. Correspondence had never been his strong suit. "Because I'll write to you often. Every day, even."

"I know you will. And I'll write you back."

"Every time?"

My voice quivered and Papa's eyes softened. "We aren't all obsessed with letters, my dear Iris."

I forced myself to smile. "It's the penmanship I love."

"Why didn't Winston come?" Hope asked in a groggy voice without lifting her head from Papa's shoulder.

I had worried she would comment on Winston's absence, for he had quickly become her favorite person in London. Before her health had declined, she loved nothing better than window shopping on Regent Street or ice skating on the Serpentine with Winston.

"He wanted to come." I reached for her and willed myself not to cry as her twig arms encircled my neck. "But he had to go away for work and won't return until late tonight."

"He promised we would find a tiger swallowtail," she said with a cough. "But we never did."

"Is Winston up north?" Papa asked.

I nodded. "He has been for the past few days. He's overseeing a new glass production method in the factory. He wants to perfect it before inviting Mr. Paxton up for a tour. But he returns today. And . . . " I smiled as I remembered his surprise for Hope. "He sent something for you."

I balanced her on one hip and dug into the hidden pocket in my dress. I retrieved a mint-green box from Hope's favorite chocolatier.

"Chocolates!" Hope exclaimed, pulling the gift close. "Are you excited to marry him?"

"Of course! But we won't marry until you come back," I promised.

"Spring," Hope said. "Papa says we'll be back for spring. Are you sure you can wait until then?"

"Easily," I said. "You'll need time to get stronger first before you return."

The conductor yelled for the Dover passengers to board. Papa gave me a rushed hug and pulled something from his own pocket.

"This belonged to your mother," he said as he placed something in my hand. I lifted the gift. A heavy rectangular ruby hung from a tangled gold chain.

"When did she get this?"

"On our wedding day. She never wore it. She always feared she would lose it."

My fingers closed tightly around the treasure.

"Don't you do the same now. You wear it. She'd like that."

"I will, Papa."

"And take care of yourself. Stay with Winston when you go out. Don't wander the streets by yourself."

"I'll do my best."

"If a man gives you trouble, you give him a solid knee right between the—"

"Papa!" I cried as I placed my free hand over Hope's ear. "That's enough! Now hurry and load your things."

Hope and I waited on the platform while Papa found a place

on board for their trunk. He returned and reached for Hope, but I did not hand her back.

"You have the address of the doctor in Nice?" I asked.

"Of course I do. You wrote it down for me three times."

"Perhaps you should memorize it on the train ride. In case you lose it."

"I am not going to lose all three copies."

"And you must call on the doctor as soon as you arrive in Nice. He does not know when you are arriving, so he is counting on you to reach out first."

Papa eyed me. "Anything else?"

"Winston has hired a man to meet you at the station and take you to his flat. The man has a small yellow pug."

"And a black mustache. We've been over all this before, Iris."

"You've memorized the address of the flat in Nice in case you can't find him, haven't you?"

"Iris." He reached for Hope again.

"Nine . . . " I prompted.

Papa sighed. "The flat is number nine on the Avenue Sauvan. The driver is named Auguste Benoit. And the doctor, Samuel Solemar, is at Avenue Sainte-Marguerite number twelve. I will take care of her, Iris. She's my daughter. I'm fully aware of my new responsibility to be all she has."

Hope looked up at me and blinked. "Will there be butterflies in France?"

I nodded heartily. "Many."

"Because you promised there would be butterflies in London."

"I know I did."

"And there are hardly any."

We had discussed this a hundred times.

"Yes, but France will be different. You won't be in a large city anymore, so the butterflies will love the air. Just like your lungs will love the air. You'll see."

Hope wrapped her skinny arms around my neck. Her breath warmed my shoulder, and in that moment, I would have readily sworn off Winston and the rest of the world if it meant I could always keep her so close. I wiped my eyes before I handed her to Papa and forced a smile, but fresh tears betrayed my heart.

I stayed on the platform and waved as the train started to rumble, Mama's necklace clutched in my hand. When the train began its slow crawl out of the station I jogged alongside Hope and Papa's window, chasing the pillows of steam the engine breathed, until its speed became too much for my heeled boots. I stopped at the edge of the platform, but I continued to wave. Just in case Hope was still watching.

CHAPTER 7

For the first time since our move to London, I awoke to a quiet flat: no sound of Papa rocking in Mama's chair or Hope calling for a drink of water. The silence carried a reverberating sadness, as if it could knock endlessly around one's empty heart with no distractions to soften it. I found I even missed the sound of Hope coughing, for it had signified her presence.

I left for Winston's house immediately. When I arrived, he was taking his last bite of breakfast.

"Stanley, bring some for Miss Sheffield," Winston ordered as he pushed his empty plate aside. "It's sausage and fruit this morning. Does that suit you, my dear?"

"It sounds lovely." I had been too sad to eat by myself last night.

"How did you sleep? I worried about you, all alone in that house."

"The flat was painfully quiet." I fingered the fork set before me.

"Stay here as long as you wish. I'm sorry I can't keep you company, but I'm heading to the London factory this morning and then going up north again this afternoon to prepare for Paxton's visit. I'll be there for a few days."

"But you've just returned," I said as Stanley set my meal before me. Three sausage links and a row of thinly sliced pears, arranged on a blue and white dish. "Surely you could wait another day or two?"

"I really should not have left Birmingham in the first place, but I had to return for an inspection in London this morning—and to see you, of course. But we're up to our elbows smoothing out this new sheet glass method for producing the windows. Stanley and the cook will help you with whatever you need. I'm sure you can find something to occupy you in this house. Stanley, fetch my coat and bag."

I swallowed a bite of pear and frowned at the china plate before me. A pastoral scene was painted on it—a shepherd beneath a tree with his sheep. Something in the pattern was familiar, but I could not place it.

"We just had the pianoforte tuned. I know you play a bit."

I had not played the pianoforte since we sold ours with our home in the country. Winston stood and crossed the room to the mirror hanging over the buffet.

"You're welcome to stay the night here," he said as he straightened his cravat. "Or any night, for that matter. You could sleep in the turret guest room. I'll have Stanley give you a house key."

"Thank you," I said, my cheeks warming. Something about the thought of staying in Winston's home before we married seemed premature. "I'll sleep in my flat, though. I'd hate to impose."

"It would be no imposition." Winston glanced at me. My mouth opened, though I had no response.

A knock at the door saved me.

"Who could that be?" Winston murmured, then widened his eyes. "It must be the artist!"

The artist. Blast. I had forgotten about the portrait.

Winston hurried to the door, too excited to wait for Stanley's return. I stood and trailed Winston to the parlor, my napkin twisted in my hand.

I had hoped Winston might forget about, or at least delay, the painting. I leaned against the frame of the open parlor doors. I did not mind Winston's portrait, or even his parents', but I had no desire to spend the remainder of my life under the eye of a painted version of myself.

Winston fiddled with the knob, which tended to stick, and opened the front door. I heard the hum of male voices from the porch. When he reappeared, an older gentleman followed, not bothering to shut the door behind him.

"Iris," Winston said, "may I present Mr. LeBrun. Mr. LeBrun, this is Miss Sheffield, my fiancée."

"It is a pleasure, Miss Sheffield."

I studied Mr. LeBrun. The artist. My prison master for the next few weeks or months, depending on how slowly he worked. A fringe of white hair encircled his pointed head, and when Winston ushered him forward, the man shuffled slowly with stiff, uncooperative knees.

Months. I suppressed a sigh. This portrait would surely take months.

I forced a smile. "Pleased to meet you, Mr. LeBrun."

"Please," Winston said, "have a seat. I am on my way out but can chat for a moment. Iris, would you be so kind as to join us?"

As the bald man stepped into the parlor, a second man appeared in the foyer. At the sight of him, my twisted napkin dropped from my hand and fell silently at my feet.

"And this is Mr. Thomas James," Mr. LeBrun said as he glanced behind him. "Though he prefers to be called simply James."

Looking at me was a man whose appearance grabbed my attention most unexpectedly. Perhaps it was his generous build.

Or his hair, which fell across his brows, ears, and neck in thick nut-brown waves. Or maybe it was his dark, brooding eyes, which studied me with simultaneous intrigue and contempt. Whatever its source, something within me shifted at the sight of him, as if a bottle of ink had been knocked over in my chest and was now spilling, cool and slick, to the pit of my stomach.

The guests settled themselves on the matching bergères. I joined Winston on the Aston bench opposite them and allowed myself another glance at James. He looked to be about thirty, rather old for an apprentice. His eyes shifted toward me and I made a point of examining a loose pearl button on my wrist. I turned it around and around with my fingers. With each turn I silently chided myself for noticing a man other than Winston. I hoped that, as an apprentice, James would not be needed at every sitting.

"I persuaded James to come," Mr. LeBrun explained. His consonants curled around his vowels as only the French can manage. "James is, how would you say, reluctant at this moment about portraits and very particular about his sitters."

Particular? Surely apprentices did not have the luxury of being particular.

"I represent James," Mr. LeBrun continued. "And while I can encourage him to accept certain commissions, the decision, ultimately, is his."

The pearl snapped off its thread and jumped from my fingers to the floor.

So James was not an apprentice at all. James was the artist—my artist, possibly. The pear and sausage breakfast twisted in my stomach.

Winston squinted at Mr. LeBrun. "Does that mean he is not willing to paint Miss Sheffield?" he asked, as if neither James nor I were in the room.

"It means that he must observe her and come to his own conclusion," Mr. LeBrun explained.

"Ah. Very well, then," Winston said. He waved an open palm toward me, and the observing, I suppose, began.

I stared at Winston, hoping to find safety in his gaze, but he was closely watching the artist, who—I could feel—was watching me. From the library clock I heard the seconds tick by, each moment seeming longer than the last. With each click I became more and more certain that sitting for James would be misery.

Stanley—dear, blessed Stanley—interrupted us.

"I have a cab waiting for you, Mr. Carmichael," he announced, holding Winston's coat and bag.

"Thank you, Stanley, I'll be but a moment. Leave my things here and I'll load them myself."

I risked a glance at James. He stared at me, a slight scowl upon his face. He said nothing but finally turned to Mr. LeBrun and gestured with his head toward the door.

"I must speak to the artist outside," Mr. LeBrun announced. I wondered if the artist was capable of speaking. "Mr. Carmichael, would you care to join us?"

"Yes, let me get the door. The knob is stubborn. You have to push, then twist." Winston picked up his coat and bag, then lingered to kiss my forehead.

"I'll be back by Monday," he promised, "and I'll miss you every moment until then. Don't hesitate to stay here. It would ease my mind if you weren't in that flat by yourself at night."

He opened the front door and the three men filed outside. When he pulled the door closed behind him it did not catch completely. I stepped silently toward it and held my breath.

"Well, what do you think?" came Winston's voice from the porch.

"Absolutely not." The artist—James—had an American accent, slow and confident. And bored. "I told you, Mr. LeBrun, I don't paint this genre anymore."

"Oh, come," said Mr. LeBrun. "It would be a wonderful opportunity. Don't be so stubborn."

"I am done with society portraits. I shouldn't have let you convince me to come in the first place."

A throat cleared. Winston spoke.

"Gentlemen, I am afraid I must excuse myself, and I will not be in town again until Monday. James, of all the artists I have considered, I have been informed that your reputation is the most . . . What was it I heard? Widespread?"

"That is an accurate description." Mr. LeBrun chuckled.

"So I will double my offer for the commission in an attempt to persuade you," Winston continued. "But I am anxious to begin, so I insist you start immediately. If I return to find you have not yet started the portrait, I will hire another artist straightaway. The decision is yours. Good day, gentlemen."

They were silent as the sound of Winston's footsteps receded. I heard the cab door open and shut. James and Mr. LeBrun waited until the horse's hooves began clacking before they spoke again.

"Double the commission!" boomed Mr. LeBrun. "That's decided then."

"I told you, I'm not doing another high-society portrait. I learned my lesson after *La Donna*. I don't care what the commission is."

"But you need the money. And this Carmichael fellow, he seems the type who would let you submit the portrait to the Academy. If it were a success—"

"Of course it would be a success." James's tone turned prickly.

"*When* it is a success, then, the Academy will love it, and it will secure your acceptance to the Barbizon School."

"High-society sitters bring drama. I can't handle a scandal."

"The sitter is engaged!" Mr. LeBrun cried. "You will be

painting her in her fiancé's home. The only way there will be a scandal is if *you* create one."

There was a beat of silence.

"You saw her," continued Mr. LeBrun. "She would be perfect. She is even more beautiful than *La Donna*, no?"

Again, James said nothing.

Mr. LeBrun sighed. "Fine, I will tell her you pass."

"No." The word was so quiet, I barely heard it. "No, I'll paint it. Tell her to be ready at eight o'clock tomorrow morning."

"Tomorrow's Saturday," Mr. LeBrun pointed out. "You never work Saturdays."

"I'd like to put this commission behind me as soon as possible. Tell her to find something to occupy herself for a few hours every morning. If she's looking for conversation, she won't find it from me."

I stepped away from the door and hurried back to the parlor, absorbing what I had just heard. Winston would be relieved, as it meant he did not have to search for another artist. And I now knew how I would occupy part of my time with my family away and Winston at work.

My company, however, would be a brooding artist who would not deign to talk to me. I knew little of Mr. James, but my first impression left me wanting nothing to do with him, nutbrown hair and broad build aside.

CHAPTER 8

$\mathcal{M}$y second night alone was no better than the first. Solitude was a constant buzz in my ears: I was aware of it all night as I drifted in and out of waking moments.

I awoke before the earliest bird's song and arrived at Winston's by six o'clock, much too early for my sitting with the portraitist.

After letting myself into the mansion I stood in the foyer and surveyed the parlor on my left and the library on my right. Winston's home was as silent as my own flat, I thought with irritation. I had said goodbye to my family one day, only to see my fiancé depart the next. I wandered downstairs to the kitchen, my only hope for activity.

Stanley was nowhere to be seen.

Anna, however, was standing upon a stool, reaching for a basket from the highest kitchen shelf.

"Good morning, Anna," I said.

She jumped at my voice, causing the basket to fall. She fumbled for the shelf in front of her, barely catching herself from tumbling off the stool.

"Criminy!" she yelled as I rushed toward her. "What in the world are you trying to do, knock me over?"

"I'm so sorry, Anna," I said as she took my offered hand and stepped carefully from the stool. She refused to look at me but heaved a deep breath before she spoke again.

"My apologies." Her meek tone sounded forced. "I should not have spoken to you so informally."

I waved her apology away. "I shouldn't have startled you. I was thrilled to find someone else here. My house is so lonely, and now Winston's is just as quiet."

Anna bent to retrieve the basket from the floor. "I won't be much help if you're looking for company. I'm on my way to the market."

"At Covent Garden?" I could not hide the excitement from my voice. "Are you going soon?"

She looked at me warily and, without any hint of sincerity in her voice, asked, "Would you like to come?"

Anna clearly hoped I would decline. And Winston would disapprove of my outing with a servant. But I did not care. A crowded marketplace would surely ease the sense of loneliness I had felt since my family left.

"I'd love to join you. Come, we'll hail a cab together."

Anna gave me an unsure look but followed me outside to hire a carriage.

I felt it important to spend time with Anna. Once I became Winston's wife, she would help me dress and would run my errands for me. Together we would plan menus for the household suppers. I had given her a list of meals last week, though she had seemed unimpressed by it. She seemed unimpressed with me in general.

All the more reason to become better acquainted with her.

"Don't you love Covent Garden?" I asked half an hour later, as we fell into step with the Saturday market crowd.

Anna raised a pale eyebrow at me. "I am surprised you have been here before."

"I used to come here often," I said proudly. We had had cooks at Pembrooke until our debts grew, but by the time we moved to London I had been shopping and cooking for our family for years. My weekly market visits were always a welcome escape from the obligations of home, if only for an hour.

"We'll start with the produce," Anna decided. She pulled her faded green bonnet low on her forehead, as if she feared being recognized. "I'll lead the way."

The market was crowded and filthy, just as I remembered it from the days before Winston began sending groceries to my family.

"You'll have to walk faster, Miss Sheffield," Anna called over her shoulder.

My heeled boots teetered on the flagstone path as coster-mongers shoved past me toward hazelnuts, roses, and carrots. Everything to be sold along London roads on Monday could be found here today.

I wove my way around a woman with a basket brimming with turnips and caught sight of Anna's green bonnet. She had stopped in front of the theater steps, where vendors sold a rainbow of produce. Emerald kale, crimson apples, and violet cabbages spilled from baskets and crates.

She waved her hand toward a pile of Brussels sprouts the size of chicken hearts, their leaves as tight as secrets.

"Do you care for Brussels sprouts?" she asked. "Perhaps some potatoes too?"

"Yes, that would be lovely," I said as a donkey cart passed, piled high with lilies. Its wheels rolled a stripe of mud across the hem of my dress.

"How much for the sprouts today?" Anna asked the vendor seated on the steps of the theater.

His gray apron stretched across his knees as a table for shelling peas. He gestured toward a board propped against the bottom step.

"It's all written right there."

"And how much is that?" she asked without looking at the writing.

The man huffed. "Two pence per pound."

"Anna," I said. She examined a potato and ignored me. "Anna, do you not know how to read?"

She scowled, whether at me or the potato I did not know.

"I could teach you. It wouldn't be any trouble at all."

We could have a lesson every day, after the artist left. Teaching Anna to read would easily occupy an hour of my afternoons, perhaps two. A smile overtook my face at the thought of it.

Anna dropped the potato into her basket. She looked up, her scowl still in place.

"I have no need to learn how to read, Miss Sheffield," she said as she picked up another potato, red this time.

"What about the sign?"

"I figured it out, didn't I?"

"How did you read the menu I wrote for you?"

"I can recognize some words on my own. Stanley helped with the rest. I always find someone willing to help me."

"But if I taught you, you could read the menus without Stanley's help. You could even read books, or the newspaper."

"I have no need of the newspaper. I hear the Bible read aloud every Christmas, which is all the books I need. As for the menu . . . " She reached for another potato. "Your menu was so short I am inventing the rest of it myself right here. I'm to learn to read for that?"

"But suppose you wanted to write a letter. To your family, perhaps."

I wondered if she had heard me until she finally mumbled, "What do you know of my family?"

She waved her finger over her basket to count its contents and yelled at the vendor.

"Six potatoes! And I'll take a pound of Brussels sprouts. Are you impressed?" she asked me with a grim look. "I counted the potatoes all by myself. Come, I need to buy fish."

We pushed through the crowd toward the fish stalls. Their stench hit me long before I saw the rows of slippery mackerel and speckled cod.

"Do your parents know how to read?" I asked as she shoved her way to the front of the stalls.

"If they did, don't you think they would have taught me?"

She asked the fishmonger for cod and watched intently as he wrapped it in old newspaper.

"And none of your siblings ever learned to read?"

"My sister did," she said, her words clipped, as the fishmonger handed her the cod. "Didn't do her any good in the long run, though. Do you want to look at anything here, Miss Sheffield? I have what I need."

We stopped at the flower stands, where I bought a miniature orchid in a blue and white porcelain pot. We hailed a cab on Bedford Street and rode in silence, the basket of food at Anna's feet, the potted orchid on my lap.

I feared I had offended Anna with my enthusiasm to teach her to read and my questions about her family. Stanley had tried to warn me that Anna would not delve into her past. I had plenty of time to regret my actions, for Anna did not speak a word to me until the streets widened beneath the carriage and we were turning onto Kennington Road.

"My sister," she said suddenly, her face to the window, "always thought herself superior to me. Learning to read and write only made it worse. I have no intention of ending up anything like her."

"If you ever change your mind," I said gently, "I would be happy to help you."

Anna said nothing. She leaned her head against the window and closed her eyes for the remainder of the carriage ride, though I suspected she was only feigning sleep.

CHAPTER 9

*a*nna and I returned to the Carmichael mansion half an
hour before the artist's scheduled arrival. I headed
straight to the conservatory at the back of the house, orchid in
hand.

The conservatory was the brightest feature of the house and,
consequentially, my favorite. When I had asked Winston the
story behind its construction, he simply told me his father built
it. Winston's father had passed only six months before we met
and I assumed his grief was too raw to elaborate. Winston later
told me that his father had been brilliant at the things he
deemed worthy of his time. I sensed resentment more than
admiration in the comment. I would probably spend much of
our marriage picking up pieces from the stories Winston gradu-
ally shared of his father. Perhaps one day, if given enough
pieces, I could put them together and better understand.

Whatever the reason for its construction, I seemed to be the
only one who appreciated the conservatory. Amid the stifling
gray of London, it was a small piece of the country, an opportunity for green life. Many London homes had boxed windows
filled with shelves of ferns, but to have an entire greenhouse at

the rear of one's house was magical. In the spring I had grown pots of daffodils and tulips, followed by snapdragons and dahlias. Three potted rose trees were at the end of their season, their crimson petals dropping and their leaves browning. I added my orchid to the collection and made a note to buy allium bulbs to plant. By the time they began growing next spring, I would be Winston's wife.

A soft knock sounded behind me.

"Miss Sheffield." Stanley stood in the doorway. "The portraitist is here to see you."

I brushed dirt from my hands and looked down.

"Oh dear," I muttered. I hadn't bothered to change after the market. I frowned at the stripe of mud, now hardened across the hem of my dress. But it was too late to do anything about it now.

"Please tell the artist I'll be there in a moment, Stanley."

I knew I would need something to occupy me for the next four hours. I was not accustomed to sitting idly. There had been a time when I listened to long performances on the pianoforte or smiled politely as our neighbor, Mrs. Darby, droned on about her travels. But then Mama died, and Hope needed me, and I was forced into the responsibilities of an adult long before Mama finished making a young lady out of me.

I stopped in the library and pulled *Jane Eyre* from the shelf, then approached the parlor, my steps wary. The artist was setting up an easel in the corner, so intent on pushing its legs straight that he did not notice my arrival.

I lowered myself into an upholstered seat and cleared my throat.

"Miss Sheffield," he said to his easel.

"Good morning, Mr. James," I said. "Is it all right if I sit here?"

"It's just James. And yes, that is fine."

I brushed a patch of dirt off my sleeve and shifted my skirt to hide the stripe of mud.

"I'm not sure which gown Winston wants me to wear."

"What you're wearing is fine," he said without looking at my dress. He slipped a smock over his head. "I'll only be studying your face today."

Studying my face. The thought set my cheeks on fire. But James, of course, did not notice. He tied the smock strings around his waist, filled its pockets with a variety of pencils, and leafed through a stack of thick, clean pages. He decided on one, which looked identical to all the others from where I sat. He placed it gently upon the easel and, finally, looked at me.

Strangers often looked at me. Perhaps it was my wide-set eyes, my unruly curls, or my plump lips. Whatever the reason, I had grown accustomed to strangers studying me and long ago learned to ignore them. But the way James studied my face was unlike anything I'd ever experienced. He looked directly at me, yet it was as if I weren't even in the room.

He studied me with as much objectiveness as if he were working out a math equation. I could have been the Parthenon, and he assigned to measure the distances between my columns. His face gave no sign that he was looking at a human. He scrutinized my features, studying me closer than anyone ever had, without making the slightest emotional connection to me. Even when I could sense him staring at my brows, the bridge of my nose, or the pinch of skin between my eyes, he never looked at me as an entire person. I was merely a combination of features for him to transfer onto the page.

His gaze embarrassed me at first, but when I realized he did not actually see me at all—not the complete me—I felt at liberty to study him in return.

His brows were thick, his nose straight. He had a square jaw and eyes the shade of coffee beans. I watched them move from his easel to my face and back again. They landed on my nose, then my lips, chin, and cheekbones. His gaze buzzed about my face like a gnat, always threatening to land but never touching my skin.

After a quarter of an hour of silence, I cleared my throat. "Do you always begin portraits by studying the face?"

He started, as if he had forgotten I was in the room.

"Yes. I always spend at least a week studying only the face."

"I enjoy your accent," I said with a smile. "I take it you are not from here."

"No, I'm not."

"Does any of your family live in London? Or are you here by yourself?"

His gaze flicked toward me. "My sister's also an expatriate. She lives in Brighton."

"I have a sister as well. I wish she lived as close as Brighton." Hope's absence suddenly pressed against the back of my eyes. I blinked back tears. "My sister, Hope, just moved to France. Ever since she was born, I—"

James turned toward me so abruptly that he knocked half a dozen pencils from the tray of his easel. The clatter tore me from my thoughts.

"Miss Sheffield, this portrait I am to paint, it is to be completed by your wedding, is that correct?"

My mouth hung open at his rude interruption, but he continued before I could answer.

"Which wedding is to take place in May?"

I gave a slow half-nod.

"Then I kindly ask you to remain quiet so I can do my task." He set his jaw and returned his sharp gaze to the easel. "As fascinating as the details of your history must be, your fiancé is not paying me to socialize with you."

I sat frozen in my chair as his pencil scratched upon the page before him. In London one inevitably crossed paths with inconsiderate men, those who let the door slam in a woman's face, who sprinted ahead of the corseted to reach a cab first. I had learned not to take such actions personally. Fortunately, such men were always in a hurry and tended to disappear quickly.

But James would not be leaving. He had no door to walk through, no cab to catch. I was his destination and would be for four hours a day, every weekday, until he completed my silly portrait. I scowled as James pushed a lock of hair from his eyes.

He, of course, did not notice my anger. Instead he scratched away at his paper and ignored me effortlessly—along with the pencils scattered around his feet—for the remainder of our portrait sitting.

CHAPTER 10

*W*hen James arrived Monday morning, I had nearly finished *Jane Eyre* and refused to let him spoil the satisfaction of the book's completion. I kept my eyes on the pages as Stanley admitted him into the mansion. I turned to the next chapter when James entered the parlor. I did not look up as I heard him pull out a fresh sheet of paper.

James was not the only one who could ignore his company.

But my focused reading meant that the book's last sentence came much too soon. I closed the cover, my mind alive with Jane's descriptions of her life with Mr. Rochester:

Supremely blest! and *bone of his bone and flesh of his flesh* and *I am my husband's life as fully as he is mine.*

To my surprise, Jane's confidence in her choice of a companion awoke my longing for Mama. I always missed her, but sometimes the ache was acute, and what bid it constantly changed and surprised me. Sometimes a breeze carried her smell, fresh and citrusy, and pulled her into step with me as I walked through the park. Once it was the hands of a seamstress, her long fingers and shell-pink nails evoking forgotten memories of Mama positioning my hands at the pianoforte.

Just when I thought I had missed Mama in every way possible, a new dimension of my grief opened. Now, as I turned *Jane Eyre* in my hands, I longed for her presence so I could ask her how she had felt when Papa proposed. Had she been drawn to Papa, like Jane Eyre was to Rochester? Had they been in love? Or had their marriage been a comfortable, amicable love, like that which Winston and I shared?

I was fortunate to marry my best friend. At Pembrooke, a neighboring family had seven daughters, and the parents all but forced marriage upon them, sometimes to near-strangers. Whether intentionally or due to his scattered nature, Papa had always let me be when it came to my relationships. He left me to my own judgment, and I knew he would never find fault with Winston.

I swatted at a fly on my wrist and it buzzed to the window, searching for an opening to the outside world.

I did not doubt my decision to marry Winston. The arrangement would bring about my happiness and restore my sister's health. I would be a fool to decline his offer. But when I decided to marry him, I had to release a sliver of possibility, a pinprick of hope. My love for Winston was sincere and warm, but not irresistible. In my decision to marry him I was closing a door on the forceful, if tumultuous, love which Miss Brontë had described to me over the past two days.

As if summoned by my thoughts, the front door opened and Winston's voice rang out.

"Iris? Are you here?"

I rose from my seat, not caring that James was in the middle of studying me.

"There you are!" Winston stepped into the parlor doorway, his face brightening at the sight of me. Had anyone ever looked so happy to see me? I could look all my life and never find anyone so thrilled by my presence as Winston.

I tossed *Jane Eyre* onto the bergère and ran toward him.

His own arms were free—Stanley entered behind him with the luggage—and he wrapped them around me and lifted me off the ground. I broke into a smile.

"I missed you," I whispered into his ear, my feet dangling above the floor.

"And I you." He gently lowered me back to the floor and, to my surprise, kissed me.

We had not kissed in front of anyone since our engagement. Though my back was to James, I imagined he was watching us with a condescending smirk. I pushed a curl behind my ear.

"Did you finish all your work in Birmingham?"

"No, but I came home anyway so I could see you—and bring you this." He gestured toward Stanley, who handed me a box from the top of Winston's luggage.

It was a hat box, its wood painted emerald green. I slipped its leather handle aside and lifted its lid to find an ivory silk bonnet. Beneath it lay a pair of cream kid gloves.

"Do you like them?" he asked, watching my reaction carefully.

"I love them—though the better gift is your presence."

He grinned. "Stanley, bring me the mail that arrived while I was away. And take my things to my room."

Winston held both my hands in his and took a step back.

"You are lovelier than ever. Have you been out in the sun? Your cheeks are red."

I placed a hand over my right cheek. Sure enough, it was warm beneath my palm.

"Or perhaps you're just blushing," he laughed.

"It's been terribly embarrassing to have my portrait painted," I admitted in a low voice. "Sitting there and being stared at all morning." And James wasn't making the process any easier, I thought, as Winston led me by the hand to the parlor.

"So the American has decided to accept the commission!" he boomed at James.

"Mr. Carmichael." James straightened behind his easel, careful not to look at me. "Yes, I began on Saturday. I promise to finish as quickly as possible."

"Fine, fine," Winston said with a disinterested wave of his hand. "As long as you're finished before the wedding it hardly matters. Perhaps it will keep Miss Sheffield out of trouble. She has little else to do during the day—isn't that right, dear?"

I pricked with resentment at his words. "I've read a book since I last saw you. And I went with the cook to Covent Garden on Saturday."

"You did?" Winston's brows furrowed. "Whatever for?"

"I bought an orchid for the conservatory. I enjoy the market, to look around, watch people, you know."

Winston cocked his head. "I'm afraid I don't know, but then again, that's never really been my cup of tea."

I ignored the stare I felt from James. "Actually, I've been meaning to ask if you might have any family records that I could read during my sittings."

Stanley returned, carrying a silver tray with four envelopes spread across it. Winston grabbed them and tore open the first.

"What type of records do you mean?" he asked, his attention quickly slipping to the letter before him.

"Journals, letters, a Bible with family names written in it. You know how I love to study penmanship. Remember when I learned to replicate yours so well? Anything handwritten is a treasure to me."

Winston nodded vaguely as his eyes ran down the page before him.

"There's nothing from my family, is there?" I assumed Papa and Hope would have mailed their letters to the townhouse, but nothing had arrived from them. It was probably too early to expect anything, but the silence still worried me.

"No," he said with a subtle shake of his head. "I'm afraid it's all for me. And I don't think we have any family journals, but you may search the library. You're welcome to anything hand-written you can find. If you'll excuse me, I must attend to some things. James, it's a pleasure to see you again."

James nodded. "Perhaps we can discuss the details of the commission after my day's work."

"Of course," Winston said, already halfway across the foyer. "Knock on my door before you leave."

Winston closed the library door firmly behind him, leaving me alone once more with James. I returned to my bergère and placed *Jane Eyre* in my lap, eyeing the cover with a new skepticism.

I had had my fiction: heat and passion, arranged for the most dramatic effect. Now I craved something true, something as honest as my warm affection for Winston. I knew of nothing more real than a record written by hand, whose penmanship attested to the writer's presence as much as the meaning of the words. I wedged *Jane Eyre* into the cushion of my chair and wondered if, somewhere inside this mansion, I might find the honest record I sought.

CHAPTER 11

*J*ames and Winston discussed the details of the portrait commission for so long I found myself standing outside the closed library door, tempted to knock. Did James intend to occupy Winston's entire afternoon?

"Miss Sheffield would not mind, I assure you," Winston's voice came from the library. "We would be most delighted."

"The portrait will have to be admitted to the exhibition first," came James's voice, "assuming I am satisfied with it upon its completion."

"That sounds wonderful," Winston said. "Write your address here and I'll have the payment sent to you. I'd be happy to introduce you to some colleagues of mine who might be interested in commissioning family portraits. I could arrange a meeting at the public house. If your wife wouldn't mind, of course."

"Thank you," James said, "but actually I'm not—"

"Fine, fine," said Winston before James could explain himself. "But if you ever change your mind, you need only say the word."

Winston's interruption caused a flicker of irritation in me.

Had James nearly admitted he wasn't married? If so, what had prevented him from selecting a wife?

I heard a shuffling of feet as the men stood, their conversation finally at an end. I slipped into the parlor just before Winston emerged and led James to the front door. Watching the two of them together, I felt a surge of confidence in my decision to marry Winston, even though Mama was not here to confirm my choice. Maybe it was the smile Winston flashed me, the warmth in his eyes when he saw me. Perhaps it was merely the juxtaposition of my caring fiancé next to the coldest individual I had ever met.

Whatever it was, the concern of finding passion like that of Jane and Edward suddenly seemed childish. As Winston wished James a good day, I bid a final farewell to such shallow notions. They were worth sacrificing for the care and security I was welcoming into my life—and, more importantly, into Hope's life.

"Would you fancy a carriage ride with me?" Winston asked. "I must return to work, but it's been much too long since we've spent time together. And there is something I'd like to show you."

I smiled at him, which felt wonderful; James had been studying my mouth for the past two hours and had ordered me not to move it.

"It's a nice day out. We'll hire an open carriage."

Within two minutes I was wearing my new ivory bonnet and gloves and we were making our way down the walk, my hand on Winston's arm. When we found an open carriage for let, Winston directed the young driver toward Hyde Park.

"All the way to the park?" I asked as the carriage began to roll. "That's a bit of a drive."

"Thank heavens," he muttered as he rearranged his hat upon his head. He tilted it forward to cover his tuft of white hair. "I could use some distance from Kennington."

"It could be worse." I thought of the few times I'd ridden past the tenement houses of London's East End, where multiple families crammed into flats meant for one.

"I'm just anxious to move to Park Lane." We rolled past a ratcatcher with a terrier at his ankles. The wooden cage in the man's hand rustled.

"Aren't the homes on that street expensive?"

"If I can secure this commission from Paxton, Park Lane will easily be within our reach." Winston grew quiet. Perhaps Mrs. Carmichael wasn't the only one afraid of the family mansion.

The driver took my favorite route, over Westminster Bridge. We rolled past the Palace of Westminster, still not yet rebuilt after its fire over a decade ago.

At Hyde Park we joined the file of carriages rolling down the dirt path, the trees clustered around us with leaves as dense as broccoli heads. Winston directed the driver to take a right, where the trees grew so close I worried we would become stuck between them.

Suddenly we broke into a vast, oval clearing. Its center bustled with activity as hundreds of navvies ran about, pouring a concrete foundation in the middle of the field.

My eyes widened at the site. "Is that—"

Winston did not need to hear the rest of my question. In his mind, every question, every answer revolved around what was unfolding before us. He leaned forward in the open carriage.

"Yes, it is. Prince Albert's dream."

"They've started it already?"

"They had to begin immediately to be ready by May of next year. The papers are beginning to call it the Crystal Palace, now that they have seen Paxton's sketches of the glass building."

I blinked at the vastness of the foundation. "I didn't realize it would be so large."

But of course, it would have to be large. The Crystal Palace would house the Great Exhibition in the spring, and visitors from countries all over the world would gather inside it to show off their industrial achievements.

"Soon they'll be raising the cast-iron columns. Paxton tells me that from there it will be a quick process. The frame will be up before you know it, and then thousands of panes of glass will go in."

"Is Paxton selecting the glass manufacturer?"

Winston nodded. "He picked the iron supplier as well. I'm sure he could pick the refreshments they'll sell inside if he wished. Prince Albert is so pleased with the design there's speculation Paxton will be knighted over it."

I watched Winston, the faint smile upon his lips, the far-off look in his eyes as he stared at the opportunity before him. But then, without warning, his features fell.

"I received a letter from a reporter I know at the *Times*. He's heard that Paxton has met with the Chance Brothers."

I frowned. "The Chance Brothers? As in the glass company?"

Winston nodded. "They were the first to use the sheet glass production method that we are perfecting in Birmingham. If I had known Paxton was in touch with them, I would not have left Birmingham so soon."

I looked forward and stifled a sigh of disappointment. This was not the ride through the park I had anticipated. I needed close conversation in the wake of my family's departure, not plans of Winston leaving me yet again. But Winston's heart was set on the commission, and an equal opportunity might never present itself again.

"Perhaps you had best return to Birmingham, until the work is done and the method perfected." It was the right thing to say, but I hoped Winston would protest.

He was silent for a moment, then reached over and took my gloved hand.

"I think that would be best."

We watched the navvies pour the foundation, a bustle of

movement and indiscernible yelling. Neither of us spoke. When I grew tired of the scene's slow progress I turned and watched Winston, who could not pull his eyes from the dream taking shape before him.

I knew he was picturing the finished palace, envisioning what he might be a part of, anticipating the heartache if he weren't involved. And perhaps Winston was seeing his father in all of it, grieving over the knowledge that this moment was lost to the only other person who could truly appreciate it. Maybe Winston was fearing the disappointment he would cause his departed father if he failed to gain the commission.

The longing on Winston's face made my bones ache, and I had to turn away. He looked the way I felt at the possibility of losing Hope, at the thought of letting Mama down.

CHAPTER 12

"Will I see you again before you leave for Birmingham?" I asked as the carriage stopped in front of my townhouse.

"I'm afraid not," Winston said. "I have to check on the factory here and try to speak with Paxton today, but I plan to be on the train to Birmingham tonight."

I nodded and did my best to keep the disappointment from my face.

"What's wrong?" he asked.

I fingered my engagement ring through my glove. "I have hardly seen you since we became engaged. And spending all day in your house without you is strange. I feel out of place."

"It's about to be your house too."

"Yes, well." I lifted my brows. "It doesn't feel like it yet."

Winston climbed from the carriage and offered me his hand.

"Why don't you bring a few of your things to the house tomorrow? To help it feel more like home."

I could not envision Winston's mansion ever feeling like home to me. Not in the way that Pembrooke once had. But moving in a few of my things couldn't hurt.

Winston left me on my doorstep with a kiss on the hand. As he climbed back into the cab, I noticed a dark coach ahead of his, making its way back to the main road. Its undercarriage and wheels flashed a brilliant red, and it bore the royal arms upon its door. The sight of it caused my heart to jump. I turned to see the letter slot in the door slightly ajar, and when I stepped into the entryway, an envelope lay on the chipped black and white tiles. The mail coach had not left me disappointed.

Writing came unnaturally to Papa and I recognized his stiff, boxy handwriting before I picked up the envelope.

Dearest Iris,

I pray this finds you well. We have arrived in Nice. The flat provided by your generous fiancé is a short distance from the Promenade des Anglais and the sea. We walk there daily when Hope is able, as instructed by Dr. Solemar.

Hope is still tired, but her spirits are better already, and her coughing has lessened slightly. The doctor predicts we shall see a gradual improvement in her over the next few weeks.

Hope sends her love and requests I inform you that she saw a monarch on our morning walk.

Lovingly yours,

Papa

I ran my fingers over Papa's writing, feeling the slight indentation left by the nib. Mama had never left dents in her pages. In all her letters, her words flowed effortlessly from her pen.

I folded the paper gently, following its original creases. In the front room, beside the large window facing Kensington Gardens, sat a Davenport desk. I pushed back its lid to reveal a neat pile of letters, organized by date, the most current on top, all tied together with a lavender ribbon. I pressed the stack to my nose, though it had lost its scent years ago.

I slid Papa's letter to the top of the pile. Sixteen letters from Mama, and now one from Papa. I had read Mama's letters so many times that their pages had grown soft. Letters in hand, I climbed the stairs, which creaked beneath my feet, the only sounds in an empty house.

My sleepless nights suddenly weighed on my eyelids. I set the stack of letters on my bedside table then lay on the bed facing them. The room was deathly still around me. The afternoon light spilling through the window could not prevent my eyes from drooping. Before I knew it, I was dreaming.

I was small, perhaps five, running through a garden thick with indigo blooms. Behind me loomed an estate, all its blue shutters thrown open. Before me stood a woman with hair as dark as mine, her eyes shadowed by a lavender bonnet. She stood in front of an easel, squinting at the house beyond me.

I ran to her and threw my chubby arms around her leg. The force of my hug sent her paintbrush in the wrong direction, but she laughed at the wild streak across her canvas and leaned down to hug me. She pushed the curls from my face with her warm hands, but the wind quickly whipped my hair back to its original mess. She laughed again and untied the silk ribbon from her bonnet.

I wriggled as she used it to pull back my curls. The moment she finished, I ran to the garden, then around the house. The wind picked up and the sun slid behind a cloud, chilling the air around me.

But I could still feel the warmth of my mother's hands on my face. And I could smell her in the lavender ribbon in my hair.

CHAPTER 13

$\mathcal{M}$orning light seeped through my window. It was the first time I had slept straight through the night since my family's departure. The realization made me sigh with contentment, until I remembered that Winston was in Birmingham again. I would take a cab to the mansion. And then I would spend four hours in silence with James.

I would need a distraction this morning. Jane's love for Rochester would no longer do. I grabbed the collection of letters from Mama, as well as the new one from Papa. I would spend this morning imitating the handwriting of my parents. It was a pastime I developed shortly after my mother passed away. I had read and reread her letters so many times the shape of her writing became engraved in my mind, which had made me wonder if I could reproduce it. With time, my imitation of Mama's slanting, looping letters became a part of my understanding of her.

Once I was at the Carmichael home, Stanley pulled a small desk to the middle of the parlor, where James could study me. I leaned a framed landscape—the only item I had brought from home besides the letters—against the desk legs. James arrived as I was pulling out my writing supplies.

"What have we here?"

I did not look at him as I twisted the lid from my inkwell. "I am practicing penmanship."

"This will make it more difficult to see your face."

I dipped my pen into the ink. "Will that be a problem?" I asked coldly.

James paused, considering. "I meant to study your mannerisms today, so I suppose it's fine for now, if it does not become a habit."

I did not care if my position made James's work more difficult. I busied myself copying a letter my mother wrote to me when I was eleven years old, on the day she discovered she would have another baby. She was quite sure, her letter said, that it would be a boy.

When I was halfway through my work I sat back to compare the two pages. I saw little difference, other than the yellowed, softened paper that betrayed the age of Mama's letter. I was so immersed in comparing the original version with my own that I did not notice James watching me until he cleared his throat.

"The painting is quite lovely." He nodded at the frame at my feet. "Don't you fear you'll kick it over?"

I set my pen across the open inkwell.

"This? You like it?" I lifted the small frame and held it at arm's length.

James stepped around his easel and crossed the room toward me, his paintbrush still in hand. He studied the landscape over my shoulder, its indigo flowers in the foreground, the sprawling country home, the stretch of blue sky.

"It is a bit naive, granted, but the proportions are good, and the overall feeling is quite charming."

"Naive." I pulled the painting to my chest and out of James's sight.

My mother's painting was not naive.

"A friend of mine teaches ladies' art classes in the basement of the National Gallery. Perhaps you'd like to attend."

"No, thank you," I said shortly, not mentioning I was not the artist. I returned the painting carefully to its spot against the leg of the desk. When I looked up, James was studying me. I could not decipher the meaning behind the flash of his eyes.

"You're quite stubborn, you know."

I scowled. First he thought my mother's painting naive, and now he was calling me stubborn.

"Who are you to tell me about myself?" I asked sharply. It felt nice to finally use a harsh tone with James.

"I had no intention of insulting you. It's beneficial, though, for me to see different aspects of your behavior. It helps me paint the portrait."

"Even if I were stubborn, which I am not, I do not see how that would help you with my portrait."

"Paintings—all paintings, including portraits—are about sending a message. I am trying to capture the essence of you. That is what Winston has hired me to do."

"Winston has merely hired you to carry on a family tradition," I muttered as I dipped my pen into the inkwell and tapped the excess against the rim.

"If that is what you believe, Miss Sheffield, you are missing the purpose of art."

When I copied the next line of my mother's letter my curves were too sharp.

"You are distracting me." I nearly growled the words.

"The Mona Lisa, the Sistine Chapel. Even your naive little landscape here," he said as he gestured his brush toward the painting at my feet. "They all leave a story, a history, for everyone who sees it. My job as an artist is to tell the story of Miss Iris Sheffield as best I can through this portrait."

"Our sittings were more pleasant when you did not talk so much."

"Yes," he agreed, undeterred by my insult. "But they have done little to help me understand your character. I must convey your nature in your portrait. Until you showed me a glimpse of your stubbornness, however, I have had nothing to work with. In all the portraits I have painted before, never have I come across someone with so little personality. It is like excavating for the fossil of a shrew."

I felt my cheeks flare.

"If I were painting your portrait, Mr. James," I said, slowly and clearly so he would not miss a word, "its story would be of a cold, judgmental man who makes no attempt to convince his sitters he cares at all for the work he is doing."

James nearly smiled at me when he said, "What do you know, you are a bit fiery as well. Does your fiancé know this side of you?"

My cheeks continued to burn as I tapped my pen on the desk. It sent a light spray of ink across my paper.

"My fiancé has never been so ungentlemanly as to provoke a fiery response from me. And now that you have discerned so much about me, I kindly ask you to leave me to my work. It has been disappointingly slow this morning, as I have been repeatedly distracted by a most inconsiderate person."

James raised his eyebrows. Surely he was making note of one more characteristic to add to the portrait.

I bent over the desk and lowered my head to such a degree that I hoped James would find it impossible to paint my face. The few times I glanced up at him, however, he was working away and ignoring me completely, as if he had already deciphered my story.

CHAPTER 14

*T*hat evening, I took a walk through the nearby pleasure gardens. As I watched a rehearsal of Handel's *Water Music*, a burst of wind scattered the musicians' pages, and I noticed a sea of dark clouds swelling in the sky. I hurried back to the mansion, arriving just as the rain started.

"I'll wait out the storm here, then hire a carriage," I told Stanley as I slid off my kid gloves.

Just then the wind began its crescendo. It rattled against the windows and howled down the chimney. At the sound of a large crack, Stanley went to the parlor windows.

"A limb broke off the oak tree," he said. "I fear the storm is just getting started. You'd best plan to stay the night here. I'll send Anna to prepare the guest room for you."

As much as I wished to argue, I knew Stanley was right. I gathered my letters and landscape from the parlor then climbed the stairs slowly. They were steeper than the stairs in my townhouse, their spacing unfamiliar beneath my feet. One day, after the wedding, I would ascend them regularly. But I felt out of place doing so now, as if I were forcing myself upon the house prematurely.

I paused at the top of the stairs and peered down the wide hallway. It was my first time seeing the Hall of Mirrors, which Mrs. Carmichael had fashioned after the famous hallway at Versailles. My reflection bounced around me. I felt watched from infinite angles. It unsettled me, though not nearly as much as James's single, pointed stare. At the thought of James my nerves pricked in agitation. I pushed him from my mind and, ignoring my reflections, quickened my steps down the hall.

The guestroom door was on the right, flung open in anticipation of my arrival. Inside, a scarlet spread adorned a four-poster bed. Thick velvet drapes of the same shade hung from the turret windows. A walnut armoire stood in one corner, a secretary's desk in another.

Anna stood at the windows, a pocketed white apron around her waist, watching the wind toss the trees in every direction. When she noticed me, she pulled the drapes shut.

"You can borrow that for the night." She nodded toward a gray nightgown draped over the desk chair. "Mrs. Carmichael won't know the difference. I'll get you some fresh bedclothes." She opened the armoire and pulled out squares of crisp white sheets.

Anna stripped the bed and unfurled a clean sheet. She arranged it across the mattress, then frowned when the sides grazed the floor.

"I can never figure out which direction these things go," she muttered.

"I'll help you." I placed my stack of letters and the small painting on the corner desk. "It's sideways. Bring your side to the foot of the bed."

We shifted the sheet and Anna pulled it smooth. I worked my way around the bed, tucking the bedclothes beneath the mattress.

"You have to push them in deep," she instructed. "Or it'll all come undone on you."

I resisted the urge to roll my eyes, for I had, in fact, made up a bed before. But I followed her instructions and shoved the bedclothes even deeper.

That's when I felt it. A sharp corner of something wedged beneath the mattress. When I yanked my hand from beneath the bed, I found a long, red line trailing across my palm.

"Something wrong, miss?" Anna asked.

I looked up. "I think I scraped my hand on the bed."

She blinked slowly. "Why don't you return to what you were doing and let me finish. Thank you for your help."

I crossed the room to the desk and sat, rubbing my thumb over the scrape in my palm.

Anna was quick in her work—I had probably only slowed her down by helping—and with a soft thud she closed the guest room door behind her. I listened for the sound of her shoes tapping down the marble hallway. Only once their echoes faded did I return to the bed.

I shoved my hand deep beneath it until I found the source of my scrape. My fingers curled around something boxy and smooth.

It was a book: a small book, hardly larger than my hand. Its leather cover was the green of an aspen leaf, and its exacting corners were sharp enough to leave a mark. A gold fleur-de-lis engraved the cover. When I held it to my nose, the smell of leather was deep and luxurious, a faint echo of saddles and shoes. I ran my fingers along its thick pages. Its spine was stiff, as if it had rarely been opened.

The pages were blank, or so I thought the first time I riffled through them. I began again, this time careful to start with the inside cover. That was where I found the first writing.

Journal of Miss Penelope Ann Bromley, 1849.

A journal. My heart pounded with possibility as I flipped through the book once more. Only three of its pages were filled. The penmanship was large but careful, with little flourishes and embellishments. Something about it seemed dreamy and youthful.

A young woman, I thought immediately. Someone who felt deeply about what she was writing.

A small card fluttered from the book and landed on the freshly made bed. I picked it up carefully by its corners. It was a daguerreotype of a woman who seemed faintly familiar. She had protruding eyes and lashes so thick I wondered how she blinked without them becoming entangled. Her cheeks were plump and her forehead broad. Despite the black and white picture, her milky complexion made me think her hair must be red. A deep, bleeding red. She was stunning.

On the back of the image, in the same embellished writing, read *Penelope Ann Bromley*.

The bell in the hallway rang, a signal for supper. Anna would come fetch me if I delayed. I ran my hand over the journal's cover. Expensive, my fingertips told me. Perhaps the journal had been a gift.

I stuffed the small book deep beneath the mattress and said a silent prayer that it would remain undisturbed until I could return. Suddenly my forced evening in the mansion held a sliver of light. The small green journal was a delicious treasure. I could not wait to delve into its few, precious pages of handwriting when the moment was right.

CHAPTER 15

$\mathcal{I}$ dined alone the night of the storm, imagination my only companion. My mind wove explanations for the journal, stories of its owner and how it had arrived in the guest room—all while the wind cried at the windows and the trees cast swaying shadows on the carpets.

My imagination was so thrilled by the possibility of the journal that, when I retired for the evening, I dared not read it. I would save it one more day, I decided, and draw out the anticipation, for once I began reading I would not be able to stop. Then the delight would be over all too quickly and I would again find myself out of place in a house that was not mine. Instead of reading I went to bed early, though between the wind tearing through the night and the journal stuffed under my mattress, I did not sleep well.

Breakfast in the morning was as quiet as supper the night before. Stanley occasionally stepped into the dining room to ask if there was anything I needed. Only after I had assured him that I had plenty of strawberries, and the scones were delicious, did I ask him what I had wondered.

"Stanley?" I tried to subdue the eagerness in my voice. "How long have you worked here?"

Stanley's forehead creased. "Three . . . no, nearly four years now."

"Have the Carmichaels had many guests during that time?"

He squinted. "Guests?"

"You know, relatives visiting, or passing through and needing a place to stay?" I wrapped an arm around the back of my chair.

"I don't recall anyone meeting that description. As you know, the Carmichaels have very few extended family members."

"The turret guest room, though. Has it ever been used? It is intended for guests, isn't it?"

Stanley frowned. "It is a guest room in name, but I'm afraid I can't say to what extent it has been used for that purpose."

I suppressed a huff of impatience at his lack of helpfulness. "Well, when Mrs. Carmichael comes into town, does she stay in that room?"

"No." Stanley shook his head. "She never stays here overnight. She used to on occasion, but she always slept in her old room. It is just as she left it."

"You mean that in the past four years you've worked here, you can't recall anyone ever spending the night in the turret guest room?"

Stanley took a breath, as if he were trying to be patient with me.

"I'm not here every night, Miss Sheffield. I go home to Agnes whenever the Carmichaels can spare me. I'm afraid I don't know everything that goes on here."

"Of course. I'm sorry, I did not mean to press you." Since the day I first stepped foot in the Carmichael home, Stanley had been most welcoming. After Winston, he was my strongest ally in the house, certainly more welcoming than Anna—or Mrs. Carmichael, when she made a rare appearance.

Stanley crossed the room and placed his hand gently upon my shoulder.

"I do remember the important things," he said, his impatient tone gone. "I still remember the day Winston met you."

I smiled at the half-eaten blueberry scone on my plate. "It was the same day I moved to London, which was overwhelming. I was a complete mess."

"Not to Winston. He came home and couldn't stop speaking of the lovely woman he had met with the curly hair and wide hazel eyes—how beautiful and kind she was, exactly what he had always looked for. I had much to do that evening but Winston wouldn't stop chattering away about you. When I finally met you, I understood. You were every bit as lovely as he had described. You look much like my Agnes did at your age. Did I ever tell you that? Winston was convinced you were perfect from the day he met you."

"Perfect?" I laughed. "Certainly not."

"He would disagree wholeheartedly with you. It was the same when I fell in love with my Agnes. Of course, she wasn't really perfect, but we overlook a great deal for those we love."

I shifted in my chair. Was Winston in love with me? Did he assume I was in love with him—and was I?

"I'd like to meet Agnes one day."

"If she feels well enough, perhaps you'll meet her at the wedding. Her pains are getting worse, though, so I would not count on it."

I touched Stanley's hand on my shoulder. "All my best to her."

"Thank you, Miss Sheffield. Would you like more to eat?"

"No, thank you, Stanley."

"Of course, Miss Sheffield." He cleared my plate and his words echoed in my mind long after he left for the kitchen.

We overlook a great deal for those we love.

CHAPTER 16

*J*ames would arrive for my sitting in half an hour, which was surely enough time to read the three written pages in the journal upstairs. Perhaps the enjoyment of reading them would carry me through the upcoming hours of awkward silence. I headed for the stairs with a wide grin on my face. I made it as far as the parlor before a knock sounded at the door.

James.

Why was he early today, of all days? Anger heated within me, as if he were purposely delaying my dive into the journal. Of course, he knew nothing of my plans, but I still glared at the door with all the resentment two eyes can manage.

There was no chance I would delve into the journal around James. I did not need his presence tainting my pleasure. I was craving a morning with a handwritten record, though, so I sat at the desk in the parlor and returned to my mother's letters as Stanley answered the door.

As James organized his paints, I pulled an envelope at random from my pile. I knew which one it was before I opened it. Mama's hand had bounced when she wrote my name across the front, so her *s* at the end of *Iris* ran off the envelope in a long, wild tail.

4 May 1841

My dearest Iris,

I feel a bit silly writing this, for you are outside on a birthday adventure with Papa, collecting rocks and searching for snails. I could simply step outside and catch up with you on your walk, but the baby is growing, and rising from my chair is increasingly difficult and I become winded so easily. You will know what I mean one day. I also hate to infringe upon your time with Papa, for you are getting older and may soon tire of foraging for nature's smallest treasures.

But my brain seems to remember less and less the larger I grow, so when you return I will likely have forgotten what I wanted to tell you. That is the beauty of pen and paper. Fleeting thoughts, emotions that time threatens to erase . . . all become permanent if written down and passed on to someone who cares enough to preserve them.

I wanted to tell you that I just felt the baby move, and it reminded me of when you first kicked me. It was nothing more than a flutter, light as the pulse of a butterfly wing, and so subtle that I nearly missed it. But as time passed, your strength grew and grew, as this baby now does, and it makes me so grateful that you are already in the world to blaze the trail for your new sibling and show him or her the way.

I'm not nearly as young as I was when you were born, but I know that with your help this child will lack nothing. How fortunate this baby will be, not only to have adoring parents, but also a brave and generous older sister.

I now hear you and Papa returning, so I shall close this and prepare to see what tiny treasures you have found on your walk. Happy birthday, my dear Iris. This day is my favorite day because it brought you to me.

All my love,

Mama

I wiped my eyes and realized that James was no longer

painting. I turned my head from him, unable to tolerate his gaze. Not now.

He said nothing for a moment, and I wondered how long he would stand there, unmoving.

Finally, he cleared his throat.

"Miss Sheffield?" he asked hesitantly.

I said nothing.

"Miss Sheffield, are you all right?"

I swiped a finger under each eye and sniffed as quietly as I could manage.

"Whatever is upsetting you is not my business, but I intended to paint your eyes today. First they went all teary, and now you're turned so I can't even see them."

He stepped away from his easel and toward me. After a moment of hesitation, he lowered himself onto the bergère beside my desk. I silently scolded myself for unleashing tender emotion before a person so devoid of compassion.

When I risked a glance at James, he was staring at the smock across his lap. I wondered what he could be thinking, until he grimaced and said,

"I desperately hope I'm not getting paint on this chair."

I laughed without meaning to, loud and unladylike. Our eyes met, and there was a softness to James's gaze that I had never seen, as if he were looking at me and actually seeing me. It was because of this unexpected softness that I decided to explain.

"I was reading some old letters." I lifted the page in my hand. "I should have known better than to start with this one. It is from my mother."

"Is she unwell?"

"She passed away when my sister was born. She had written me letters for a year and half before she died, just on a whim. Now they are all I have left of her."

I raised the letter to my face.

"They once smelled of her. And of my childhood. I don't

know what the smell was. Something fresh, a little sweet. Similar to wine, but we rarely kept wine in the house, so it couldn't have been that. But now I can't smell her anymore."

"Do you read her letters often?" James asked quietly.

I nodded. "They caused me to love penmanship. It's a piece of someone that lasts longer than they do."

James said nothing.

A sound escaped my chest, part laugh and part sigh. "That probably sounds crazy to you."

"No," James said softly, "not crazy at all." He opened his mouth as if to say more but decided against it.

"She painted the landscape I showed you the other day, of the estate with the blue shutters."

"I thought you had painted it."

"I was about to tell you." I narrowed my eyes at him. "But then you called it naive."

"It was not an insult," James said. "Did she study with a professional?"

"No, she was self-taught."

"That makes her work all the more impressive, then." He hesitated and looked toward his easel. We had shared more words in the last three minutes than he probably spoke in a day. Surely the duration was torture to him.

I waited for him to stand, to say he must return to his work. Instead he ran his knuckles along a spot of dried paint at his jaw.

"My mother wanted me to be a doctor."

My eyes widened in surprise.

He laughed in agreement. "Can you imagine? No, it was never a good fit for me. I wanted to paint people—not rich people in their mansions, though. I never wished for that."

Obviously. "What did you want to paint?"

"If I could choose? Genre painting."

My lips twisted. "Pardon?"

"Everyday life. People working: gleaners, stonebreakers, peasants kneading bread, that sort of thing." He sighed and put his palms on his thighs. "I fell in love with genre painting in art school. I could paint the working class all day. But I was tight on money, and peasants kneading bread can't pay you for painting them."

"So you began painting high-society portraits."

He stared at me, intent on my eyes, and I felt the pulse in my chest quicken. He waited a beat before he spoke.

"There's a group of artists in France called the Barbizon School. They paint the working class. I'm hoping to join them soon."

"That sounds lovely," I said. It seemed the proper response.

"It's not as glamorous as society portraits. But if this one turns out the way I hope it will . . . "

His voice trailed off. I leaned forward, curious to hear what would happen if my portrait turned out as he hoped.

"Well." James nearly smiled. "It still wouldn't make up for the fact that I never became a doctor."

I grinned, grateful to James for providing a small distraction from my tears. He stood and returned to his easel.

"It's for the best," I said, feeling I owed him for his kindness. "With your bedside manner, you would have made a terrible doctor."

He looked at me strangely, and my cheeks blazed. I had gone too far. My teasing had crossed over into insult. But before he slipped behind the easel again and out of view, I saw a smile curl half of his mouth, if only for a moment.

CHAPTER 17

$\mathcal{L}$unchtime was drawing near, which meant James would soon depart and I could retrieve the journal from upstairs. But as he gathered his paintbrushes there was a knock at the door. Stanley's steps came quickly across the foyer. I heard him rattle the knob for several moments before the door yawned open.

"I am here for Miss Iris Sheffield."

I stood quickly, recognizing the high, eager voice before I ever saw the face.

Margaret Darby, my closest childhood friend, swept into the foyer, wide skirt swishing about her. Her honey curls were swept high off her neck and a grin consumed her face, pushing her rounded cheeks to their limits.

"Iris, the bride-to-be!" Margaret squealed as she rushed past Stanley and captured me in a squeeze.

"Margaret," I said, laughing, "it has been over a year! What are you doing here?" I gestured toward James. "And allow me to—"

"I can't believe you are to be married!" Margaret cried, ignoring my attempted introduction. No matter. Margaret was a bloodhound around men. She would notice him soon enough. "Father still does business in London, you know. And once you moved, I asked him to keep an eye open for you. He read of your engagement last week in the *Observer* so I decided to join him on his next trip to London. I had to congratulate you in person."

I wrinkled my nose. "Our engagement was in the newspaper?"

Margaret laughed. "Of course! You can't marry the owner of Carmichael Glass and expect no one to take notice."

Strangers across London had read of my engagement? It seemed unnecessary, never mind embarrassing, but I did not say as much to Margaret, who loved attention and would never understand.

"I am glad your father noticed if it brought you to me. How long will you be in London?"

"Only for the day. We must leave first thing in the morning. I told Father I'd return late tonight, so we can spend the day together."

I smiled and tried not to think of the journal upstairs that would have to wait yet another day. But I could not pass up a day with Margaret. She had once been my dearest friend, and I wrote her regularly for a year after moving to London. But letter writing was not her strong suit. She did not have the attention span for it, and I knew when she hugged me goodbye on the steps of Pembrooke that the impending distance between us would weaken our bond.

James, in his corner, was shifting his eyes back and forth between Margaret and me like a birdie in a game of badminton. When I raised my eyebrows at him he resumed wiping his brushes.

"Is Mr. Carmichael home?" Margaret asked. "I'd love to make his acquaintance. Does he have a brother? Or a male cousin, perhaps?"

"No brothers," I said as straight-faced as I could, "nor male cousins, for that matter. Though he does have an elderly uncle."

She scrunched her nose. "Do the men in his family age well?"

I nodded toward the fireplace. "That's his father. Judge for yourself."

"Not bad," she mused. "Particularly when you consider—"

Her gaze swept across the room and she caught her first sight of James. Her eyes widened. She gave a half smile and lowered her chin.

"I beg your pardon. I did not know you had company."

I stretched my hand toward James. "Miss Margaret Darby, may I present Mr. Thomas James. The portraitist."

I watched carefully as Margaret approached James and accepted his hand. When she cocked her head to the side and raised her shoulder, I couldn't help myself.

"Please," I muttered, just loud enough for her to hear. Margaret ignored me, fixated upon James.

"Miss Darby," James said politely, "pleased to make your acquaintance."

"An American!" Margaret's dimples deepened. "You have the most charming accent, though I'm sure Iris has already told you that."

"He speaks very little," I said, though neither Margaret nor James paid me any attention. Why was James grinning at her? And why did he not release her hand?

"Miss Sheffield generally keeps her opinions of me to herself," James said, "out of politeness, I assume."

"Come now," Margaret gushed. "Even though she's happily engaged, I'm sure Iris must not be immune to your charming accent. Which part of America are you from?"

"Boston." He released her hand. "Though I haven't been there in ages. I went to art school in New York, then Paris."

"And now you're a portraitist," Margaret said. Behind her batting eyelashes I could almost see her mind searching its deepest recesses for common ground with James. But art held as much interest for Margaret as letter writing. She would come up empty-handed, and then she would have to lie to carry on the conversation.

"I prefer painting the working class, but they don't pay as well as the upper class, so yes, I am a portraitist."

"Is it really so bad, sitting in mansions and painting beautiful women?"

"It becomes tedious after a while."

I glared at James.

"Do you sell your paintings?"

"On occasion." He began wrapping his brushes in their cloth case. "Typically, I am commissioned before I begin a painting. Obviously, this is the arrangement for all my high-society portraits."

"I've always wanted to invest in art." There it was: the lie. "I don't suppose you have any works for sale? Perhaps a self-portrait I could purchase?"

Margaret placed a hand on her chest and laughed her classic laugh: head thrown back, wide mouth showing all her teeth.

And James, the man with the stiffest upper lip in London, joined Margaret in her laughter. I gaped at him in astonishment. What in the world had come over him?

"Really, though," she said when she finally calmed, "I would love to see some of your work."

James placed his wrapped brushes in his bag and shrugged its strap onto his shoulder. "Most of my art for sale is displayed in a small gallery in the West End. I'm afraid I have commitments the rest of the day, but I can give you the address if you'd like."

It wasn't the tête-à-tête invitation Margaret had been hoping for, this much I knew. But she kept her expression as pleasant as if James had just offered to take her to the gallery himself. I buried all hopes of an afternoon activity Margaret and I might both enjoy. Any plans of my own would not stand a chance against Margaret's determination.

"That sounds lovely," she said. She waved a hand toward me without taking her eyes from James. "Grab your hat, Iris, and a shawl and gloves. It is a bit chilly out there today, and you and I have an art gallery to visit."

CHAPTER 18

ames's gallery was tucked at the top of a narrow cobblestone street. Margaret's driver pulled the reins at the bottom of the road.

"I'm afraid you'll have to disembark here and walk up to it," he called to us. "I'll get stuck if I try turning around up there."

We descended the carriage, which was particularly challenging for Margaret given the breadth of her skirt.

"I hope this is worth it to you," I said once she had maneuvered herself from the carriage, "considering you don't truly care for art."

Margaret shrugged, undeterred. "Father has considered collecting paintings for the estate. Maybe I can talk him into buying one."

We hobbled up the uneven path together, two friends reunited for a day. Above the quiet road loomed two-story shops painted schoolhouse reds and delphinium blues. The gallery was the last shop on the right, with *Pendleton Fine Arts* painted in gold letters across a black sign. In the window sat three still-life paintings in intricate gold frames.

"How fancy!" Margaret stage-whispered as we entered.

"May I help you?" A wiry man with a monocle sat behind a desk overflowing with papers.

"We're here to see paintings by Mr. James," Margaret announced.

"Thomas," I added. "Thomas James."

"The American?" Mr. Pendleton studied my dress, then shifted his gaze to Margaret's wide grin. Deciding we were trustworthy, he waved us toward the rear of the shop.

"His works are along the back wall. Help yourself to a look. Let me know if you have any questions."

We walked through the narrow shop, its stone walls lined with framed paintings, each a window into a different world—cows grazing in pastures, children blowing soap bubbles, sunflowers bursting from vases.

The entire back wall was dedicated to paintings by James. They were all small, not much larger than a piece of stationery paper. *Studies*, they were labeled. There was a study of a boy on the Waterloo Bridge, a study of a beggar on the steps of Westminster Abbey, and one of a young woman selling nuts, clutching a plaid shawl around her shoulders. The work that intrigued me the most, however, was not a painting but a framed sketching. It was of a woman's hand, her long, tapered fingers splayed across the top of a table in an elegant pyramid. I wondered to whom that hand belonged.

"Five pounds for a sketch of a hand?" Margaret laughed as she studied it with me. "Whose hand is it, Queen Victoria's?"

"It's a study from *La Donna*," Mr. Pendleton called from the front of the gallery. I blushed, reliving past visits with Margaret to the ribbon shop or the bookstore, her voice always booming wherever we went. Stepping out with Margaret meant drawing looks from everyone within earshot of her generous range.

"What is he like?" asked Margaret as she squinted at the

sketched hand. "James, I mean. Is he always as charming as today?"

"The opposite," I said. The vehemence in my voice surprised me. Then, remembering his reaction when I had read my mother's letter, my voice softened as I added, "For the most part."

"I find it surprising that your fiancé is not threatened to leave you alone with such a handsome man."

"He's not that handsome," I said. Margaret raised her brows. "And we're not alone. Stanley is always nearby—and Anna, the cook." Besides, Winston was far too busy with his commission to worry about things at home. And he seemed to assume that James was married, though I had my doubts.

She stepped toward the single window in the shop to catch her reflection in the glass. "It's all right to admit he is handsome, even if you are engaged. You don't have to pretend that you don't enjoy looking at him."

"I don't enjoy it," I said flatly. The only thing more awkward than sitting in silence with James was, perhaps, sitting in silence while Margaret flirted with James.

She turned from her reflection and shook her head.

"Your portraitist is dashing," she said as we made our way out of the gallery. "But his drawing of that hand will never sell."

I hesitated at Mr. Pendleton's desk while Margaret stepped outside. He lifted his eyes toward me without raising his face from his papers.

"Do you have *La Donna* for sale here?" I asked, knowing this might be my only chance to learn about the painting without asking James directly.

Mr. Pendleton's face twisted. "*La Donna?*" he repeated, raising his head. "For sale? I don't think Mr. James would sell that painting for all the money in the world. That is, if it is still in existence."

Now it was my turn to look confused. "What do you mean, if it is still in existence?"

"I mean that I would not be surprised if Mr. James destroyed that painting himself. It hasn't been seen in years, not since it caused him so much trouble."

CHAPTER 19

*M*argaret loved to talk more than anything in the world. It was the means to her two favorite pastimes—flirting and gossiping. Having squeezed in a bit of flirtation this morning with James, she was now ready for gossip, so she suggested that we stroll through the pleasure gardens and chat.

"When will I meet Mr. Carmichael?" she asked. "I feel that, as one of your dearest friends, this marriage requires my approval."

At her words, gratitude bloomed inside me. Margaret may have forced me away from the mysterious journal I had found, but her company had distracted me from the absence of Winston and my family, and her interest in my engagement touched me.

"Soon, I hope. He is traveling a great deal right now."

"And tell me more about James," she said as we skirted a couple kissing on the path, Margaret's eyes trailing after them.

I frowned. Had we moved on from Winston and back to James so quickly?

"What do you know about him?" Margaret pressed.

"Little. As I said, he rarely speaks."

I had gleaned a bit of information about James here and there. He had one sister, whom he never saw despite her recent move to Brighton. He was too busy with his art to make the trip south. And there was his dream of moving to France to study with the Barbizon School. But that information had cost me hours of awkward silence. I would not hand it over to Margaret so easily.

"Do you think he would paint my portrait?" Margaret asked as we neared the Turkish Tent. "I would not mind staring into those brown eyes for weeks on end."

"He said mine is the last high-society portrait he will be painting." I was not sure why telling Margaret this gave me a small amount of satisfaction, like when I signed Mama's name just right.

"And what is Mr. Carmichael like?" Margaret indulged me.

I smiled. "He's loyal. And dependable."

"You've just described my dog."

I frowned. "He is also hardworking and incredibly responsible."

"Wonderful qualities," she allowed. "Particularly desirable in one's *father*."

I quickened my pace, hoping she would struggle to keep up. But she easily matched my stride, even in her wide skirt.

"He'll be the father of our children one day."

"And an excellent one, I have no doubt. Don't be cross with me! Just tell me more of the excitement." She tugged playfully on my arm. "What made you fall in love with him? What makes you yearn for him?"

"Margaret! I can't discuss such things."

"Come now, if you can't discuss them with your best friend then you and I both are missing out. Does he kiss well?"

"I will not answer that," I said without looking at her.

"He doesn't kiss well?" she exclaimed. "And you're still going to marry him?"

"I did not say he doesn't kiss well. I said I would not answer."

"Which is equal to saying that he does not kiss well. Otherwise, you would happily say yes!"

I groaned. Kissing was nothing more than one person's lips against another's. Why did everyone pretend there was a great deal of variation in how well it could be done?

"Winston is also kind and generous, and he takes good care of me," I said, not proud of the edge in my voice.

I did not need to prove anything. Margaret was surely of the Jane Eyre persuasion, seeking a Mr. Rochester to set her heart blazing. One day, she might find him. Or, perhaps, she would come to realize the worth of a love built on friendship and caring and the comfort in planning a future with someone she knew and trusted so well.

"Caring and generous are wonderful qualities," Margaret allowed, no doubt to calm my ruffled feathers. "I wish the two of you all the best, and you seem truly happy, which delights me. No one deserves it more than you, my dear friend. If a man who matches Winston's description proposed to me, I suppose I would accept as well. Who wouldn't want a man who was wealthy, kind, and eager to care for you? I am glad you have found that in Winston."

She paused.

"Though I would have to give it some serious thought if he kissed poorly."

CHAPTER 20

*W*hen I awoke the next morning I hardly noticed the silence of my townhouse. I thought of nothing but Penelope's journal. When I arrived at the mansion, Stanley and Anna were in the basement. James was not due for an hour. I flew up the staircase and through the mirrored hallway to the empty turret guest room. I pushed my hand beneath the mattress. When I felt the sharp corner of the journal I breathed a sigh of relief.

Now to find a place to read.

The conservatory would be nice, though Anna or Stanley might interrupt me there. Anywhere inside, for that matter, I ran the risk of seeing them. It would have to be outside, then. I let myself out the front door. The knob, which often stuck, yielded graciously under my hand, as if it understood how anxious I was to begin.

Winston's front courtyard was small, little more than a few square yards of brick. But it was gated and had a black metal bench. The street was quiet and the air crisp as I stepped outside with the journal under my arm and a shawl around my shoulders. I had mentioned to Stanley last week how chrysanthemums were one of my favorite things about October, and now three pots of them—amethyst, topaz, and citrine—clustered around the feet of the bench like a miniature jewel garden. I sat and made myself as comfortable as I could on a metal bench while wearing a crinoline.

I studied the journal in my hand, my insides crackling with anticipation. Not another soul knew of my discovery. I would tell Winston as soon as he returned, but for now the gift was mine alone. I slipped my finger behind the front cover and held my breath as I gently opened it.

That was when I heard the footsteps. I froze, as if I had been caught, though their sound was still at a distance. I looked up to see James, attired in a black coat and hat, coming down the walk.

I puffed out the breath I had been holding and clapped the journal shut.

"James," I snapped when he reached the gate. His eyes widened at my tone. "What are you doing here so early?"

"I came to express my apologies to you, as I won't be able to attend our sitting today." He spoke in his usual bored manner, though I sensed an undercurrent of amusement at my foul mood. "I have been asked to substitute for an art class this morning. The usual teacher is unwell."

"I am sorry to hear that." I wasn't. I did not care about anything in that moment other than ridding myself of James.

"As am I. I don't care for teaching. But few artists can avoid it at some point or another. And I owe this particular teacher a favor."

"I'll see you tomorrow then."

"It's a class you might enjoy if you take after your mother. It's held in the basement of the National Gallery."

Why was James choosing now, of all times, to be chatty? I should have tempered my terse answers, I realized; they only revealed my desire to be rid of him. When he let himself through the gate, I was sure he did it only to irritate me.

"I apologize if I am interrupting you," he said as he eyed the journal in my hand. I quickly placed a palm over it.

Please don't ask me what I'm reading, I silently begged.

"What are you reading?"

Blast. Now what would I tell him? I was a terrible liar. It would be easier to tell him the truth than to convince him otherwise.

"I've found a family record," I admitted reluctantly as he peered down at me. "Well, I assume it's a family record. I'm about to find out." As soon as I said the words aloud a small smile tugged at my lips, my irritation yielding to excitement. "It's a journal. I found it in the guest room upstairs. Nothing delights me more than handwritten records, as you know. I was about to dive into it."

I did not expect excitement from James, as I did not think him capable of it. But I also did not anticipate the scowl that formed on his face.

"You don't know whose it is, and yet you still plan on reading it?"

My hands tightened around the journal. "Why shouldn't I?"

He took the liberty of sitting beside me and held out his hand. I hesitated.

"I'll give it back," he promised.

His palm lay open, broad and rough. The journal seemed particularly small when I placed it in his hand. He examined the gold fleur-de-lis on the cover and turned the book over.

"It's a beautiful journal—rather a work of art." He returned it to me. "But if it's not yours, do you really think you should be reading it?"

"I don't see what business it is of yours," I said curtly.

"None," he admitted. "But that's my point. You're about to

stick your nose where it shouldn't be. Journals are meant to be private."

His logic irritated me.

"Perhaps," I allowed, "but by writing, one creates a record. The point of *records*, after all, is that they are meant to be permanent, to live on past the life of the recorder. What is the point of making a permanent record if you don't want anyone to read it? Wouldn't it be better simply to keep it in your head and never write it down if you were intent on it remaining secret?"

"This isn't one of your mother's letters," he said gently.

"It's an innocent journal. There's no harm in reading it."

"How do you know it is innocent?" he asked. Something in his tone made me look at him differently—as if he had seen things that weren't innocent.

"I can't imagine it wouldn't be."

James swallowed. I had made him uncomfortable.

"Everyone has skeletons in their closets," he said softly.

"I don't."

His gaze shifted away from me. "Sometimes people have a history that they prefer remain hidden. Best not to go digging it up."

His shadow passed over me again as he stood and walked to the gate.

"I'll be back at the regular time tomorrow," he said. "I apologize for breaking our appointment."

I held my breath as he left, anxious to be rid of him. He closed the gate behind him, then left in the direction he came. Only when he was out of view did I open the journal to the first page. The handwriting was already familiar after my first, brief glance at it.

Journal of Miss Penelope Ann Bromley, 1849.

I would not be able to copy Penelope's hand yet, but perhaps with a little further study . . . I leaned closer. The letters were rounded and looping, the handwriting of a young woman who was still a bit of a child, I decided.

The journal's single entry began on the fourth page. It was dated a mere five months before Winston and I had met.

15 March 1849

I smiled to myself. Winston's street lay silent and empty, and even the birds in the commons across the road were quiet, as if they knew the significance of opening a long-awaited gift. The mums smelled earthy at my feet and the chilly metal bars of the bench merely enlivened me.

But when I continued reading, my smile disappeared, and something sour twisted in my stomach.

Winston Carmichael came to me today.

CHAPTER 21

I blinked hard, as if doing so could change the sentence on the page before me. But when I read it again, the same six words stared at me in their rounded, looping strokes.

Winston Carmichael came to me today.

I looked over my shoulder, afraid someone was reading the awful revelation with me, but the courtyard was empty. There was not a carriage on the street nor a soul on the sidewalk. I gathered an unsure breath before venturing on to the next line.

Winston waited for me in a carriage parked along High Street, stewing, I am sure, over my tardiness. At that moment, he was the busiest and most successful man in Moreton-in-Marsh. And he was waiting for me, a mere barmaid who has never been to London.

It had been so long since I last heard from him that I was sure he was through with me. But I was wrong. He has invited me to move to London so we can be close to each other. We shall be particularly close when his mother is away, I dare say!

I always knew I was meant for more than life in Moreton. When I begged our neighbor to teach me to read and write, my family mocked me, as they did when I spent all my earnings on dresses. But I was destined for more than the circumstances into which I was born, and I had to be ready. They wouldn't laugh if they knew I'm to be carried from this dull town, and that the heir to Carmichael Glass will be the one carrying me.

I forgot about analyzing the handwriting and appreciating the quiet of the fall morning. I forgot about everything as my world shrank down to the words on the three pages before me. I reread them twice more, slowly studying every word, hoping I had misunderstood. But every reading confirmed that Winston had kept Penelope a secret from me.

I closed the journal and held it between my palms, unsure what to do with it.

It felt like fire between my hands.

CHAPTER 22

"Can you go any faster?" I yelled to the carriage driver through the window.

"And hit the cab in front of me?" the driver hollered back.

I did not know how long James's art class would last. Perhaps I had missed him already. I had no interest in art lessons, but I needed to find James. I needed him to tell me what to do about the journal, about the terrible entry I had just read.

I cursed the slow row of carriages stretching before us. I watched for Nelson's column and the spire of St. Martin-in-the-Fields to appear. As we neared Trafalgar Square, I hovered above my seat, ready to jump out as soon as we were within running distance.

"Stop here!" I cried.

The driver pulled the reins so hard that I fell to the carriage floor. I scrambled out and paid him then joined the locals and tourists pushing their way toward the entrance of the National Gallery.

I ran up the wide steps and past the Corinthian columns. Once inside, a museum guard pointed me toward the basement.

I flew down the stairs, one hand lifting my skirt from my steps, the journal wedged safely beneath my arm.

At the bottom of the narrow staircase lay a long marble hallway. At its end stood an open door. A voice came from it, deep and rumbling.

I was so desperate for advice regarding Penelope's journal that I was turning to James. In whom else could I confide? Anna wanted nothing to do with me, and Stanley had acted strangely when I questioned him about the guest room. Margaret had left, and Papa and Hope were gone. And I certainly couldn't ask Winston.

Perhaps it was due to James's stubborn silence during our sittings that I knew I could trust his discretion. He would not gossip about his sitters. He cared too little for them.

My heels clicked in rapid staccato until I neared the end of the empty hallway. I stopped to catch my breath and sank into a chair beside the door.

He had been right about the journal. How had he known to be suspicious of it? It was such a beautiful book, its writing so youthful, I would never have guessed its words could bite. But maybe, because James had predicted its danger, he would also know how to treat its damage.

Footsteps sounded from the stairs. Then came a voice, female but low. It slid easily over the marble floors.

"I hear he's from Boston, and he's not married," the voice hummed. "All of London's richest women want him to paint their portraits, but he refuses them all."

"Fortunate for their husbands," came a second voice, soprano and light. "If I were a man, I'd never let James paint my wife. Especially after all that happened with *La Donna*."

"Did you hear Miss Eliza before class? She was speaking of the handsome artist in the square, sketching the man who feeds the pigeons. Then her face went white and she said *That's him!* as he walked in to teach the class."

Both erupted into a flutter of giggles that halted as soon as the women reached the bottom of the staircase and saw me sitting at the end of the hallway. I turned my face toward the door, avoiding their eyes as they walked past me into the classroom.

The hallway was narrow, its ceilings low. I had not eaten this morning and my head began to spin. I was not sure how long I could last here, hovering outside the classroom in this stuffy corridor.

The deep rumble of words returned, and in it I recognized James's voice. Perhaps he was almost finished. I stood and inched toward the open door and peered into the classroom. Easels were scattered everywhere. They faced various tables that held bowls of crimson apples and golden pears, and vases filled with drying chrysanthemums.

James stood at the far end of the room beside a seated blonde woman, bending over her and waving his hand across her canvas. She looked up at him with eager eyes, nodding occasionally, not missing a word.

All the students—about fifteen in total—were young women. Some were intent on their work, but most—even from across the room—were watching James. A cluster stood near him, listening to his critique of the woman's painting.

Suddenly my need for James's opinion seemed foolish. I had no business being here, interrupting his work, demanding he advise me on a subject he cared nothing about. James had never given me reason to suspect he was interested in my personal affairs. In fact, he had gone out of his way to make the opposite clear. Why would he help me now, when I had ignored his advice to leave the journal alone?

James had not caught sight of me yet, and his students were oblivious to my presence. I turned to leave before he saw me, before he knew I had tracked him down like a madwoman.

I had forgotten about the wooden chair behind me. I crashed

into it, knocking it sideways and hitting my knee against its leg so sharply that I cried out in pain.

The room behind me fell silent. When I straightened and turned, all eyes were on me, including James's. I pressed my lips together and swallowed.

"I apologize for the interruption." My brain went vacant as I searched for an excuse for my presence, but with the weight of thirty-two eyes on me, I could think of nothing but the truth.

"Mr. James, I need to speak with you after class, please."

He did not pull his eyes from me as he told the blonde woman he would be with her in a moment. He crossed the room to me in six long strides.

"I'm sorry," I muttered as he closed the classroom door behind him. "I didn't mean to cause a scene."

"Is everything all right?" he asked. He searched my face, not unlike when he was painting me. It felt different this time, though, with him standing so close.

"We can talk later, once your class is over."

Beyond him I saw several young women eyeing us through the glass of the door, whispering to one another.

"Your pupils seem to be missing you already."

"I was in the middle of explaining perspective to them."

"A topic they find fascinating, by the looks of it."

"Miss Sheffield," he said, his voice quiet but firm. "Tell me what is wrong."

With a bite of my lip, I pulled the journal from under my arm.

"Ah, Miss Sheffield," he sighed. "You didn't."

I felt as if smoke were pressing against the back of my eyes. The spinning sensation in my head returned.

"I did," I confessed. "And it is so much worse than I could have imagined."

He leaned against the wall beside me. "Would you like to talk about it? Is that why you are here?"

"Yes, but it doesn't have to be right—"

"Come." James gestured toward the end of the hallway. "We have no privacy here."

I stuffed the journal under my arm again. We took the stairs to the main floor of the museum, then stepped outside, overlooking the bustle of the square. There were people everywhere, so I slipped between two of the grand columns and James joined me. The space was narrow enough to provide privacy.

He waited for me to speak.

"Winston had . . . " I was not sure how to say it. "He had a . . . I don't know what she was. A mistress."

"Does the journal say that?" James asked.

"Practically."

"Did you read the whole thing?"

"There is only the one entry."

He offered me a handkerchief. I dabbed my eyes with it.

"For heaven's sake, don't think about it, Miss Sheffield. You'll only torture yourself."

"I can't help it." I swiped the handkerchief beneath my nose. "What if they were engaged, or even married, and he never told me?"

"Surely they could not have been married. He couldn't hide that with how well-known he is in London."

"Well, perhaps they never married, but she sounds desperately in love with him. Why wouldn't he have told me about someone who meant so much to him?"

"I wouldn't worry, Miss Sheffield. It was probably long ago—"

"It was last March." I pulled the journal from under my arm as if for proof. "Only five months before I met him."

James shook his head. "Mr. Carmichael is a grown man. Did you think you're the first woman he's ever courted? He probably didn't tell you because he knew you'd make a fuss over it."

"I wouldn't have made a fuss over it if he had told me himself," I said, my jaw tight.

"I am sure he simply did not want to risk hurting your feelings."

I did not reply.

"He's clearly committed to you. After all, he's having your portrait painted." James cast a glance at the doors of the museum, no doubt thinking he should return to class.

"It's just a portrait," I muttered as I fingered the corner of the journal.

James fell silent. When I looked up, he was facing me, but his gaze was distant, his eyes staring past me.

"Just a portrait?" He sounded on the verge of laughter, yet I could tell he was not amused.

"I mean no offense to your work," I said quickly, crumpling his handkerchief in my hand, as if my hold on it could ward off the incredulity on his face.

"Just a portrait?" he repeated, his voice louder, his jaw twitching.

I tried to step back, but with the pillar behind me there was nowhere to go.

"Do you know what Mr. Carmichael is doing by *just* having your portrait painted?"

James took two steps toward me so we were practically nose to nose. The cement column shot cold through the back of my dress. He leaned toward me, placing his hand on the column behind me. This close, I could see that his irises were flecked like amber. A faint white scar cut vertically through his bottom lip.

"He is capturing you, Iris Sheffield." He said it like an accusation. "He is freezing you in this very moment, and then he will hang that moment in his home so he can gaze upon you anytime he chooses."

My stays squeezed against my ribs as James inched his face closer to mine.

"He is memorializing you in paint. For the rest of his life, he wants to remember you as you are now." He paused for a moment and his face softened. "He wants to remember the subtle point of your chin and the twin peaks of your top lip. When he is sixty, and seventy, he will sit by the fire and instead of reading the paper he will take in the small knob at the end of your nose and the green and gold of your eyes. He is keeping you as you are now, forever. He is making you his."

James pressed his lips together. As if to confirm his descriptions of my features, his flecked eyes darted to my eyes, my chin, my nose. As his gaze rested on my lips, my breath locked hard in my chest. He opened his mouth slightly and I waited for him to say more. Instead, he stood unmoving before me, both of us frozen by the charge in the air between us.

The journal slipped from my fingers and landed at our feet. The softness passed from James's face, and he dropped his hand from the column behind me. I forced my breath out.

In. Out.

James bent to retrieve the journal.

"If it's just a portrait," he said as he handed it to me, "I'd like to know why he never had a portrait painted of this mistress you've discovered."

"He . . . " I cleared my throat and opened the journal. "I found this daguerreotype."

"A daguerreotype? You mean a portrait taken by a machine?"

I handed it to him. He studied it for a beat, then two. I could not read the look that passed over his face. Was it attraction? Recognition? Finally he looked up and, at the sight of me, remembered his lecture.

"Tell me, Miss Sheffield. How meaningful would your beloved letters be if, instead of written by the hand you love, they were made by some impersonal instrument?"

He had me there.

"Allow me to do you a favor, Miss Sheffield."

He crumpled the picture of Penelope in his hand and shoved it into his pocket.

"If you are happy with Mr. Carmichael, if marriage to him is something you desire, then don't sabotage that happiness over a . . . a daguerreotype." He nearly spat out the word. "Show me a man who goes out of his way to have a woman captured in paint, and I'll show you a man who's serious about the subject."

I couldn't help hearing James's words from our conversation on the porch, that everyone had skeletons. And Mr. Pendleton's words at the gallery, that *La Donna* had given James so much trouble.

"I'll see you on Monday at the usual time." He turned and disappeared into the museum.

For a moment, I forgot about the journal and the beautiful woman in the daguerreotype. As James walked into the museum and the iron doors slammed behind him, I could not help but wonder whose portrait James had painted when given the liberty to choose his own subject.

CHAPTER 23

*M*y eyes were shut. We were in a carriage, and beyond the closed curtains it was night. Darkness enveloped us, a deep, velvet presence.

We had started out beside one another on the carriage bench, seated an appropriate distance apart, not speaking in the darkness. There was nothing in our actions to cause the slightest degree of suspicion. But he had shortened the distance between us, and now he was kissing me as if he had never done it before—and had no intention of stopping. My face was tilted up toward him and he leaned over me, scarcely giving me opportunities for breath.

When my lungs finally threatened to burst, I pushed him away and took a hungry breath of air.

"Winston," I gasped. "Wait."

He was silent beside me save for his breaths, which were deep and rushed. I froze when I heard them, for they were not Winston's. It was like hearing a different voice, though he said nothing. His tone, his timbre, was not that of my fiancé.

Breath, I realized, had its own distinct voice.

"Winston?" I whispered into the darkness.

There was no answer, only the breathing, quieter now.

"Winston?" I asked, more forcefully this time. I reached out a hand and he quickly grasped it and pulled it toward his chest, bringing me close to him again. I felt his warm breath on my neck. He slipped his nose against my cheek and I felt his lips move against my earlobe as he whispered my name.

"Miss Sheffield."

I recognized the voice immediately. He began to kiss me again, this time starting with my ear, then trailing to my neck. I pushed my fingers through his hair.

"Miss Sheffield," he murmured again, his voice a soft rumble against my neck, his hands spanning my waist.

"Stop," I whispered, because I knew we should. But he pulled me closer. His fingers dug into my back, pressing until they hurt me, and I cried out.

"Stop!"

My yell echoed through the silence so loudly that I sat up with a jerk. I panted and blinked until my eyes adjusted to the strip of moonlight slicing between the curtains. My bedroom was as it always was, my mother's tulip quilt upon me, the washstand in the corner, the unlit candle and glass of water on my bedside table.

I reached a hand behind me to where the fingers had pressed against my back. My palm hit the corner of something solid. My fingers closed around it and I brought it to my face.

Penelope's journal. I should have known better than to make it my bedtime reading. I tossed it onto my bedside table, embarrassed by the dream it had caused—and about James, of all people.

I took a long drink of water. My pillow was warm under my cheek when I returned to it. I lay on my side and stared at the spine of the journal, its aspen cover two shades darker in the night.

The room was silent save for the sound of my breathing,

which had not yet returned to normal. Why had my brain conjured up such a scene? Was it a futile attempt at revenge, to pay back Winston for the past he had kept from me?

James had insisted I forget about the journal, but by reading it I had brought Penelope into my life. Such was the power of penmanship for me. Now that I had read her thoughts and feelings, all inked onto paper, she was a new presence, whether I welcomed her or not. I knew my mind would not rest until I asked Winston about her. I had to learn what had happened between the two of them and why Winston had hidden her from me.

My body ached with exhaustion. I stared at the journal until its edges blurred. My eyelids drooped, then closed, and I finally fell asleep.

CHAPTER 24

*W*ould Winston sense something different in me when he returned the next evening? Perhaps he would know I had found Penelope's journal simply by looking at me. I had felt a small change in myself upon finding it, a sliver of skepticism sliding its way into my mind. I cared deeply for Winston, that had not changed. I loved his loyalty, his generosity, the way he made me feel I was the most important thing in his life. Of course, the glass company was proving to be competition, but this was a rare time for Winston. He still possessed all the qualities I had mentioned to Margaret.

And yet, Penelope's journal had cast a shadow behind him, a potential darkness in his past that I had to understand. I had no choice but to ask him about it. I was not afraid of my fiancé, but my chest tightened at the possible direction the conversation could take.

"I'm going to pick up Winston at the station," I announced to Stanley an hour before his train was due.

"I'll help you hail a cab, Miss Sheffield."

Outside, the trees look disheveled from the recent storm and several had lost large limbs. I saw no sign, however, of the Carmichaels' broken oak branch.

"Did you clear away that large branch already?" I asked.

"No, Miss Sheffield," Stanley said with a hint of a smile. "Anna cleared it out early this morning."

"Anna? That wisp of a woman?"

"I was shocked myself. When I saw her in the wee hours of the morning she mumbled something about frustration to burn, and the next thing I knew she had an axe and was whacking away at it. Within thirty minutes she had chopped the whole thing into firewood. Makes me wonder what else she's capable of."

* * *

WHEN WINSTON STEPPED off his train at Euston Station, I was waiting at the platform. The smile he gave me was tired, the kiss upon my cheek brief.

"I've hardly slept the past three nights." He shifted his suitcase to his other hand. "But the Birmingham factory is nearly capable of producing all 900,000 square feet of glass for the palace."

He offered me his arm and I showed him back to my hired carriage. I had never seen him so spent.

It was dusk, the gas street lamps not yet lit. I could still make out the familiar London scenes rolling past our windows. A young man sleeping against a brick building, his arm draped across a scarred lap harp. A woman hovering in the doorway of a shop, calling after a passing couple for money.

The journal lay tucked inside my fur muff, clenched between my hands. It was not the best time to ask Winston about it, as exhausted as he was. But I had to know about Penelope, and if I waited he would leave town again before I had the chance. There would never be a perfect time, I told myself.

He stared at the *Times* on his lap. I took a slow, deep breath.

"There is something I want to tell you, Winston."

He turned to me, his features weary. My heart hammered inside me.

"It's silly, actually." I ran my thumb along the edge of the hidden journal. "But I'd like us to be without secrets. I thought you should know that three men proposed to me before you, when I lived at Pembrooke. Matthew Crane, Simon Beauregard, and Clarence Danes. Of course, I refused them. Matthew had courted me for a month, but Simon's and Clarence's proposals surprised me completely." I had had little time for courting when we lived at Pembrooke, between caring for Hope and looking after our estate.

Winston said nothing. He stared at me a moment through squinted eyes, his lips tight. Soon, though, the intensity in his face eased and his mouth pulled into a tired grin.

"Is that all, my dear? You did not need to tell me that, much less worry. Your past is your own, not mine."

My heart sank. If he thought so, how could I expect him to tell me about Penelope?

"Perhaps it *was* unnecessary," I admitted, "but I wanted you to know. I'd like you to know all of me, including my past, for isn't that also a part of me?"

"If your innocent confession brings us closer, then I gladly accept it." He leaned over to plant a soft kiss against my cheekbone, then returned to his newspaper. I watched him, frustration brewing inside me. I had shared, and now it was his turn. But he would not even look at me.

"Winston?"

He did not look up. Kennington Road was only six blocks away. I was determined to pull answers from him before we arrived.

"Winston," I repeated.

He finished the sentence he was reading and placed his thumb on the page before looking at me.

"What about you? Was there anyone?"

"Was there anyone where?" Confusion clouded his face. He had forgotten our conversation already.

"Was there anyone before me, whom you courted?"

Winston cocked his head, as if he did not understand why I was bothering him with something so trivial. Then, deciding I was determined, he suppressed a yawn and looked to the carriage ceiling.

"Let me think. Father went through a spell where he invited a friend's daughter over in hopes I would take a liking to her. I did not care for her, if for no other reason than to displease my father, but we ended up spending several afternoons together over a chessboard at his insistence. I can't even recall her name."

"Anyone else?" I pressed.

"I met Alfred Fox's niece at a ball several years ago and found her charming, but then I danced with her and discovered she was visiting from Italy, so I abandoned that pursuit. In all honesty, my dear, I rarely had the ambition for courting until I met you."

"Two women? You're sure that's all?" I took a breath, then a plunge. "Didn't you mention a Penelope once?"

"Penelope?" He frowned. "I doubt it. I know no one of that name—that is, no one of consequence."

"What do you mean?" I asked as calmly as I could, resisting the urge to grasp his lapels.

He hooked a finger into the knot of his silk cravat and loosened it with one swift tug. "I once knew a Penelope. We were friends before I moved to London, and she eventually moved here herself. She called on me once or twice at the mansion, but nothing ever came of it. I could never have married someone like her."

"What do you mean, someone like her?"

Winston ran a hand over his jaw. "You would have to meet her to understand. I can't believe I ever mentioned her name to you."

"Does she still live in London?"

"No," he said slowly. "She was rather forward, and I had to be frank with her that nothing would come of us. I'm afraid it broke her heart. She said she did not wish to see me again. She left London and returned to her family."

Winston allowed himself a full yawn and leaned back.

"Does that answer your questions, my dear?" he asked as he closed his eyes, his face still and calm.

My fingers loosened around the journal in my muff and my pounding heart dulled to its regular rhythm.

That was it, then. Penelope was nothing more than an admirer who had proved too ardent for Winston. She had desperately wanted everything Winston offered me, and now she was little more than a blink in Winston's past, a name not worth remembering.

As sleep overcame Winston two blocks shy of his house, I knew that James had been right when he brushed off my worries. Penelope meant nothing to Winston.

That knowledge should have reassured me.

CHAPTER 25

"*W*here have you been?" Mrs. Carmichael demanded as Winston and I entered the mansion. She stood in the foyer, her face scrunched in impatience, Cleo draped in her arms. "I have been waiting for you for thirty minutes."

"I've just returned from Birmingham." Winston removed his hat and pecked his mother's cheek. "Had you mentioned you were coming?"

"You wrote to me and told me to come today."

"Did I?"

It came as no surprise to me that Winston had forgotten. He thought only of the Crystal Palace these days.

"You said you needed to discuss something urgently," prodded his mother.

"Ah, yes." His eyes shifted toward me. "Perhaps we should eat first."

Mrs. Sheffield gave a huff of impatience. "We'll discuss it over supper. Then I would like to leave before it grows darker."

"Already, Mother?" Winston shrugged out of his coat. "Why don't you stay the night? You've only just arrived."

118

Mrs. Carmichael shook her head. Her gray chignon trembled. "I don't sleep well here," she said. "I haven't since . . . " She trailed off and I suddenly felt sorry for Mrs. Carmichael, unable to relax in a house she once called home. She set Cleo down and watched her climb the stairs. "I hope she doesn't wander off. She runs upstairs and hides whenever I visit. I may have to stop bringing her."

Stanley appeared from the kitchen with Anna behind him, both carrying plates of stuffed quail and poached apples. When they set the meal on the table before us, Mrs. Carmichael did not touch her fork.

"All right, Winston, we are seated. Supper is here. What did you wish to discuss so urgently?"

Winston swallowed a bite of quail before he spoke. "I've been thinking about the wedding, and I am afraid that spring will be too late for it."

Mrs. Carmichael nudged her plate aside. "What do you mean?"

"The Great Exhibition is in May. If I provide their glass, my schedule will only worsen as the date draws nearer."

"That's true," Mrs. Carmichael admitted.

I cut my quail into tiny pieces, not looking at Winston and his mother. Why hadn't he discussed this with me first? He was a grown man, the head of a large company, and yet he seemed afraid to make decisions without his mother's approval.

He turned toward me. "It also has occurred to me that it would be nice if I could bring you with me on my trips to Birmingham. I suppose I could do so now . . . "

"Absolutely not," Mrs. Carmichael interrupted with a frown. "It would look inappropriate."

"We wouldn't *be* inappropriate," he said.

"I won't have people making speculations about my family. But I do approve of a December wedding, considering how busy you will be with the commission."

"What do you think, darling?" Winston asked, reaching for my hand. "Would you be opposed to a December wedding?"

His need for his mother's approval aside, an earlier wedding would minimize the days we spent apart. I had only one concern.

"I would agree to a December wedding if Hope is well enough to return to London by then." Her presence, and my father's, were not negotiable.

"Of course," Winston said. "We would never proceed if they could not be here. We shall write to your sister's doctor in Nice and make sure he approves the voyage."

He released my hand to spear a sliver of apple with his fork. "Which reminds me, have you heard from your father?"

"Not recently." I fingered the silver handle of my knife. "He is not the most dependable correspondent, and perhaps the mail service in Nice is slow."

Mrs. Carmichael glanced at me. "If your family and the doctor sent their letters here, that might improve the communication."

"It's worth a try, I suppose. I'll tell him the next time I write to him."

"Excellent," Winston said. "We'll wait to hear from them before moving forward with a December wedding."

"That's settled, then," Mrs. Carmichael said. "Stanley, bring me my things. My driver is waiting outside. We won't announce the new wedding date until we hear from Iris's family, but we'll need to start preparations immediately just in case. The church, the flowers, the music. These things can't be arranged at the last minute."

Stanley entered with Mrs. Carmichael's accessories. She took the gloves and stuffed her fingers into them. "Not to mention the ball I must plan."

"The ball?" I had never heard any mention of a ball.

"The engagement ball," Winston explained.

"It's usually held a few weeks before the wedding, so we won't have much time," Mrs. Carmichael said. "We'll hold it here, in the Hall of Mirrors. It will be a small affair, just a hundred people or so."

A hundred people. Was that all?

"You'll need a new dress for it," Mrs. Carmichael continued. "Stanley, have Anna arrange an appointment with Sarah Jameson on Regent Street. She can make you a dress for the ball, Iris—and a wedding gown."

"I have a wedding gown," I said, louder than I intended. "It belonged to my mother."

Mrs. Carmichael paused a moment before she nodded. "Very well. Anna can accompany you to the dress shop tomorrow. Sarah may already have a dress you can buy. If not, tell her it must be ready in three weeks. We will need her to begin immediately if this wedding is to take place in December."

CHAPTER 26

"I have a hired carriage waiting for you," Stanley announced as I buttoned my petticoat. "I left Anna waiting with it at the curb."

"Thank you." I wriggled my fingers into my gloves. "Walk me there?"

He followed me outside and down the front steps. I let him open the courtyard gate, then shut it behind us, before I cleared my throat.

"I must ask you a question, Stanley. I don't know if you'll be able to answer it."

"I'm happy to be of service if I can."

I glanced over my shoulder. Anna stood several yards off, hand on the carriage door, waiting for me.

"It is regarding someone who was once very close to Winston."

Stanley held his smile. "You are the only person I know who meets that description, Miss Sheffield, besides his mother."

"No, I don't mean her." I lowered my voice. "I learned of a woman from Winston's past. She loved him not long before I moved to London. You were working at the mansion when they were acquainted, only five months before Winston met me. Did you know her?"

Stanley's features hardened as much as doughy cheeks and fading eyes can. I was being direct, much more so than when I had asked him about the guest room. But I needed a direct answer, and Stanley seemed my only chance.

"It's not my place to say, Miss Sheffield, particularly if Mr. Carmichael has not spoken to you himself."

"You needn't tell me any details about her," I assured him. "Even just knowing whether or not you had met her—"

"Mr. Carmichael has always been good to me," Stanley said, his white brows angled over his eyes. "Particularly while Agnes's health has been so poor. I've made it a point to respect his privacy as a matter of gratitude."

How convenient for Winston, I thought, that his money allowed him to buy Stanley's loyalty.

As if he could read my thoughts, Stanley's face softened.

"I *can* say that Mr. Carmichael has never loved anyone— including any woman you may be speaking of—the way he loves you. For if he had, he would have married her. As you may have noticed, Mr. Carmichael has a way of getting what he wants."

Then I am fortunate he wants me, I thought with a frown. I turned from Stanley and headed toward the carriage, too distracted to bid him farewell.

Winston had said that Penelope visited him at the mansion a couple of times. Surely Stanley had waited on the woman. But I would learn even less from Stanley about Penelope than I had from Winston.

"Are you all right, Miss Sheffield?" Anna asked as I reached the carriage. "You look troubled."

I studied Anna, the fair brows and lashes, the protruding eyes. If only she had been in the house when Penelope visited, perhaps she could have told me something—anything—about the woman who had loved my fiancé so ardently.

But she had arrived at the mansion more recently than I had, so I told her all was well. We climbed into the carriage and rolled toward Regent Street, off to find a ball gown.

CHAPTER 27

"*P*ut your arms up, please. Higher."

Sarah Jameson circled around me, frowning at the swath of rose fabric I wore.

"The skirt would fit better if you wore a crinoline," she said around the pin between her lips. She pinched the sleeve. "And I could take it in around the arms. But it would require so much altering that I don't think it would turn out well. Would you like to look at other dresses? Some closer to your size?"

I had been looking at dresses for an hour. The rose gown was the prettiest one I could find among Sarah's collection. Mrs. Carmichael's dressmaker of choice, I discovered, had similar taste to Mrs. Carmichael.

I lowered myself from the stool before the mirror and headed to the back of the room, where dresses hung in rows. Anna, who had been ordered to accompany me for no reason known to either of us, followed me obligingly.

"Do you see anything you like?" I asked Anna as I returned to the sparse row of pastel dresses.

"Balls were never of much relevance to me," she said as I swiped through the gowns.

"But surely you occasionally shopped for dresses with your mother."

She shook her head. "My mother was never around for dress shopping. I've always worn hand-me-downs, but even I know these dresses were all likely rejected. Why else would she have so many here?"

"I'm afraid you're right." I pushed aside more dresses. "I would ask her to make me something, but I don't know that she would understand what I—Oh!"

I had just parted the heavens. Wedged between a pea-green frock and a black crepe mourning dress hung a gown that was far from hideous. In fact, it was lovely. Made of white, gauzy fabric, its ruffled collar was long and loose. The skirt was chiffon and too narrow for a crinoline. A lavender sash circled the waist. Its shade perfectly matched the ribbon my mother once tied in my hair.

"I'll help you into it," Anna offered.

We stepped behind the paneled screen in the corner. I lifted my brown curls as Anna unfastened the pearl buttons on my dress.

"I don't believe Mrs. Carmichael would like this one," I admitted as I eyed the white gown. "It is not gray enough."

"No, I'm sure she would not like it. But she seems to have taken a liking to you, so I don't believe it will matter. There, you're all unbuttoned now."

I shook off the dress and stepped carefully from its pile of fabric. Anna held the white gown open as I stepped into it. Then she began tackling another long trail of buttons.

"There must be an easier way to pull fabric together," she muttered as she tugged at the back of the dress.

"If you create such an invention, you should take it to the Great Exhibition next year," I said over my shoulder with a smile. Then I grew serious. "Why do you say Mrs. Carmichael has taken a liking to me? I do not think she cares for me at all."

"I rarely see her," Anna admitted. "But if she agreed to advance the wedding, she's hardly trying to be rid of you."

She reached the top stretch of buttons. The dress fit well and would only need minor alterations. I wrapped the lavender sash around my waist.

"Do you think she would try to be rid of me if she did not approve?" I had wondered this at dinner last night. In truth, I had wondered since Winston told me that Penelope was all wrong for him. Had he come to that conclusion on his own? Or had his mother persuaded him?

Behind me, Anna said nothing.

"Surely she wouldn't forbid Winston to marry me, nor would Winston allow her to make such a decision." I did not know if I was trying to convince Anna or myself.

She finished the last button and her hands dropped from my back. She led me around the screen to the full-length mirror.

"Found one you like?" Sarah asked.

"Yes, with some slight alterations I think it will do perfectly."

Sarah pinched and pinned the fabric at my shoulders, bust, and waist. When she was satisfied, I slipped out of the dress with the same care I used when trimming a rose tree without gloves.

After arranging for the dress's delivery, we rode home in silence. Anna sat with her hands in her lap and her elbows tight against her sides, as if trying to make herself as small as possible.

"Anna."

"Yes, Miss Sheffield?"

"Do you and Stanley . . . chat often?"

"Chat?" Her fair brows lowered.

"I mean, are you friendly with one another? Do you tell each other things?"

"I'm not the chatting type," she said, eyes avoiding mine. "But he likes to talk so I listen sometimes."

"Has he ever . . . "

Anna's eyes met mine and their sudden intensity made me stop.

"Has he ever what?" she asked quietly.

I shook my head. "It's nothing. Never mind."

Anna cared nothing about my personal life, and though she was quiet, that did not necessarily mean she was discreet. I trusted Stanley not to relay my inquiries back to Winston, but if I asked Anna for the downstairs gossip she might tell Stanley— or even Winston, or his mother.

Disappointment settled, heavy in my chest. Penelope would remain a mystery to me. A single daguerreotype and one journal entry of looping letters were all I'd ever know of her. Perhaps she had sat in this very carriage, dreaming of a future with Winston, wishing for the life that was suddenly mine. It was a life I had never imagined for myself, particularly after Mama died. Until Winston, I had not had time for such dreams.

Penelope's journal entry made it clear she did not come from money, and I wondered how similar our histories were. Perhaps she had lost a parent early, had been overwhelmed by life and responsibility. Had she dreamt that Winston was her best chance at love—not only to give it, but also to receive it?

Perhaps she had been confident in his love for her.

Maybe she never anticipated that he would break her heart.

I supposed I would never know.

CHAPTER 28

*T*he first scream, the one that told me my life was about to change, came one August afternoon in the garden when I was twelve years old.

Mama was picking seeds from the face of a sunflower, then handing them to me. I placed them in a burlap sack for safekeeping until next year.

I was attempting to chew a sunflower seed, but its shell was as stubborn as a rock. I attacked its woody exterior with my back teeth, but it refused to yield its mellow center. I finally spit it out and reached a hand out to Mama, ready for more, but no seeds appeared in my outstretched palm as they had each time before.

Mama's hands were on her knees and the sunflower head lay at her feet. A small puddle soaked the dirt beneath her.

"Run for Papa," Mama said between labored breaths. "Then tell Lincoln to ride the horse to Dr. Patterson's. Bareback, as fast as he can get there. Run."

I dropped the sack and forced my scared legs toward the house. Mama withheld her scream until I was nearly inside. The sound of it doubled my speed until I found Papa in his library, where I knew he would be. He did not ask what the matter was. He looked at my face and asked where Mama was, then declared we must move her into bed.

Mama cried as Papa carried her into the house, stopping only to tell him how quickly the baby was coming. I trailed behind helplessly.

Dr. Patterson arrived in his leather smoking slippers, with bread crumbs in his beard and a woman behind him. She carried his medical bag in one hand and a pile of blankets in the other.

"You can wait in the hallway," the doctor told Papa as he disappeared into the bedroom. "Send in your daughter to help."

Papa ignored the doctor and followed him into the bedroom.

"Stay in the hallway, Iris," he ordered over his shoulder. "I'll tell you when you can come in."

I paced the corridor, wearing down the pale pink roses in the carpet and running my hand back and forth across the toile wallpaper. Mama's screams stopped occasionally, like she was catching her breath, only to resume more loudly a moment later. I forced my mind elsewhere, pretending I was still spitting sunflower shells outside or chasing grasshoppers off the tomato plants in the kitchen garden. I did not like to think that that terrible noise was coming from Mama.

The screams escalated until I could stand them no longer. If I descended the staircase and walked out the front door, then ran far from the house, would anyone notice?

Suddenly Mama's noise gave way to a different cry. It was a high, pulsing sound, filled with question more than pain. *Why?* it seemed to squeal. *Why? Why? Why?*

When Papa opened the bedroom door his face was red, but he was smiling.

"Come meet your new sister."

Mama lay in her bed, her dark hair plastered to her forehead and her dress damp. She held an impossibly small bundle, wrapped in a yellow blanket.

"Her name is Hope. You can hold her. Support her head, like this. That's right." Mama lay back on her pillow and closed her eyes. "Be careful. Take care of her."

"Of course," I promised without looking up. "Of course."

I was so mesmerized by Hope—her rosebud lips, her tiny fingers folded against the soft flesh of her palm, her lashes resting against the rounds of her cheeks—that I hardly noticed when the doctor ordered me to leave immediately. Papa pushed me into the hallway and once again shut the door.

I sat on a bench with my sister in my arms, never taking my eyes from her miniature face. It did not occur to me that Mama should be the one holding the baby, that she should be feeding the baby. The sounds behind Mama's door were hushed and frantic and then dropped to where I could not hear them at all. To my young ears, the quiet was a relief after all the screaming. I was merely a twelve-year-old girl, thrilled by my first and only sibling, holding a baby for the first time in my life. I had not yet learned to worry about everything, to feel the weight of having to always make things right for the child in my arms. I was ignorant and joyful as I sat on the opposite side of Mama's door —just a child holding another child in a silent, peaceful home.

CHAPTER 29

"*L*ook at me."

James sat on his stool in the corner of the parlor, a brush poised in his hand.

"I am looking at you," I said as I stifled a yawn. I was not in the mood to deal with James today.

"No, you're not. You're looking to the right of me."

I glared at him. "Fine. How is that?"

"Did you not sleep well last night?"

"I slept fine, thank you." In truth, I still struggled to sleep in my silent townhouse, though it had been two months since Papa and Hope left. But James need not know that.

"You look glazed over. Come, Miss Sheffield, I'm trying to paint your face. But you must give me an expression I can use."

I sighed. "I don't know what you mean."

James gestured with his paintbrush to the hand mirror beside me. He had brought it this morning but had yet to explain why.

"Keep that expression on your face. Now pick up the mirror and look at your reflection."

My face appeared in the oval glass. No wonder James had

asked if I was tired. There were faint circles beneath my hazel eyes, and my thick brows were disheveled. But my curly hair was pinned back in as smooth a chignon as I could manage, and my cheeks were slightly pink. I had done all I could to look presentable.

"As I've told you all morning, I need you to look at me as if I were Winston."

I put down the mirror and tried.

"No, that's not it. You're looking at me like you are a pigeon in a park. This portrait is going to be a testament to my skill as an artist. The Academy doesn't want portraits of pigeons! Now, I need you to look a little bolder. Come, Miss Sheffield, really look at me."

I bulged my eyes out at him.

"Quite amusing." He tossed his paintbrush aside and stood. "Very well then, you leave me no choice. Grab your shawl. And your hat. And any other accessory you need to survive the November air."

"Whatever for?"

"We're going on an outing. Now don't look so scandalized, Miss Sheffield, it is for the sake of the portrait. I promise to be a complete gentleman."

At the front door, I fiddled with the knob only for a moment. (*Push, then twist*, Winston's voice sounded in my head.) When we stepped outside, I pulled my bonnet as far over my face as possible and kept my head down. A sharp wind pricked my cheeks, and I wished I had brought my shawl.

As if reading my mind, James chided me. "You should have grabbed your shawl, it looks like it's about to start snowing. Go inside and fetch it."

"I'm not cold," I lied. The sooner we were in a cab the less likely anyone would see us together. And I would not take orders from James that did not relate to the portrait.

He hailed a hansom cab, small and fast, not well-suited for a lady. But it was either that or risk being spotted alone with James by Winston's neighbors, so I climbed in as quickly as I could. Only moments after stepping out of the Carmichael mansion, we were clipping down Kennington Road, the small, enclosed space slowly warming me.

CHAPTER 30

We rode in silence, crammed inside the cab, my left arm and leg pressed against James's right side. I pretended not to notice.

He peered out of his window wordlessly. How he could sit so closely to someone without feeling the need to converse was beyond my understanding. I refused to tolerate such rudeness, particularly when he was the one who had insisted on this outing.

"Studying the working class out there?" I asked as we passed three men repairing a stone wall. I was quite sure James would rather watch them than talk to me—all the more reason to force him into a conversation.

James turned toward me, a confused look on his face.

"You did say members of the working class are your preferred subjects, didn't you?"

He smirked. "I didn't know you were paying attention."

"Why wouldn't I?"

James shrugged. "Many of my sitters don't. Most prefer not to speak to me, truth be told."

I can't imagine why. His derision for his sitters—who were the source of his success—was becoming tiresome, and I did not bother restraining the irritation in my voice when I asked, "Why did you become a portraitist in the first place?"

He shifted in his seat so he was facing me. "When I was studying art in Paris, I took a portraiture class from a man who had connections with the London socialites. Once I moved here, he began recommending me to them for portraits. One family hired me, then they all began hiring me. It was not long before I found regular work painting them."

"And is it really such an awful profession? If art can be both your passion and your occupation, then what reason have you to complain?"

He faced straight again and his shoulder shifted against mine. I wondered if he would ignore my question. But after a pause he spoke, his words slow and serious.

"When I was growing up in Boston, we had a book of artwork by Vermeer. Do you know him?"

I narrowed my eyes. "I may not be a professional artist, but I have certainly heard of Vermeer."

He suppressed a smile. "When I was twelve, I opened the book and, for the first time, saw his painting entitled *A Maid Asleep*, of a young woman seated at a table. She has nodded off and is sleeping with her head against her hand. Behind her is a door, slightly ajar. And from the moment I saw the painting I wondered what lay beyond the doorway. Or who. Is it the source of her exhaustion? Is she content in her situation? She is dressed in fine silks. Her table is covered in imported rugs. But is she happy? Or is her nap to escape, perhaps to escape what lies behind her?"

His description unnerved me, as if I were actually seeing the woman asleep in front of the ominous doorway. A shiver tickled my arms. I pulled them close to me and wrapped my fingers around them, wishing again for my shawl.

"There was a story in that painting, though I did not fully

understand it. I merely knew that it was there. And that was enough to pull me in. Ever since then, my objective when I paint has been to tell a story." He paused. "Painting the wealthy does not allow me to fulfill that objective."

"You told me all art could tell a story," I reminded him, "and that your society portraits capture the essence of the sitter. Or were you merely making small talk?"

As if James would bother with small talk.

"When I paint rich sitters in their parlors, their story is their wealth. There is nothing new there. Everyone is already familiar with it. What contribution am I making, then? I am simply reinforcing what everyone already knows."

The carriage paused at an intersection. A woman sat on the corner crocheting, a pile of scarves for sale across her lap.

"But you see a story there," I said, nodding toward the woman. We watched the tangle of her working fingers until the carriage pulled through the intersection.

"When I moved to New York, and then Paris," he said, "my parents cut me off financially. They had been intent that I become a physician, like my father. When I began my life as an art student, I was suddenly poor for the first time. Since then, I have become interested in a class of people I was taught to ignore all my life."

"There is still a wide gap between you and that woman back there," I pointed out.

"True. I never did have to beg. But even when I began to make a name for myself in London and knew I would not starve, I still felt a pull toward the lower class."

"Enough to move to Barbizon."

He turned toward me with a look of surprise.

"I listen when you speak, James. Not all your sitters are as heartless as you'd like to believe. Some of them might even have stories of their own, if you took time to learn them."

He did not respond.

"Are you willing to forgo the reputation and security you've built here in London to move to Barbizon?"

James nodded, a distracted look on his face. "I may never match my success as a portraitist. But it will be worth the price."

I squinted at the cab ceiling, recalling his words on the subject. "Because there are stories to be told amongst the gleaners and stonebreakers and peasants kneading bread."

I felt his eyes on my face. When I turned to him, he was watching me intently.

"There certainly are," he said.

We stared at each other for a moment, then two. I looked away first.

CHAPTER 31

"Speaking of stories." I leaned away from James and folded my hands neatly in my lap. "I finally asked Winston about Penelope."

James's stare weighed on my face as I studied my gloves.

"I know you think I shouldn't have, but I had no choice. He is going to be my husband. I don't want there to be secrets between us."

I glanced at James. He watched me, unmoving.

"Winston hardly blinked when I asked him about her. Apparently, he knew her before he moved to London. She loved him, but he never loved her."

James spoke quietly. "Perhaps it's best you didn't follow my advice then, if your discussion with Winston brought you peace."

"If anything, it has brought me guilt. I was so upset that there was someone from Winston's past he had never mentioned to me, but now I think Penelope merely wanted what I ended up having: Winston's complete love and commitment. I feel terrible that Winston broke her heart, yet I am the direct beneficiary of it."

James leaned toward me until his arm pressed firmly against mine. "That is how love works. You're not to feel guilty about it. It's a universal pattern much bigger than you are."

I picked at a thread on my glove. "What do you mean?"

"Degrees of affection rarely balance. Nine times out of ten, one partner is Penelope. Smitten with love. And the other is Winston, not invested enough to make it work. That is why we go to such lengths to celebrate when the affection is equal on both sides. It is a miracle, in my opinion, that it ever happens at all."

I looked at James's knee, resting against my skirt.

A universal pattern. "You really think so?"

His shoulder nudged mine gently, only for a fraction of a moment. But it was enough. I took it to mean that I was not a completely terrible person.

"Trust me," he said as he straightened, our shoulders no longer touching. "As one who has seen the universal pattern unfold time after time."

I glanced through the window to find we had reached an industrial neighborhood. The cab stopped by a whitewashed brick building. James climbed out and helped me down.

"Welcome to my home away from home, Miss Sheffield."

At the building's front door, James's key clattered in the lock for a full minute before it fit. He held the door open for me and I stepped inside to find myself in a large, open space. The leather soles of my boots tapped quietly on the cement floor. The air was dusty and somehow colder than outside. When I shivered, James removed his jacket and placed it around my shoulders.

"Thank you." I slipped my arms into the sleeves then pulled off my bonnet for a better look.

"An abandoned factory," he explained. "Though I'm sure they'll find use for it soon, and then I'll be left to find another studio."

He headed toward a metal staircase. I hesitated. When I did not follow, he called at me without turning around.

"Still fretting over your deportment?"

My cheeks burned.

"Don't worry, there's no one here to rat on you. Think of it as a favor to Winston. I'd like him to get his money's worth out of your portrait."

Reluctantly, I followed James up the stairs to the third floor, where he fiddled his key in another doorknob. "This was once the office of the factory manager," he said as we stepped into a large room littered with easels and chairs.

Deep cupboards covered one wall. Another wall of glass overlooked the factory floor. Windows lined the back of the room, bathing the space in morning light. A large table sat in the middle, cluttered with crusty brushes, dried pigments, and murky jars of water.

"Do you teach here?" I asked, my bonnet dangling from my hand.

"No, this is where I store my works I don't want to sell. I paint here as well—when I'm not painting tragically beautiful sitters in London mansions."

I crossed my eyes at him.

"Sit down," he said with a laugh, motioning to a chair and walking toward a corner of the room. He unbuttoned his cuffs and rolled his sleeves to his forearms. He stopped at an over-sized easel tucked into the corner, its back to us. The canvas on it stood slightly taller than James, and he slowed as he approached it.

"You mustn't tell anyone what I am about to show you."

I grew nervous at the seriousness of his voice.

"Thomas James, are you about to confess to me that you are an art thief?"

He placed a hand on the frame, then looked at me for a moment, debating. He eased the painting out of the corner and turned it. The easel wheels squealed in protest until the canvas was facing me.

"I'd like to introduce you to Isabella da Messina. Or, as I call her, *La Donna*."

CHAPTER 32

*I*sabella—*La Donna*—stood before us, slightly larger than life. She posed in profile, one hand on her waist, the other resting with splayed fingers on a table beside her. Her head was tilted up, her ebony hair pulled back from her face. Her red silk dress slipped lazily off one shoulder and tapered dramatically at her tiny waist.

A shot of envy pulsed through me. She was stunning.

"She's beautiful." My voice was calm, almost reverent, but my mind scrambled to make sense of the painting before me. She must be the skeleton in the closet to which James had alluded. I tilted my head as I studied *La Donna*'s dress, her generous hourglass figure.

Skeleton was the wrong word for her completely.

"She *is* beautiful. And she knows it. Can't you tell?" James walked around the canvas, studying it as if he had never seen it before. "She exudes confidence. Look at her expression. She knows her place in society, and it is at the top."

Was James engaged? Had he brought me here to introduce me to the painted version of his fiancée? I was impatient to know, but I did not dare ask. Instead, I picked an obvious question.

"Did you paint her?"

He nodded. "About ten years ago, for a portrait exhibition. I was making a name for myself in London, and this painting was to seal my fame. It is my favorite of all my paintings. She loved it too. But the public disapproved of it, and the critics hated it, which devastated her and turned her against me. She never spoke to me again."

I studied the bonnet in my hands. "Were the two of you . . . "

I couldn't finish. James studied Isabella's face a moment before he answered.

"I fell in love with her as I was painting her, if that's what you are asking. My portraiture teachers had warned us never to fall in love with a subject. But I was young and had found success early, and I thought myself immune to the rules. Isabella was older than me, rich, and charming. I fell for her quickly and completely. She seemed smitten with me too, until the art critics hated her portrait. They decided her pose and her dress were too suggestive. The moment she read the reviews she went from adoring the painting to despising it, and me. She demanded I keep it out of the public eye. I was reluctant. Nobody approved of the portrait, but it garnered me a great deal of attention as an artist. But I honored her wishes, though I never knew what to do with the painting."

"Did her actions affect your future work?" I asked, thinking of how reluctant James had been to accept the commission from Winston.

"I stopped painting portraits of women as a rule. Over the years I have made very few exceptions to that. I have set other rules for myself since then as well—safeguards, one might say."

Before I could press him for details, he stepped closer to the painting and beckoned me to follow. Isabella loomed before us. James reached out a hand and gestured at the profile of her face.

"Look at her expression, Iris. She is confident. She owns the painting."

"Because she is a confident person."

"No." James shook his head. "She was feigning confidence. As soon as a few critics hated her portrait she lost all belief in herself. She left the country out of shame. It was all a show. Come."

He led me to a table covered in art supplies. Above it hung an oval mirror, its surface tarnished with silver speckles. I saw my wide eyes, my brown curls, and James's jacket hanging loose around me. He stood behind me and placed his hands gently on my shoulders.

"Now I want you to study your face. This is the face that Winston Carmichael wants to look at every day for the rest of his life. He wants generations after ours to continue to look at it. He is paying me a ridiculous sum of money to make sure that happens."

I turned toward James. "He is?"

"Don't look at me. Look at the mirror. Now, show me the face of a woman who knows she has that type of influence over her fiancé."

"We already had this conversation when you first started painting me. Don't you remember? You informed me I was stubborn and fiery—"

"And you told me that I am cold and judgmental. Yes, it's a conversation I will not soon forget. But I am not painting your portrait for myself. I am painting it for Mr. Carmichael, so I need to capture the look you would give him, not me. I need you to show me confidence. And I need at least a degree of desire in your expression if this portrait is to accomplish what I intend."

My shoulders slouched in his grip. "I can't, James. I understand what you're trying to do, but I really can't."

"Miss Sheffield," James said, his voice rough with frustration. "I have looked at you nearly every day for two months."

He paused, and when he spoke again his tone was calm and steady.

"I have mastered every curve of your face, the small bump at the end of your nose, the way your top lip rests gently upon your lower lip. But you scowl at me when I paint you, and I would prefer not to capture that forever in your portrait. Show me the look you would give to the man with whom you'll spend your life."

He searched my cheeks, my forehead, and my eyes in the reflection. But he must have come up wanting, because his face dropped in disappointment.

He released my shoulders and went to the window. He leaned against it, staring at the road below, the bustle of London life.

"I shouldn't be surprised," he said, without looking up from the street.

I tossed my bonnet onto the table. "What do you mean?"

His eyes trailed something below, perhaps a carriage or a running child.

"I've seen how Winston kisses you. I shouldn't expect such a look from you if that is all you have to work with."

My mouth dropped and I lowered myself onto a chair beside the table. It was bad enough that Margaret had asked me about kissing Winston, but to hear it from James's mouth was so inappropriate it left me speechless.

Strangely, though, when I found my voice, it was not to call out his impoliteness, but to question his judgment.

"Surely you can't know how well Winston does or does not kiss me merely by watching."

James shrugged. "Sometimes, one simply knows."

"In the first place, James," I stammered, "such details of my relationship with my fiancé are none of your business. But, if you must know, there is nothing wrong with the way Winston kisses me."

James did not bother to look at me when he said, "Only because you've had nothing better for comparison."

A mixture between a laugh and a huff escaped me. "You are inappropriate beyond belief."

"Miss Sheffield." He turned to me. "Once in your life, you deserve the experience of kissing a man who knows how to do it properly."

"A man such as yourself?" I challenged, my words crisp.

James gave a subtle shrug. "Anyone would do, as long as they could pull a more meaningful look from you. But yes, I am sure I could kiss you in a way that would produce better results than Winston."

"That is absurd. Surely there would be little difference between Winston's and your . . . " I swallowed the final word.

"There is only one way to know for sure."

I scowled. "You can't possibly be proposing that we—"

"No, Miss Sheffield. No, I am not proposing that we kiss." He folded his arms and leaned against the wall of windows. "I promised you that I would be a gentleman on this outing. It is a shame, though, because if we were to kiss it would benefit the portrait."

I shot an icy glare at him. "In one breath you tell me of your falling-out with Isabella, and in the next you speak of kissing me. Do you not see the incongruity of your words?"

James looked at Isabella's painting. "I told you that after painting her I set up safeguards. I began putting a wall between myself and my sitters. No matter what they do, I don't allow it to affect me. If we were to kiss, it might enlighten you to the lack of magic between you and your fiancé, but it would not affect me. Now don't look so scandalized. I'm not proposing to you, Miss Sheffield. I am not suggesting I am the better man for you. On the contrary. My love is my art, and always will be. That is what allows me to put up my wall."

"Is that why you always seem so pained to talk to me, and why we spend so many sittings in silence? Because you are incapable of caring for your sitters?"

"Don't misunderstand me, Miss Sheffield. I am not heartless, nor am I indifferent to your happiness. You are a kind person. You deserve a life of contentment, of enjoyment. If we were to kiss it would not only benefit the portrait, but it would be pleasant for you."

"But not for you," I scowled.

"No. Because of the wall I have built around myself."

Suddenly I could not stand the feel of James's jacket against my skin. I struggled out of it. "I highly doubt that a . . . a kiss . . . from you . . . "

The jacket sleeve caught on my arm and I wrestled with it for a moment before freeing myself.

" . . . would cause any look other than repulsion to cross my face."

I crumpled the jacket and threw it onto the table next to my bonnet, my breath heavy from the effort of removing it.

James smiled, amused by my anger.

"Trust me. With Isabella as my witness, it would vastly improve your expression."

"I am confident that it would not affect my expression in the slightest."

James returned to the view of the street and leaned an arm against the window.

"Be careful, Miss Sheffield." His voice was lazy and indifferent. "Your words nearly sound like a dare."

I studied the angle of his arm against the glass, his rolled sleeves, the cords of his forearm. Even his stance was overly confident. Why were some people born with such an obnoxious level of self-assurance? In that moment, I hated Thomas James. I hated him for dragging me here and insulting my fiancé, for inflicting two months of awkward sittings upon me, and for his derision for my class. Mostly, though, I hated how sure of himself he was, and I felt a sudden urge to kick his legs out from under him. This hatred fueled me to challenge him, and I blame that hatred for what transpired between us next.

CHAPTER 33

"**Y**our wall is a lie," I declared. "Such a thing is not possible unless one is a heartless person. And even you, James, are not heartless, as you just admitted."

"I realize it's terribly difficult for someone as open and caring as yourself to understand," James said from his spot at the window. "But sometimes, out of self-preservation, it becomes necessary to shut oneself off."

"It's impossible."

James shrugged.

"Even more importantly, though, you are wrong about . . . " I took a breath. "About Winston and me. I am so confident in my choice that nothing you could do would lessen my heart's commitment to him."

James slowly turned his head from the street below and looked at me.

"Are you suggesting what I think you are suggesting?"

I frowned. "What do you mean?

"Do I have your permission to . . . experiment?" he asked. "For the sake of the portrait?"

My mouth dropped open. Part of me wanted to protest, but

James was so sure of himself that I longed to prove him wrong. I could imagine the disappointment on his face when the experiment did not change my expression at all, when it only confirmed my commitment to Winston.

"Fine," I said with as little emotion as possible. "On one condition. When the kiss does not improve my expression, then you must stop pestering me about the look I give you for the portrait."

"*If* it does not improve your expression." He smiled. "But it will."

He was wrong about kissing. I knew he was. Since my engagement to Winston, I had learned that it was what the kiss represented, not the kiss itself, that mattered. Winston's technique in putting his lips against mine held little, if any, importance. The meaningful part was that it signified he loved me, he cared for me, he promised to look after those dearest to me. That was the significance of a kiss—everything it symbolized.

James straightened beside the wall of windows and watched me. He moved toward me slowly, like I was a bird he meant to catch before it could realize it was prey. When he stopped before me, a faint smell reached me, of oil and paper and old leather. He held out his hands: palms calloused, fingertips stained with amber and cerulean and burnt sienna.

My love for Winston was real, but calmer than the love I always assumed I would feel for a fiancé. But the gap between what I had expected and what I had found did not matter. My feelings for Winston were different from what I had imagined, but those feelings were still significant. I reminded myself of all this as I studied James's stained fingers. Slowly, I put my gloved hands—which suddenly looked so small—in his.

We stood only a foot apart, but James pulled me gently to him until my nose skimmed his collar. My eyes trailed to his mouth and its faint white scar.

"What happened to your lip?" I asked, trying to keep my voice steady.

"My lip?" He lifted his right hand, which held my left hand, to his mouth, then used my index finger to gently trace his scarred lip. "Right here?"

His lip burnt through my glove. I nodded, trembling on the inside, hoping he could not tell.

"I was playing hockey on a frozen pond in Boston. I was thirteen. I slid into a rock and it split my lip in half."

I felt the pulse of each word he spoke.

"Winston took me ice skating once. I hated it."

James smiled under my finger. "He probably just hasn't taught you how to do it properly."

His hand released mine, and before I could miss its warmth, both his hands were at my waist.

Bringing his face close, he brushed his nose against mine. My breath was hard in my chest but I did not dare release it.

His nose trailed to my cheek. Then his fingertips traced their way up my back until they reached my bare neck. A wisp of curls lay at the base of my neck, always too short to pull into my chignon, and his fingers studied the stray hairs as if they were the most important thing in the world, as if he were trying to memorize them.

My insides felt like a violin string tuned tighter and tighter, threatening to snap. The feeling was familiar: I recognized it from my dream of the dark carriage. It all rushed back—the carriage, the dream, James—solid and immediate, only a millimeter before me. I knew what James's hair would feel like between my fingers, how warm his lips would be against my neck. It was real, I suddenly understood with a burst of excitement and fear. This was real. I had not imagined something impossible. I had only been looking for it with the wrong person.

A faint noise sounded from the street below the window. I

would not have heard it but for the silence in the studio. It was a laugh, high and light, undoubtedly that of a child—a girl, running outside, laughing and yelling as children should. As Hope should.

The moment I thought of Hope my eyes flew open and I put a hand on James's chest.

"Stop," I whispered.

His lids flicked open and our eyes met, causing something sharp to shoot through me. Before he could put on his mask of indifference, I saw it in his eyes. Longing, just as I had felt only a moment before. The longing gave way to a flash of disappointment, only for an instant, but I saw it. I had been right about at least one thing, then. James's wall was a lie.

He took a quick step away from me and shook his head, as if trying to rid himself of a troubling thought. He busied himself with pushing *La Donna* back into her corner, his movements unsure.

"That's enough for today," he mumbled as the easel wheels squealed into place.

"It's only . . . " My words came out breathless. There was not enough air in the studio. "I didn't mean to—"

"That's enough," he said sharply.

I pulled my shoulders back and stood straighter. "We should return to the mansion anyway, before Stanley starts to wonder where we are."

He began to gather loose brushes, gripping them into a tight bundle. "I have some things to finish here. I'll hail you a cab, though."

I grabbed my bonnet and pulled it over my hair, relieved to put some distance between us. "Thank you, but I can manage myself."

"No, no," he insisted as he moved toward the door. "I'll show you out."

We headed for outside, but he rushed ahead of me. By the

time I stepped out of the factory he already had a cab waiting for me and was holding open its door.

"Will I see you tomorrow for the usual sitting?" I asked before he could shut me in. He was avoiding my eyes. Thank heavens. Otherwise they would betray me, show him how a mixture of excitement and dread was whipping against my ribs like a rosebush in a windstorm.

"I may miss tomorrow's sitting," he said. He worried himself with an invisible spot on the carriage door. "I should take a few days to step away from the portrait. I've been working on it so constantly. Sometimes an artist must pull back and . . . " He swallowed. "Regain perspective."

I tied my bonnet beneath my chin and nodded. Something dormant within me had awoken and now buzzed inside me. Could I ever share the same space with James again?

"Then I shall see you once you've gained some perspective."

James gave a half nod. "Good day, Miss Sheffield."

"And to you, James."

I pulled the door shut myself. He stood in the road as the carriage clipped into motion, his sleeves still pushed to his forearms despite the cold. He was still standing there when the carriage turned the corner.

Twenty minutes later, I returned to the Carmichael home. I sat alone in the parlor and stared at James's easel in the corner, his work for the day left unfinished.

What in the world had I done?

CHAPTER 34

"Why can't we attend the exhibition tomorrow?" Winston asked.

James and I had experimented with fire, but I would not do it again. I had made my decision. Winston trusted me. Hope depended upon me. When memories of James, or of us in his studio, came unbidden, I forced my attention toward Winston—which was how I now found myself in the dining room, staring him down and holding him to our date.

"Today is the last day. If we don't see it now, we'll never have another chance."

"I have work I'm anxious to complete tonight." He studied me, his jaw working in agitation, but I held his stare squarely.

"You will always have work to do." I handed him his new beaver-fur top hat.

And I've seen so little of you since our engagement that I dream of kissing my portraitist. As much as I initially wanted to see the exhibition at the British Library for entertainment, it seemed as if our relationship, our ability to stay together, depended upon this outing.

Winston sighed. He turned to the mirror above the buffet

and put his hat on while I headed toward the foyer. "What is the exhibition about again? Stamps?"

"Handwritten documents from the royal family."

"I hope there's not a long line." He followed me to the curb to hail a cab. "I'll have to finish my work later tonight."

"Of course," I said, then clamped my mouth shut. I was in no mood to encourage discussion of the glass commission this evening. Had it not been for Winston's ridiculous work schedule, we would have seen the handwriting exhibition when it first opened, and perhaps several times, rather than fitting it in now, on the evening of the last day, a few hours before the library was to close.

Once in the carriage we quickly ran into London traffic. By the Vauxhall Bridge it was at a standstill.

"Why are we stopped?" Winston asked, as if I knew the answer. He pulled back his own curtain to see the situation before us, then behind us.

"The driver couldn't turn around if he tried. We're blocked from all sides. Wait here."

He opened his door, letting in a late-autumn draft. I pulled my shawl tighter around me and wished I had worn my peacoat.

He disappeared for five minutes then returned with a dusting of snow on his jacket and hat.

"Is it snowing out there?" I cried.

"It just started." He settled onto the bench and closed the door behind him before wiping the flakes off his shoulders.

"Why aren't we moving?"

"Someone climbed the bridge wall and is threatening to jump. A crowd has gathered to persuade him otherwise."

I pressed a hand to my mouth, suddenly embarrassed by our impatience at the queue of carriages. Winston had once told me that jumpers preferred the Vauxhall Bridge for its low wall, but I had never heard of anyone actually going through with it.

"Threatening to jump? Are you serious?"

"As death," he said, fighting a grin.

I frowned. "Perhaps you should return to the crowd and talk some sense into him." Winston could persuade a celibate priest to buy a honeymoon cottage.

"Very well," Winston sighed, lifting his collar to his neck before ducking out of the carriage once more.

I endured ten more minutes of silence. At one point, I opened the carriage door and leaned out to watch the scene unfolding, but from our position at the far end of the bridge I could see nothing.

I imagined the man on the wrong side of the bridge, his freezing fingers gripping the low wall. I could almost see his blue fingernails and the white lunulae above his cuticles. The thought of those fingers releasing their grip and the earth pulling his helpless body toward the water below twisted my insides. I buried my head in my hands and prayed that the stranger would change his mind.

The carriage began rolling again. I jerked my head up and wondered if I should call out for the driver to stop. But we were only at a slow roll, and Winston's door soon flew open. He hopped in as the carriage dragged along.

"Success!" Winston declared.

I gave a cry of relief and reached my arms out to Winston to embrace him.

"Oh Winston, thank you." I took his gloved hand in mine and planted a kiss on the back of it.

"I know this exhibition means a great deal to you," he said. "Hopefully we will arrive in ample time."

"Never mind the exhibition, thank you for helping that man. What did you say to him?"

Winston shrugged. "He wasn't capable of holding a conversation. He seemed quite unwell."

"And how did it end? Was somebody willing to take him?"

Winston frowned at me. "Take him?"

"You know, to take care of him."

He gave me a patient smile. "They would have to find him first."

"What do you mean?" I asked.

"It can take some time for a body to resurface in the Thames."

I gasped. "You mean he jumped?"

Winston glanced about the carriage. "Did I bring a copy of the *Times* with me?"

"Winston!" I clutched at his shoulder. "He jumped? That is terrible!"

"It happens all the time, my dear." As if that somehow made it any better.

"Did you try talking to him?"

"Of course I did, but he didn't understand a word I was saying. He was rambling on to himself in some strange language."

My eyes heated with tears. The carriage inched forward at the pace of a funeral procession. When we neared the midpoint of the bridge, Winston pulled his curtain to hide the view.

"Please don't worry about it, my love. This happens all the time. The men who jump from bridges are never missed."

I raised a hand to my cheek. This man had had a life, a history. He had once been a baby, born to a mother who surely loved him fiercely, even if she were no longer here to care for him. I felt a sudden urge to know more about this lost stranger, to read his story. I wondered what his penmanship looked like, how he signed his name.

"Do you think we will be able to read about him in the *Times* tomorrow?"

Winston shook his head. "If they wrote an article every time a lonely immigrant jumped from one of London's bridges, that is all we would ever read."

The Thames drifted beneath us, murky and brown. I held

my breath until we were off the bridge and was grateful when we were past the river. The remainder of our ride was spent in silence. Winston, with no paper to read, dozed off while I stared out my window.

Throughout the exhibition, with the signatures of Henry VIII, Elizabeth I, and George III spread before me, I wondered what that man's name was, which country he came from, which language he had been speaking.

Papa and Hope had never wished to leave our home at Pembrooke. They now found themselves living in France, without knowing French nor hardly another soul in the entire country.

I could not stopping thinking of them, and of the man who jumped from the bridge. And I thought of how everyone who passes away is missed and mourned by someone, even if the mourner is nowhere to be seen.

CHAPTER 35

"Don't tell Hope that we are selling Mama's bed. It would only upset her," Papa warned me as we prepared to move to London.

I was twenty years old and finally looked the adult I felt I had been for years. Papa sat at his library desk and rubbed his beard, which had grayed significantly in the eight years since Hope's birth and Mama's death.

Behind him, his library shelves held only a quarter of his book collection. He had already given away most of its volumes to friends and neighbors.

On the desk before him lay a list—in my handwriting—of everything we could sell before we moved from Pembrooke: the china, the horses, the pianoforte. Papa had added a few items to the list, the last being Mama's bed.

"We'll handle Hope's disappointment when we arrive at the townhouse and she realizes it isn't there."

"But Hope and I were born in that bed," I argued. "Mama slept in it as a child. We can't just sell it."

Hope and I had shared the bed since Mama passed. We would lie together at night and, beneath its high walnut bedposts and intricate lace canopy, she would tell me about her friends and fears, her dreams and her nightmares. Just before Hope nodded off, I would tell her a memory of Mama.

Papa sighed, puffing out the white down of his mustache. "It was your suggestion that we move in the first place."

He was right. I only convinced Papa to move after asking what would become of Hope and me with our mother dead and our father in debtor's prison. Papa was the sentimental one about leaving things behind, and I was the practical one.

But the bed was different. It was a connection to Mama that awaited Hope every night, a link to the parent she never knew.

"Couldn't we have it sent to London?" I asked, though I knew the answer before Papa pinched the bridge of his nose in frustration.

"We're bringing your mother's rocking chair and the desk. Between that and three steamer trunks, Lincoln has already told me the carriage will be overburdened. Besides, there are beds in the flat in London already. And the Thatchers offered to buy the bed and the armoire for their daughter."

"The Thatchers?" I frowned. "The Thatchers are buying the bed for Melanie?"

Papa nodded.

"Oh, Papa, anyone but Melanie. She can't sleep in Mama's bed, she's awful to Hope." I hadn't cared for that girl since a picnic last year when Hope tried to join Melanie in a game of hide-and-seek. Melanie had given Hope a smile and said sweetly, "You don't have to follow my friends and me around, Hope. You can play your own game."

Papa turned from me to finish sorting his books. The conversation was over. I stood and left him to find Hope. I would tell her three or four stories of Mama tonight. Time was running short.

* * *

ON THE DAY of our move to London, I woke up determined that Hope would not see her bed passed on to Melanie. The Thatchers' servants would arrive that morning with a cart to carry it away. I had to distract Hope during that time.

"I don't want to go," Hope pouted as she sat in the middle of the bed. She eyed the armoire, its doors flung open to reveal its empty interior. Her desktop was bare, all her books packed in her trunk along with her favorite dolls and dresses. Only her bed looked the same. I had forbidden Papa to strip it when Hope might see.

"Come, Hope, we could go anywhere. I'll take you to the ribbon shop, or to the pond to feed the ducks. We could see the Blackhursts' new foal."

"No." She flopped onto her back and draped an arm over her eyes. "I'm never leaving here. I don't want to move to London."

"We could visit the Darbys," I suggested. "Margaret would let you try on her dresses."

Hope didn't reply. I was running out of ideas.

"We could go for a carriage ride or look for milkweed in the fields. Or we could climb the bell tower."

My mouth snapped shut as soon as I made the last offer, but it was too late. Hope propped herself up on one elbow, her eyes bright for the first time since we began packing our steamers.

"I thought you were afraid of the bell tower!"

The medieval church was a ten-minute walk from Pembrooke. Its bell tower was the subject of much speculation among the youth in our town, and I was no exception. It began when a vagabond was found to be living in its staircase. From there, stories grew about all sorts of crimes that were committed in the windowless tower. Margaret Darby's brother had climbed it and swore it was pitch-black inside and smelled like the grave.

"I meant we could look at it, not climb it," I said as Hope shoved her feet into the boots beside her bed.

"You said climb it, which is what I want to do. Joseph Darby told me you can see all the way to the lake from the top of the bell tower. I've never climbed that high in my life!"

"There will be many high places to climb in London," I said. "I'll take you to the clerestory of Westminster Abbey."

Hope was already in the hallway. "Let's run all the way there."

Outside, the sky was iron gray and bulging clouds hovered above the horizon. I paused at the sight of them, wondering where we would find shelter on our walk if the rain started. No place came to mind. We had to catch the afternoon train to London and there would be no time for a warm bath should we get caught in a freezing downpour. I opened my mouth to tell this to Hope, but then I heard horse hoofs. The Thatchers' servants were rolling up with their cart, ready to carry away the bed.

"I'll race you there," I yelled to Hope as I ran ahead of her. She gave a cry of delight, then sprinted behind me. I waited until we were over the hill and Pembrooke was out of sight before I slowed.

The sky grew darker as we walked. By the time the tower peeked over the crest of the last hill, the clouds loomed graphite above us. I had started to pray the door to the bell tower would be locked, but Hope reached it first and it gave easily under her small hand. She turned toward me with a triumphant smile.

I suppressed a sigh. "We'll have to be quick to return home before the rain starts."

Leaving the door open provided just enough light to navigate the winding stone steps. Hope climbed ahead of me. I followed with a hand in front of me, both to catch Hope if she fell backward and to prevent me from running into her. By the time we reached the top, my legs were tight and burning. Hope pushed open the door to the belfry and the stairs grew a degree brighter. We skirted around the bell and peered over the tower wall. Hope's breaths were labored, but her smile pushed against her round cheeks at the sight of the valley below us.

It was a patchwork of emerald and jade. In the distance I saw the stream's serpentine trail and the lake, a pewter plate beneath the impending storm. My eyes followed the path we had taken here, curling over hill after hill until it disappeared into the distance. Estates lay scattered along the trail, Pembrooke third in line. Spring greens grew dense around our home, just as Mama had intended when she planted the garden. In the summer they would burst into deep blue blooms.

"Do you think this is how Mama sees us?" asked Hope, looking toward Pembrooke. She slipped her chilly fingers inside my palm.

"Perhaps," I said, though I wasn't sure.

"I like to think she watches us from somewhere high, perhaps like a bell tower. I hope she'll follow us to London."

I wrapped an arm around her. "Knowing Mama, she will find the tallest tower in London and watch us always." In that moment, I believed it myself.

"I wonder what it would look like if you saw us up here, from the ground," Hope said.

"I'm sure we'd look rather small."

"Which is all wrong, because I've never felt bigger in my life." The smile still had not left Hope's face. I watched her instead of Pembrooke. She was as content as I had ever seen her.

"Do you think they'll ring the bell while we are up here?"

"They only ring it when service is about to start, or for a wedding or a funeral."

"I heard they ring it to scare away demons. That's what Melanie Thatcher said."

"And she probably said it with a smile on her face," I muttered.

"What?"

"Nothing. Do you hear that?" Rain began to fall above us, fat drops that pelted the roof, intent on bursting through its tiles. A clap of thunder startled us both, and I pulled Hope toward the door. "We'll wait inside the church until the rain stops."

"I don't want to leave yet," she protested.

A silver vein of lightning cracked the sky.

"Hurry, Hope, we shouldn't be up here in a storm."

I pulled her toward the tower door. The wind whipped my hair into my eyes. We made it to the staircase and down three steps before a gust of wind slammed the top and bottom doors of the tower shut. Darkness enveloped us. Hope let out a yelp and I lost hold of her hand.

"Where are you?" My voice rang through the tower and echoed off the stone steps. Rain drummed outside, a million tapping fingers begging entry.

There was no response. I waved a hand in front of my face, but the blackness was too thick to see anything.

"Hope?" I called again, my voice rising in panic. I listened for the sound of breathing but the drum of the rain was too loud. Anyone could be in here and I would not hear them. The vagabond could be climbing the stairs toward us right now.

"Hope?" I cried again.

"I'm right here," came a quiet voice, hardly discernible under the rain. She sounded a step or two above me. "I don't dare move."

I didn't dare move either. Joseph Darby's description of the vagabond had been vivid, down to the stains on the old man's teeth and the limp hair that hung to his shoulders. I could practically see his face in front of me. If he were in here we would have no defense against him. I couldn't even see where to run.

"Do you think there's anyone else in here?" Hope's voice trembled. Suddenly it did not matter that I was frightened myself. For Hope's sake, I would have to feign courage.

"Of course there's not," I managed steadily. "Now hold out your hand. You're not to move until I find it."

It seemed an eternity until my fingers finally landed on Hope's plump arm and trailed down to her freezing hand. She gave a sliver of an exhale.

"We are going to take it one step at a time," I ordered. In the darkness I envisioned the two of us tripping, rolling down the length of the tower. "Don't put your weight down all the way until you can feel the step beneath you."

Hope moved hesitantly toward me. Once I could feel her on the step beside me, I moved ahead to the next step, then led her by the hand to join me. Our descent was slow and stilted, and at the back of my mind I feared we were moving closer and closer to the vagabond. I said nothing, though. I swallowed my fear for Hope, for I knew she was terrified enough for us both.

About thirty steps down I landed on something like a foot beneath my boot. It might have been a mere rock, or a bump in the step, but I froze.

"What is it?" Hope breathed in panic. "Should we turn around?"

We had to be halfway down by now. Please let us be at least halfway down, I thought.

"We've come this far," I said as I lowered myself onto the next step. "Let's finish what we started."

A few moments later my foot reached for another step but instead hit something vertical. The door. I laughed in relief. "It's the door. We made it, Hope." I reached out my free hand and, as it had for Hope, the door gave easily and the space before us broke into silver streaks of rain.

We dashed to the church, still hand in hand. Its doors were locked, so we huddled within the portal and watched the water fall from the sky in sheets, then in drops, and finally in sparkling pinpricks. When the rain ceased altogether the sun broke through the clouds in wide, golden bands.

As we began our walk back to Pembrooke, the church bell

began to peal from the tower behind us. Hope looked over her shoulder.

"Do you think they are announcing a wedding or a funeral?" I laughed.

Hope's face remained serious as she wrapped her free hand around my arm.

"Neither," she said quietly. "They are announcing the demons are gone. You scared them away for me."

I pinched my lips together and did not reply. I had done nothing more than keep my promise to Mama.

By the time we returned to Pembrooke, the Thatchers' cart was gone, as was Mama's bed. Papa and our driver, Lincoln, were loading our trunks into the carriage. I waited for Hope to say something about how little we were bringing, but she said nothing. She climbed into the carriage. When I settled beside her, she rested her damp bonnet against my shoulder and fell asleep.

CHAPTER 36

$\mathcal{J}$ ames had threatened to miss our Monday sitting. I hoped he would. I wanted to skip it myself. But Winston was in town and would question me if I did not come. I could not give Winston reason to suspect anything had transpired between James and me.

Besides, I told myself as I took the steps to Winston's front door, nothing had transpired. We hadn't even kissed. Never mind that our near kiss felt more like kissing than anything I had ever done with Winston. Nothing happened, I repeated to myself as I approached Winston's door.

It was Anna who answered my knock and ushered me inside.

"Where's Stanley?"

"He's hailing a carriage, Miss Sheffield."

I inhaled so deeply my corset pushed against my ribs. Stanley securing a carriage could only mean one thing. "And where's Winston?"

"He's upstairs, Miss Sheffield, preparing to catch his train."

Birmingham. And now I would be left alone with James,

should he decide to come. I should have stayed home after all. I squeezed my eyes shut. Winston was not making this any easier.

"The architect for that glass palace would like a tour of the Birmingham factory tomorrow," Anna explained, "so Mr. Carmichael is traveling there today. He said he will be down soon. If you'd like to wait in the parlor, you'll find a package for you."

"For me?"

"Your altered dress, Miss Sheffield. It arrived half an hour ago."

In the parlor I found a brown box leaning against one of the bergères. I sat down, but before I could reach for it, Winston rushed into the room, fingers twisting at his wrist as he fastened his cufflink. When he saw me he broke into a grin.

"My dear Iris. I have news for you!"

"Anna told me. Tomorrow is the day of the grand tour?"

"Yes, and I believe we will be ready, thank heavens. But that is not all. We have received word from Dr. Solemar in Nice. He has approved your family to travel for an early wedding."

My eyes widened. "You heard from him so quickly?"

"A neighbor was headed to France, so he acted as my messenger. I received the doctor's reply this morning. Isn't it wonderful? We shall have a December wedding!"

Winston pulled me into a hug as a bright feeling swelled within my chest. My family had been approved to travel. That meant Hope must be improving, for no doctor would allow a gravely ill child to cross the Channel. I squeezed Winston tightly.

"But can a wedding be arranged so quickly?" I pulled back to look at him. "That only leaves us six weeks."

"With my mother at the helm? Of course. I hope you take this as a good sign." He released me and straightened his sleeves. "She would never have agreed to pushing the wedding forward if she didn't care for you. What is that?" He eyed the box at my feet.

"It's the dress I chose for the ball. It just arrived."

"Perfect. Stanley's still preparing the carriage. Fetch Anna to help you put on the dress. I would love to see it before I leave for the station."

I was never one for parading myself around, but Winston had bought the dress, so if he wished to see me wear it I felt obliged. He rang for Anna, who followed me up the staircase. As I reached the top step a knock sounded at the front door.

James. He had come after all.

"Heavens," I muttered to myself.

"Pardon, Miss Sheffield?" Anna asked from two steps behind me.

"Heavy," I said. "This box with my dress inside is surprisingly heavy."

"Hand it to me, then. No need to strain your pretty hands," she said with the faintest touch of sarcasm.

It took ten minutes for Anna to take off my green dress and help me climb into the new white one, whose narrow skirt required I remove my crinoline. When I slipped my arms into its sleeves, we discovered that the neckline required I also change my corset. By the time Anna had fastened the last of its buttons, at least ten minutes had passed. Winston would be desperate to leave for the station, if he hadn't left already.

"Thank you, Anna," I said, starting for the guest room door.

"Wait, you've forgotten the sash," she said, lifting the long strip of lavender from the box. I ignored her and hurried into the Hall of Mirrors, sweeping past my reflections until I reached the top of the stairs.

Winston stood at the bottom of the staircase, tapping his foot impatiently on the marble floor and slipping his watch into his coat pocket.

When he looked up and saw me his foot stopped tapping.

I placed a hand on the iron railing and stepped carefully, lifting my chiffon skirt just high enough that I would not trip over it. I was a quarter of the way down the steps when I heard James's voice from the parlor.

"Mr. Carmichael, I've been meaning to ask what type of frame you would like for Miss Sheffield's portrait."

He stepped into the foyer next to Winston, who did not answer him. James followed Winston's gaze up the steps. When James's eyes finally reached me, he stood very still. His stare numbed my skin. I forced myself to continue until I reached the bottom of the staircase and stood between Winston and James. Winston circled me, studying the gown. James watched me, a strange look on his face.

"I have never seen a dress quite like it," Winston said. I turned to him, thinking that meant he did not approve, but found him smiling. "It is perfect on you. Don't you agree, James?"

James eyed me intently.

"James?" Winston repeated. "What do you think?"

"Yes," he said, his voice so hoarse he had to pause and clear his throat. "Yes, Mr. Carmichael. It is quite perfect."

"You forgot the best part," called Anna from the top of the stairs. The lavender sash lay smooth across her palms like an offering. She hurried down to us, not bothering with the railing.

"Raise your hands, Miss Sheffield." I put out my arms and she wrapped the fabric twice around my waist and secured it with a knot at the front—all as James continued to stare.

"There. Now it is perfect," she declared.

"James, I'd like Miss Sheffield painted in this dress for the portrait," Winston said. "That won't be a problem at this point, will it?"

James shook his head. "I have been working on her face mostly. The dress . . . " He swallowed. "It will do fine."

"Wonderful." Winston took my hands and kissed my cheek.

"I must dash, but I shall see you tomorrow night. James, I know it will be difficult, but please try to do her beauty justice."

Winston headed for the door without waiting for a response.

"Oh, I nearly forgot," he said, his hand already on the knob. "We are now marrying a week before Christmas and having a ball the first Friday evening in December. It will be here at the house. We'd love for you and your wife to attend, James."

"I'm sorry, Mr. Carmichael, but—"

"I insist. You will love it. And a colleague of mine wants to talk to you about a commission. Tell him, Iris, or Mr. Paxton will be sorely disappointed."

If Winston wanted James at the ball for Joseph Paxton's sake, he would stop at nothing until James agreed. And if I discouraged James from coming, Winston would wonder why.

"You must come," I said to the floor. "It would mean a great deal to us both."

James hesitated only a moment. "Then I shall be sure to attend."

"Excellent," Winston said. "I will tell Mr. Paxton when I see him tomorrow. He will be most delighted. Good day, James, and thank you."

Winston fiddled with the stubborn knob a moment before swinging the door shut behind him, leaving James and me alone together.

My eyes bounced around the foyer, looking for an escape. I glanced at the Axminster carpet below me, at the Dutch still life paintings on the wall, at the chinoiserie umbrella vase by the door—anywhere but at James, as I felt the weight of his gaze on my face.

He is making you his, James had said. As if the act of looking at someone's portrait could capture them, could make them belong to you.

When I allowed myself a glance at James, his jaw was clenched and his lips tight, but most intense were his eyes. His pupils nearly eclipsed his speckled irises. He was speaking to me with his eyes, reminding me of what we had done together, where it might have led, where it still might lead if we allowed it. My white leather boots did not move from their spot at the bottom of the stairs, but James and I looked at one another as if we could feel each other's breath on our lips, as if his hands were palming my waist again. All as the library clock ticked away the seconds of our portrait session.

We might have stayed like that for the entire morning had a voice not broken the spell.

"Well," Anna said from the stairs.

We jumped. I had forgotten she was there. James turned from me and ran a hand over the back of his neck. He shot me one last glance then headed for the parlor.

"I'll be in the kitchen if you or Mr. James need anything, Miss Sheffield." She curtsied and waited until she was to the basement steps before adding, "Though I am quite sure that the two of you will not be needing anything besides yourselves."

CHAPTER 37

"You have no idea how excited I was to hear you were holding a ball. It was just the excuse that I needed to return to London. Ever since the Queen married her cousin, I love the city at Christmastime."

Margaret slipped her arm through mine as we walked down Regent Street. A wreath of holly berries hung in the silk-shop window. Evergreen boughs draped around the jeweler's door, and green velvet bows trimmed the gas lamps. London winters were gray, but Prince Albert's German traditions now brought color to every December.

"Winter in the country, on the other hand, is nearly as bad as being a governess."

"You've never been a governess," I laughed as we passed the funeral monument shop, its urns stuffed with pine branches.

"I've imagined it, though. Where the only man around is married and your days are spent observing children who aren't your own? It would be worse than January!"

I pardoned Margaret's complaint of children, for I was grateful she had knocked on Winston's door only moments after the day's drawn-out portrait session had ended.

James had not spoken to me since the day he saw me in my ball gown and Anna caught us staring at one another in the foyer. I'd endured five sittings now in which James said nothing. I had read *Wuthering Heights* and reread *Pride and Prejudice*, but the silence was driving me madder than . . . well, a hatter, I thought, as the milliner's storefront came into view.

Margaret's insistence on a shopping trip was a welcome change. There was noise everywhere on Regent Street. A cluster of carolers stood outside the watchmaker's shop, hands deep in fur muffs as they harmonized "God Rest Ye Merry, Gentlemen." A bearded man pushed through the crowd selling almonds. A pair of boys stood in the middle of the road, each holding the end of a tube wrapped in purple paper. They counted down from three and tugged until the package pulled apart with a *crack!* and the winner raised his larger piece in the air with a rolling laugh.

Noisiest of all, of course, was Margaret, her chatter a trail that had not stopped since she arrived on Winston's porch.

"There are so many things I need to buy while I'm in the city. I have a dress for your wedding, but I need a petticoat to go with it and I'm desperate for a new pair of boots. Oh, bonnets! Would you mind if we looked?" she asked at the milliner's door.

Inside, the shop was small and warm. Behind the counter, the milliner bent over a crackling fire in the fireplace. The air was soft with the smell of feathers, furs, and well-worked leather.

"Is the wedding planned?" Margaret asked as she fingered the rim of a straw bonnet.

"Yes, Winston's mother did it all, which was just as well because I don't care for that sort of thing."

"I don't know why. It sounds like such fun."

"Winston's mother never speaks of any hobbies. I think she enjoyed the stress of having a wedding to plan." A row of ribbon samples hung from a rod on the wall. I ran my fingers along them as if they were the strings of a harp.

"Yes, she certainly seemed consumed with the idea of a wedding when I saw her."

My fingers froze. "You saw Mrs. Carmichael?"

"Didn't I tell you? She paid us a visit at the end of summer, and several of the neighbors as well. I hear she even toured Pembrooke."

My face burnt to the tips of my ears. She had toured my old home?

"Whatever for?"

Margaret shrugged. "I suppose to better understand you and your history. She asked me repeatedly about your character."

"Did she ask about my father's . . . about my family's . . . " I did not know how to ask if Mrs. Carmichael had been inquiring after my father's debts.

"No, she did not seem to care at all about your family's wealth." Or lack thereof, Margaret was too polite to add. "She only enquired after your family's reputation."

"She was making sure I was worthy of her son. What a horrid test."

"Perhaps, but you passed."

What a meddler Mrs. Carmichael was! Couldn't she trust Winston to make his own decision?

Margaret slipped on a velvet bonnet and studied herself in a mirror. "How is Winston?"

"He's fine. Busy, of course. He's anxious to hear who won the window commission for the exhibition. He thinks of little else."

"Mmm-hmm," Margaret murmured as she toyed with the angle of the bonnet. "And what about James? Do you still see him?"

"James?" I busied myself with the hat closest to me, a wide-brimmed number covered with yellow roses. "The artist, James?

Yes, occasionally. I mean, he's still painting my portrait. So I see him then."

I placed the hat on my head as casually as I could, not meeting Margaret's eyes. I could feel her watching me with the intensity of hot pokers.

"What?" I turned to her sharply.

"Something happened." She broke into a slow smile. "With the handsome artist. What was it?"

"Nothing." I pulled the hat from my head and returned it to its stand. I moved it slightly to the right, then to the left.

"You're lying." She shook her head. Her curls bounced. "I can tell because you're pretending to be interested in that hideous hat. And you're acting strangely, just like when I tried to talk to you about how handsome James is."

"I did not act strangely."

"You did." She lifted another bonnet, a rich violet one with a cream ribbon. "You refused to admit that he is handsome, as if you had something to hide."

I glanced toward the milliner's counter, afraid of being overheard, but he had disappeared into his workshop at the rear of the store. I leaned toward Margaret and whispered.

"We almost kissed."

She gasped and the bonnet fell from her hands.

"You kissed the artist?" she cried.

"Quiet," I hissed with another glance at the empty counter. "We didn't kiss, but we came very close."

"Thank heavens Mrs. Carmichael doesn't know, or you would have failed her test completely!" She picked the hat from the floor and exchanged it for an identical one that had not been dropped. "How does one *almost* kiss someone without actually doing it?"

"I don't know . . . we were alone, and he was being particularly arrogant and suggested that kissing him would ruin kissing Winston for me. And then it turned into an experiment..."

Margaret raised her brows.

"But it spooked us both and we stopped short of kissing. We haven't been able to speak to each other normally since. He just paints me in silence now."

Margaret twisted her lips in distaste. "The two of you never discussed what happened?"

"He hasn't mentioned it. If he insists on being silent, then I'll be silent too."

"How mature of you. Tell me, Iris, did you enjoy almost kissing James?"

I turned away to hide my blush, but not quickly enough.

"Iris," Margaret chided. "You have to discuss this with him."

"It would be improper for me to mention it first. And what could I possibly say?"

"James, I enjoyed almost kissing you. I would like to completely kiss you, and regularly."

"Funny," I said without smiling.

"You must discuss it, Iris. He might want you to choose. Between him and Winston.'"

"He would never do that. James has plans—plans that require Winston to pay him for painting my portrait. He needs the money to move to the continent."

Margaret frowned. "But if you did have to choose..."

"I would choose Winston," I said without bothering to think through my response. James's love was his art. He had told me so himself. I would choose Winston if I had to, but it would never come to that.

Margaret slipped the hat onto her head and tied the ribbon beneath her chin. "I don't know. Winston has his strengths, I'm sure, but I think you're just being practical to a fault."

"Said by one who is passionate to a fault."

Margaret raised a shoulder in agreement and admired her

hat in the mirror. "I'm going to buy it. What do you think?" She turned her head from one side to the other so I could see all angles of its narrow brim.

"It's lovely," I admitted. "What's it for?"

"Your wedding," she said as she marched toward the milliner's desk. "Though I'm still not convinced who the bridegroom will be."

CHAPTER 38

$\mathcal{J}$ ames continued to paint me in silence, his eyes so often fastened to the canvas before him that I wondered if he even needed me there.

Three days before the ball, however, his behavior began to change. Instead of immersing his attention in his canvas, he began flitting his eyes about the room. With the weather growing colder by the day, I had taken to sitting in front of the fireplace, where I wrote letters to Hope and Papa and read. When I raised my eyes from the page, I often caught him looking above me, as if making a point of not meeting my eyes.

When the day before the ball arrived, I was nearly giddy with relief. The next morning, Friday, would be spent preparing, with food, flowers, and musicians arriving early. There would not be time for a sitting, Winston had assured me. After the ball would come Saturday and Sunday. I was on the brink of three days of freedom from James's silent, awkward presence.

Winston came home for lunch just as James was finishing our last session before the ball.

"James," he cried as he handed his hat and coat to Stanley. "How is the portrait?"

"I am just putting the finishing touches on it now. Would you like to see it?"

I had not seen the portrait myself and had no desire to do so. Not only did its existence embarrass me, but now I feared it would constantly remind me of James. I would have to learn to ignore it when it hung in the Carmichael mansion.

"If you are pleased with the portrait, James, I have no doubt it will meet my standards," Winston declared. "I would prefer to be surprised when it is completed."

"I believe you will find it an accurate representation," James said, his gaze never nearing me.

"Are the two of you nearly finished? I have a few things to discuss with Miss Sheffield."

"My work here is done," James said.

"Excellent. I hope you enjoy your morning off tomorrow."

"Yes, Mr. Carmichael, thank you."

"Of course. We'll be much too busy preparing for the ball. You are still coming, aren't you?"

James, coming to the ball? I had forgotten Winston had invited him. I was sure that he would rather take a medical course than act on Winston's invitation to attend. I waited for a look of reluctance to cross James's face before he declined. Instead, he glanced across the room toward the fireplace, lost in thought, before nodding.

"You can depend upon it."

I suppressed a groan. Why did James wish to attend the ball? To share his awkwardness with Winston's social circle? To stare above people's heads and not say a word to them? I was sure he could not dance. I had an image of him attempting a gavotte, his head tilted to avoid eye contact with his partner, his mouth clamped shut in defiance of conversation.

"It should only take another sitting or two to finish the portrait, Mr. Carmichael."

"Perfect. Let's have it delivered the day of the wedding. Then Miss Sheffield and I can unveil it together after our ceremony."

"You will not be disappointed, Mr. Carmichael. I look forward to seeing you both at the ball tomorrow night."

"As do we," Winston assured him.

I bit my tongue and wished Winston would speak for himself.

CHAPTER 39

*T*he Hall of Mirrors was a dazzle of light. Candelabras lined the tables of food and flowers, and lit chandeliers hung across the length of the hallway. Amid their golden glow danced men in ebony suits and women in jewel-toned silks. A string quintet sat at the end of the wide marble corridor. The notes they pulled from their strings soared through the lofted ceiling, wound around the guests' dancing feet, and spilled down the staircase.

Margaret was my only guest of the one hundred people invited. We talked for a moment before Joseph Paxton's son asked her to dance, and that was the last I spoke to her all night. Winston then found me and led me from group to group, introducing me to bankers, shipping magnates, and traders. There were a few British noblemen as well, and a count from France whom Winston kept watching.

James was nowhere to be seen.

Winston's desire to include me was kind, but with each new group we approached, my dread grew. Their conversations revolved around the men's occupations or hobbies, which quickly turned into discussions of the upcoming exhibition and Winston's guaranteed commission for the glass. I was grateful when Mr. Charles Fox, the builder of the Crystal Palace, declared that he was tired of such talk, and might I find space for him on my dance card?

Mr. Fox and I began with a waltz, then a gavotte and a saraband. Mr. Fox's mastery of engineering was known to most Londoners. One did not need a fiancé obsessed with the Crystal Palace to have heard of Mr. Fox's genius. But his talent did not extend to the dance floor, and each time the orchestra began to play again I appreciated his distraction from Winston's mundane conversations less and less, as did my feet.

When Mr. Fox released me, I surveyed the room: still no sign of James. Winston was deep in conversation with Joseph Paxton. Convinced they would be awhile, I stole down the stairs. Ten minutes on the parlor sofa would not hurt anyone, and my feet would be most grateful.

I pulled the parlor doors closed behind me. Flames danced in the fireplace, casting a warm glow throughout the room. My corset was stiff around my ribs, but I was glad not to be wearing a crinoline as I sank into the sofa. I kicked off my shoes, lifted the skirt of my white dress to my knees, and stretched my toes toward the fire. The heat from the flames warmed them and a small sigh of pleasure escaped me.

"Don't let me bother you," came a voice from the corner.

I gasped and pushed down my dress.

James stood beside the window, his dark silhouette blending into the shadows.

"James!" I cried. "Do you always lurk in dark corners like that?"

As he approached me I saw he had shaved, and his dark suit was cut just right for his broad shoulders. The glass in his right hand was nearly empty, only a sliver of gold liquid left at the bottom.

"It started to snow. I was watching a man shovel outside."

My feet were still bare. I tucked them under my skirt and tried to hide my embarrassment.

"Would you care to sit?" I asked out of politeness, hoping he would decline. He paused a moment. His tired eyes took in the closed parlor doors, and he lowered himself beside me.

"Mr. Paxton is upstairs," I added, attempting to be a helpful fiancée. "Winston is anxious to introduce you."

"I don't believe I have another portrait left in me," James admitted, his words loose and slow.

"Perhaps you could give him a shovel and pretend he is one of your beloved working-class members." I nodded toward the window where he had stood. "You know, there's plenty of the lower class here in London. You don't have to travel to France to find them."

"It's not the same. Connections are important in the art world. It's best to go where there is a school of respected artists."

I was surprised at how much it pleased me to be talking to James again, even if I had his near-empty glass to thank for it.

"How soon are you moving to Barbizon?"

"After your portrait is finished. This commission will finance my trip there."

I already knew this, but his words—and the thought of my portrait making his departure possible—caused me to look away. Upstairs, a minuet slowed until one last sweep of strings rang out. A breath of silence. A flutter of applause.

"I'm glad this commission will have been so profitable for you, James." I meant to sound lighthearted, but my words came out like an accusation.

"After your portrait is done, it will make little difference to you where I live. We would not see one another anyway."

I had looked forward to a weekend without James and his silence, but I knew our time together was ending. How empty would my days be then? James angered me with his presence, and soon his absence would anger me as well.

"Perhaps the next time Winston's mother visits, her cat will knock over my portrait," I said half-heartedly. "And you will have to paint another."

"It's possible," James said. Then, more quietly, "Anything's possible."

No, I thought as I watched the flames undulate around the coal. No, some things are impossible.

"Winston has granted me permission to show your portrait at the Royal Academy's exhibition in the spring. I've always wanted a painting in it, and this will be my last opportunity."

"Only if the portrait is any good, though," I pointed out. The Academy would have to accept it first.

James was silent for a moment. "It will be good. I've known from the beginning that it would be."

I turned to him. "How do you know?"

He studied the glass in his hand, avoiding my gaze. "Sometimes, one simply knows."

"Aren't you Mr. Confidence," I muttered, but a smile threatened the corners of my lips.

James drained what was left of his drink, then cast a sideways glance at me.

"You look lovely in that gown. And your necklace is stunning. Have I seen it before?"

I picked up the jewel hanging from my neck. "No, this is the first time I've worn it. It was a gift."

"From Winston?"

"My father. It was my mother's. She had it since my parents were married but never wore it."

"Is it a ruby?"

"I believe so."

The muffled song of dancing feet and violin strings floated down the stairs. James set his glass on the side table and leaned toward me. He smelled like oil paints and brandy. When he touched the ruby in my hand his fingers brushed mine. I inhaled sharply. He looked up at me.

"Miss Sheffield," he whispered, his face softening. The fire crackled and its glow danced across James's cheeks. He placed the ruby against me, right above my sternum where the chain reached.

Suddenly I was back in James's studio. It may have been the fire, flicking shadows across his face, or the soft sound of strings floating down the stairs. Perhaps it was the snow, falling silently around the Carmichael mansion, or James's hand on my necklace, his fingertips brushing my skin. Whatever it was, it caused James to inch his face toward mine until he was so close that, even in the dim room, I could see the earliest stubble darkening his jawline, see the thin white scar on his lip.

"Miss Sheffield," he said again. His eyes dropped to my mouth. A single, taut inch separated us.

Suddenly his eyes dropped to his lap and he shook his head. "No."

The softness in his face vanished, replaced by the stone expression he always wore when he painted me. I pulled back.

"Oh." My voice came out loudly, a crack that split any remainder of the spell between us. "Oh, I am sorry. I didn't mean to—"

"It's not that, Miss Sheffield. I want to. Truly, I do."

I could not do this again. The awkward aftermath. The weighty silence. We had nearly gotten past all that, only to return to its beginning? I reached for my shoes, and shoved my foot into the left one.

"Let me explain, Miss Sheffield."

"Please, I beg you. You are drunk, and I am not in my right mind." I fought back tears of embarrassment. "Let's not discuss it any further."

He placed a hand on mine. His touch unnerved me, causing my right shoe to fall from my hand.

"We're at my engagement ball," I said as he reached for my shoe. "In my fiancé's house. And you are about to move to France. I am a fool."

"I'm not drunk, Miss Sheffield," James said crisply, his prior looseness suddenly gone. "I came tonight because there is something I have to tell you."

He stood and held out his hand. I paused before allowing myself to slide my fingers into his calloused palm. He pulled me up beside him. As soon as I was standing on my feet—unsteady on only one shoe—James dropped my hand.

"I was not just watching the man shoveling snow outside. I came in here to study Winston's portrait. Do you know who painted it?"

"No." I clenched my fingers. They pulsed from James's touch.

"Does Winston have any siblings?"

I frowned, struggling to follow. "He's an only child. Why do you ask?"

"I've been studying Winston's portrait, both tonight and during our past few sessions, and there's something you should know."

He pointed at the painting of Winston, then moved his finger down and a fraction to the left.

"There. Do you see it?"

The painting was no different than the hundred times I had seen it before. Winston stood tall in his dark suit, his hand relaxed on the empty chair before him. He looked identical to his present self, save there was no patch of white hair at his temple in the portrait.

"You're acting strange, James. What are—"

"To the left of Winston. Next to his shoulder, just above the back of the chair. Can you see it? The paint is different. The background there is a slightly different shade than everywhere else, and the paint of the chair is slightly thicker than the rest of the painting."

I stood behind James so I could follow his finger. He was right.

"And that is important because . . . "

James turned to me. His eyebrows furrowed.

"Miss Sheffield," he said. His voice was intense but low, as if he feared being overheard. "Don't you understand? The artist painted over it. Painted something out of the portrait. Some*one*, that is."

I shook my head. "You're not making any sense."

"What I'm trying to tell you," he said, "is that there used to be another person in this painting."

CHAPTER 40

I stared at Winston's portrait, the area where the background was slightly paler than the rest, and the chair below it slightly thicker.

"What do you mean, there was another person in the painting?"

"You can tell," James insisted. "Originally someone must have sat in front of Winston. The artist hid it well by reworking the chair, but see how much thicker it made the paint. And the artist painted out the sitter's head by turning it into the background, but he made it a shade too light."

"That doesn't make any sense," I said. "Winston is an only child. And his mother and father already had their own portraits painted. Who else could have been in his portrait?"

James shot a meaningful glance toward the front door. Surely he was thinking of beyond the door, to the porch, where he had caught me with Penelope's journal.

"Oh, please," I hissed. "Now you are suspicious of Winston? You have been defending him all this time."

"That was before I knew he had his portrait painted with someone else."

"You and your lofty ideals of portraits. Memorializing in paint and all that." I tried to make my tone light, but his suggestion scared me. It awoke the seed of suspicion I'd felt since the day I asked Winston about Penelope.

"All right, then. Who else? Who could possibly have been painted with him besides Penelope?"

"A cousin, perhaps?" My voice sounded distant.

"Do you know any of his cousins?"

Actually, I knew he had none, but I needed to buy myself time. I just needed time to think this through.

"Come now, look at how much thicker the paint is in this spot. It's been completely worked over. What other explanation is there?"

My head shook subtly, a tremor beyond my control. "But I asked him about Penelope. He told me that he didn't love her. He never loved her. He said she was . . . " What was the word he had used? "Inconsequential."

My eyes shifted toward Winston's portrait. It was so large, and now the empty chair in it dominated my attention. Even if James were wrong, I would always see the chair first and Winston second when I looked at it. Could I ignore it the rest of my life? My brain began to pound. I squeezed the bridge of my nose.

"Miss Sheffield," James said. "You have been desperate to discover more about Penelope since you discovered her journal. Why are you so quick to dismiss that she might once have been in this painting?"

Because it was one thing if Winston failed to mention someone from his past. It was quite another if he had lied about how close they actually were.

James studied me, trying to read in my face the words I refused to speak.

"Of course," James said slowly, "perhaps it's best to ignore it. After all, he is one of London's richest bachelors."

I forgot the headache forming behind my eyes and narrowed them at James. "What does that mean?"

"What will you do if there *are* shadows in his past, Miss Sheffield? Will you end your engagement? Because the evidence suggests there is at least one."

I snapped my mouth shut, though the thought of a second sitter was not what silenced me. It was the image of Hope in a French-speaking town, taking a walk along the Cote d'Azur, her bare toes sinking into the sand, the sea air sweeping deep into her lungs.

This image caused me to say to James, in a voice as steady as I could manage, "I would appreciate it if you would not mention Winston's portrait to me again, or to anyone else, for that matter."

James watched me. "You're not going to question Winston about it?"

I had no intention of asking Winston about the portrait, but I did not need to tell James as much. All I needed, in that moment, was to be alone.

"If you will please excuse me, James, I am feeling unwell," I said evenly. "And I believe it would be wise if we skipped our sitting on Monday."

"We skipped our sitting yesterday. I promised Winston I would complete the portrait soon."

"I'm sure you can manage without me. You hardly look at me during our sittings anyway."

"Miss Sheffield, I—"

"Mr. Carmichael will pay you for Monday regardless. I know you are anxious for the money so you can depart for France."

I reached out my hand for my shoe, which James still held, but he glared at me and made no motion to return it. I turned on my heel and marched out of the parlor without it, my steps uneven. I could feel his stare on my back as I walked away. I nearly made it out of the room before he spoke.

"It must be nice," he said to my back. "Having access to Winston's money. That is worth something, even if his record isn't pristine."

I spun around so fast I nearly tripped over my single shoe. "What did you say?"

"You picked up the journal." James advanced toward me. "Why did you start digging into his past if you planned to do nothing about it?"

"I must be misunderstanding you, James, because it seems you are implying that I am only marrying Winston for his money."

James tossed the shoe to me. "If it fits."

My eyes widened. "How dare you! You know nothing about me, or my situation—"

"I know enough about Winston and *his* situation to draw a well-informed conclusion."

My breaths were shrinking. "And the only reason anyone would marry Winston would be for his money, is that right?"

"I only know that your family is old money that ran dry." He stepped closer toward me. "Now you're returning to wealth thanks to a man you trust so little you are reading journal entries about him behind his back."

I turned from him and headed for the closed parlor doors. "You are nothing more than a guest here. I do not have to answer to you."

"Ah, there we have it," he said. "All talk of friendship turns to smoke when you don't like what I have to say."

"Get out," I said through clenched teeth.

"Of course! Because this mansion is as good as yours. Marriage to a liar is a small price to pay for it."

I yanked open the parlor doors and the sounds from upstairs grew: the quartet playing a polonaise; laughter; the gentle thump of dancing feet. James bowed before brushing past me into the foyer. I followed him for three steps.

"I'll see myself out," he said without looking back. He pulled open the front door, struggling only for a moment with the knob, and slammed it shut behind him.

The polonaise ended and the guests applauded.

I stayed frozen in place, one shoe on my left foot, the other clenched in my hand. I stared at the closed door and imagined James pulling his jacket tight around him in the snowy London night as he walked down Kennington Road and disappeared around the corner. I do not know how long I stood there, staring at the door, knuckles white around my shoe, but by the time I finally forced myself back to the party the dancing was over.

CHAPTER 41

I could not look at Winston's portrait. A mere glance at it made my stomach roll. The questions James had posed—*Who else could it be? What other explanation is there?*—twisted inside of me and threatened to burst their way out. If only I could ignore them, could pretend James had never told me of the second sitter in the painting. If only I could forget everything.

Such were my thoughts as I watched Winston at supper, his newspaper open before him like a map of his life.

As he turned the page, I envisioned him a month from now, sitting in his usual chair at the head of the table, his nose in the latest newspaper, scouring it for an update on the palace as his portrait sneered at us from the next room. He would be exactly as he was now, except he would be my husband.

I could see him ten years from now, ebony hair dusted with gray, and twenty years from now, the lines between his brows deep and permanent like those in his father's portrait. I imagined watching him at supper every evening for the rest of my life, trying to still the questions beating inside me like a butterfly caught on the wrong side of a pane: questions that would hammer against me if I kept them in, bruising me day after day until I could stand them no more.

I waited until Stanley took away our plates before clearing my throat.

"May I speak with you, Winston?"

He did not look up from his paper.

"Winston?" I said a bit more loudly.

"Yes, darling?" He still did not raise his eyes.

"There's something important I would like to discuss with you—perhaps over some tea in the conservatory?"

Winston lifted his head but his eyes were hazy, his thoughts still in the article.

"Of course," he said. He folded the paper and tucked it beneath his arm. "I'll be there in a moment." He pushed back his dining chair and crossed the parlor toward his library, then shut himself in without another glance in my direction.

When I opened the double glass doors to the conservatory, I was greeted by a blast of crisp winter air. The last light of day swept gray through the space. I sat in one of the wicker chairs, but my nerves were too charged to hold still. Upon the table beside me sat a bowl of pine cones I had collected from my walks through the Vauxhall Garden. I placed the bowl on the floor to make room for the tea and walked back to the double glass doors.

There was no sign of Winston.

Many of my favorite flowers in the conservatory had died a month or two ago, but I had replaced the daylilies and roses with pots of poinsettias and miniature firs. I busied myself with rearranging the poinsettias until there were a few in every corner, then lined my pots of tangled aloe vera along the back of the house, where they could hug the bricks for warmth.

Stanley brought the tea, but there was still no Winston. What was taking him so long? The sooner he arrived, the sooner we could have this conversation behind us. I sat again, eased the journal from my pocket, and opened to the first page. I had opened to it so many times it now lay flat on its own.

The door creaked behind me. I snapped the book shut and shoved it beneath my dress.

Winston stood in the doorway, his newspaper wedged beneath his arm and a perplexed look on his face. His ebony hair, always smooth and in place, was disheveled. He came toward me, the hazy look still in his eyes.

He lowered himself into his chair, neither looking at me nor addressing me. I served the tea, the tremble in my hand nearly imperceptible. After I poured, I waited. Winston did not move. Aside from a branch scraping against the window, all was silent. Neither of us touched our teacups.

"I'm sorry," Winston said with a shake of his head. "I'm a bit distracted this evening. Was there something you wished to discuss?"

I fingered the handle on my teacup. "I was just . . . I was wondering . . . "

The timing wasn't right. Winston was too distracted. As soon as I said the name *Penelope* it would be an unforeseen blow to him, hard and painful. I should wait to bring it up on a different day. But I was tired of waiting. The wedding was nearing, and I had waited for answers long enough. He owed me the truth, and now.

"The conservatory is so lovely," I said, thinking I would ease him into the subject. "I can't believe your father built it."

"My father?" Winston gazed toward the ceiling, an intersection of angled windows framed in iron the shape of a star. "Yes. He built it right after he bought the house. It was an experiment."

Winston was speaking about his father, and there was more he had to say. He studied his father's handiwork, choosing his words carefully.

"Father wanted to prove his skill as a glassmaker, though he had never built a greenhouse before. He asked Paxton to design this and told him he had spare glass to make it. This was when Paxton was designing the Great Conservatory at Chatsworth, and my father was desperate to provide the glass for it. He didn't tell me that, of course."

Winston rubbed his nose, followed by a quick sniff.

"He would never admit to being desperate for anything. But I could tell. He obsessed over it. He wanted it more than anything. Everyone around him was a distraction to his goal: my mother, me. He worked at his dream relentlessly, desperate to make it work. And then . . . "

The haze in his eyes cleared and Winston looked at me.

"He did it. Paxton loved this project." He gestured around the room. "So much that he designed the Great Conservatory after it and used Carmichael Glass for its windows. And now the Great Conservatory is the largest conservatory in the world."

"I wish I could have met your father." I had thought it often before. It might have helped me better understand Winston.

"My father was a success story." Winston paused. "And he never let me forget it."

"Pardon?"

"He had to be sure that I understood all he had accomplished, all he had prepared for me. All that I risked losing if I chose poorly. He reminded me of it nearly every day that he lived here."

Winston stared through the tea set between us.

"Surely that can't be true," I said. "He must have been so proud of you, and would be now if he could see you."

Winston said nothing. I took it as my chance to shift the conversation.

"I was actually admiring the portrait of your father this morning," I said.

"The portrait of my father," Winston repeated in a faraway voice.

"Was it done by the same artist who painted your portrait?"

"I don't recall," Winston said, shifting in his seat. "He had it painted at the factory, while he was working. He was rarely at home."

I ran my finger around the edge of my teacup.

"Your portrait, I noticed . . . " I lifted my teacup and took a sip to buy myself time. "I noticed that the way you are positioned in it . . . "

I paused. The conservatory grew still. I finally had Winston's attention. I could feel that he was looking at me, even as I studied the teacup in my hand.

I could often sense when Winston was looking at me.

"Yes?"

I set my teacup down but did not release my hold on it. I pressed my thumb into its handle, grounding myself, gathering my courage.

"Iris."

I looked up. Winston's eyes were fast upon me. When he spoke, his words were slow and measured.

"Tell me why you asked me in here."

His eyes held mine, and I stared back, resisting the urge to swallow before I spoke.

"Before we are married, Winston, I need you to tell me about your past—without leaving anything out."

Winston sat still in his chair, his mind examining my words, deciding what to do with them. Or was he thinking of something else? Was he considering all he had done for me, all he had done for Hope? Perhaps he was imagining the flat in Nice, which he had never stepped foot in yet bought so willingly for my sister, and put in my father's name so his mother would never know.

"You need me to tell you about my past," he repeated slowly.

"Yes." I spoke evenly despite the hammering in my heart. "I realize you had an entire life in London before I moved here and met you. I know there was someone in your past. I just need you to be honest with me about her."

Winston's face was stone, as calm as ever. When he spoke, though, his voice was taut.

"Are you questioning my loyalty to you?" he asked. "Is that what this is about?"

"Of course not," I said quickly. "You've never given me any reason—"

"You think there is something in my past that makes me unsuitable for you?"

"That's not what I said."

"Because my past, I can assure you, is most reputable. In fact, it might be all I have."

He stood and pulled the newspaper from beneath his arm, then tossed it onto the tea set so the china rattled.

Great Exhibition plans continue, the headline read. *Paxton meets again with Chance Brothers Glass.*

"This," he hissed, index finger on the headline, "this is *my* Great Conservatory. The Crystal Palace is my opportunity—probably my only opportunity—to prove myself worthy of my father's legacy. And what is Paxton doing? He is making plans with the Chance Brothers. Fox warned me about this last night at the ball, but I assured him he was misinformed. Everything I have been working for, all my time spent in Birmingham, away from you, apparently means nothing to Paxton. And now, on top of this unfortunate news, I have to convince my fiancée that I am worthy of her."

Winston turned toward the doorway, knocking over the orchid at our feet. A crack sounded, quick and clean, as its blue and white pot hit the brick wall.

"Winston, stop."

Without thinking, I stood and reached for his hand. The journal fell from my skirt and landed with a soft thud at our feet.

One small step and I could have hidden it beneath my dress, but Winston saw it before I had the chance. It lay open to its first written page, the spine bent with my obsession.

Journal of Miss Penelope Ann Bromley, 1849.

Winston pulled his hand from mine and stared at the journal: such a small book, yet its writing screamed throughout the room.

He bent down slowly and picked up the journal. He read the title page, then turned until he found its single, short entry. His eyes scrolled across the words once, and then he turned back to the beginning and read it again. He shuffled through the rest of the empty pages until he reached the journal's end and was sure there was no more to be seen.

When he had finished, he closed it carefully, as if its pages were as delicate as onionskin. When he spoke, his voice was hardly above a whisper.

"Is this the source of your concern?"

I did not answer.

"You find a journal from someone you've never met, and you trust it over everything we've shared?"

His eyelids glistened. He turned from me, but I followed him out of the conservatory, into the house and through the hallway.

"Please, Winston." I followed him into the parlor. "I only wondered—"

"Wondered what, Iris?" He stopped in front of the fireplace. Its flames cast dancing shadows across his cheek. "If I'm courting another woman? If I'm hiding her from you?"

"No, it's not like that." Tears burnt at the back of my eyes. "I only wondered what happened. She seems to have been so in love with you."

Winston's eyes flicked toward his portrait above the mantel, only for an instant. His gaze shifted to the fire, his black eyes brightened by the flames.

"Please," I said again. "I know you don't want to discuss this with me, but we are to be married. If there had been someone this wrapped up in my past, I would have told you."

Winston stared into the fire, selecting his words.

"My father did not find success until I was fifteen years old," he finally began. "He uprooted me from my school and friends to pursue his business. I resented him for it, but he did not care. He cared for little other than his business and reputation. I rebelled and began pursuing everything of which I knew he would not approve. And everyone."

He did not have to say Penelope's name for me to know he meant her.

"At first my father was livid about my behavior. He forbade me. He threatened me. He was unkind toward me, but at least I had his attention."

Above the glowing fire, Andrew Carmichael stared down at us. I had always been so eager to learn of him. Now, as Winston finally shared details, I missed my ignorance.

"All of that changed when the demand for his glass outgrew the London factory and he decided to open a second factory in Birmingham. He bought a flat there, intending to return home to London on weekends, but he never did. The Birmingham factory became his obsession. He had more space there than he ever could have in London and he kept making it bigger and bigger. He was building the factory, but also himself, his legacy. It justified his existence. He poured himself into it. He went from wishing to control me to caring nothing about me. I only saw my father once in the last two years of his life."

Winston's eyelids burned red against the whites of his eyes. He turned Penelope's journal in his hands, staring through it.

"I continued pursuing everything my father disapproved of and keeping company that had upset him. I even toyed with the idea of marrying someone in part because I knew my father would disapprove of her. But Father was no longer around to care, and I began to realize I did not want for myself what I was pursuing."

Now that he had started to speak his words quickened and tumbled from him.

"Penelope was a far cry from what I had always envisioned for myself. Yet I was caught in her inertia, unable to break the habits I had formed. I was trapped. I did not really wish to marry Penelope, but she had me under a type of spell, you might say. I did not have it in me to break it. I needed to change my direction, but I was barreling so quickly down the path I had chosen that nothing short of a collision could stop me. And then..."

Winston's face sank. He looked through the journal with dull eyes.

"And then your father died," I whispered.

Winston blinked hard. "It should have made little difference. He had been dead to me for two years, or so it seemed. But his death haunted me. He had come home one weekend, miraculously, but I was not here. I was with . . . her. Mother told me that Father came home and . . . " He swallowed and tried again. "He came home and his heart gave out. If I had not been with her—the woman he told me to stay away from—I could have seen him one last time, perhaps even righted things between us."

Winston pressed his lips together.

"He died disappointed in me, before I had a chance to redeem myself," he said. "So I threw myself into his business and have tried to build it—and myself—into something of which he would be proud."

This explained his obsession with the commission, all his waking hours poured into courting Paxton, perfecting things in Birmingham. It did not excuse all he had withheld from me, but it explained it.

He still had not admitted Penelope's presence in the portrait, but that seemed beside the point now. Instead of forcing him to confess that final detail I asked, "Did you love Penelope? Tell me the truth, Winston."

"No," he said quickly. "Looking back, it was never love. I can't believe I once entertained the idea of marrying her. She brought out the worst in me, and I in her. She was selfish and solitary, and I had always wanted someone maternal, companionable. I gave up on that search when I spent time with Penelope. But then, one day on a train to London . . . "

Winston looked at me.

"I found exactly what I had been searching for. And I recognized it the instant I saw it. Iris, you caused me to forget about Penelope completely. Until now."

He studied the journal in his hands, thumbed its gold fleur-de-lis. Perhaps he was remembering the last time he saw Penelope, the scent of her skin, his favorite things about her. The journal had brought her back from wherever she was.

"Penelope brought me nothing but anguish. I wish never to remember her again."

He lifted the journal a few inches in his hand and, with a swift flick of his wrist, threw it into the fireplace. I stood mesmerized, watching the flames lick at the small book. The stench of burning leather hit me as Winston brushed past me and out of the room. He was gone before the flames gained their momentum on the journal, but I could not pull my eyes from Penelope's history as it glowed orange, then blackened to crisps, and finally crumbled to ashes.

CHAPTER 42

*W*inston and I met a little over a year ago aboard a train, on the day we moved to London.

Papa, Hope, and I had stayed at Pembrooke nearly eight years without Mama. My time was spent caring for Hope and attempting to maintain an estate large enough to keep a full staff occupied. My grief for my mother changed from a stabbing pain in the middle of my heart to a constant ache. It was this grief that drove me to spend every waking moment mothering my sister or trying to keep the house and its thirteen rooms in order. Papa, who distracted himself from his own grief with constant reading, was loving but of little help.

When Papa confided in me the extent of our debts, I seized the opportunity. It pained me to persuade him to sell the estate and move to our townhouse in London. I loved Pembrooke as much as Papa did—Mama was wrapped up in Pembrooke. But it was more than I could manage on my own. Papa sold the estate and I tried to quiet my mother's voice in my head, her disappointment that we were leaving the home that had been in her family for generations.

We caught the late-morning train to London. Hope began in

the seat next to Papa but eventually fell asleep in his arms. I sat in front of them by the window, watching the countryside slide by in summer hues of gold and yellow.

Someone took the seat beside me. I assumed it was Papa, so it was several moments before I looked at him. Once I did, though, he had my full attention.

Winston Carmichael, as he introduced himself, lived in London and was returning from a visit to his aunt. He apologized for his presumptuousness in introducing himself, but his mother's birthday was approaching, and he wondered where I had bought my hat. Only later, when I had met his mother, did I realize what a fabrication this was, for the hat I wore was pale blue, a color far beyond the scope of Mrs. Carmichael's taste.

Winston did not pull his eyes from me the remainder of the voyage. He spoke comfortably, asking me about Papa and Hope, but mostly about myself.

It was raining when we arrived in London.

"I insist on giving you a ride," he said as we disembarked the train. "What's your destination?"

"Near Exhibition Road," I told him. "Across from Kensington Gardens."

"I know the area well. Have you lived there long?"

"The townhouse has been in our family for years, but it has been some time since we visited."

He secured a carriage and waited for us to file inside. The driver tied our trunks to the roof and the back of the cab. Papa leaned out of the window, ignoring the rain and taking in the peddlers and the beggars and the muck on the roads.

"It's worse than the last time we came," he informed me, still not bringing his head inside.

I smiled apologetically at Winston, but he did not notice my father's behavior. He was in the middle of a conversation with Hope who, just shy of eight years old, had more energy than anyone I knew. Rejuvenated by her nap on the train, she was practically bouncing in her seat as she spoke to Winston.

"The painted lady caterpillar is rather plain, but I think that makes it more special, don't you? The monarch caterpillar is bright yellow and black, so you'd expect it to change into something colorful. But an ugly brown caterpillar? It's a true miracle when *that* becomes something beautiful."

"Yes, I agree completely," Winston mused, keeping his face serious. "But what of the tiger swallowtail caterpillar?"

Hope frowned. "The tiger swallowtail?"

"Surely you've seen one?"

Hope shook her head, the motion sending her curls bouncing around her cheeks.

"You have seen one," I told Hope. "Last year there were a few in the garden."

"I don't remember ever seeing them," insisted Hope.

"We shall have to remedy that," Winston said. "The tiger swallowtail starts out as green as a fern leaf, but when it becomes a butterfly, its wings are black and yellow. It is, in my opinion, the most beautiful . . . " He looked up at me and smiled. "The most beautiful of them all."

My eyes darted away and heat rose in my cheeks.

"Are there many to be seen in London?" Hope asked.

"No," Winston admitted, "I'm afraid not. But I'll make sure you see one. Even if I must leave the city to track one down and catch it myself."

We rolled to a stop in front of our townhouse. The driver carried our trunks to the front door. Winston and I lingered by the carriage, shielded by the umbrella he had lent me.

"You'll need this," I said, pushing the wooden handle toward him.

"Keep it," he said. "I'll come for it another day, which will give me an excuse to call on you. If that would please you."

I blushed again. "That would please me very much. We could

take a walk through the gardens." Feeling emboldened by his attention I added, "Tomorrow, perhaps?"

"Unfortunately, I have to attend the theater tomorrow," he said. "But perhaps the day after?"

Two days later we strolled through Kensington Gardens together, past the Great Tree and the Orangery and the palace. I had taken many walks with Papa and Hope in the country, Hope always running ahead, Papa trailing behind with his nose in a book. I was always suspended between them, making sure neither became lost.

Walking with Winston was different. He offered me his arm, led me around puddles, and pulled me toward him when a Saint Bernard ran in our direction. He asked how I liked London. When I told him I found the pollution exhausting he snorted at my unintentional joke and I, in turn, erupted into unladylike laughter. How pleasant a stroll is with a friend, I realized: one doesn't worry about the people ahead or behind, but can just enjoy the person beside.

* * *

Now I stood alone before the parlor fireplace, Winston having disappeared and the journal a pile of ashes before me. I believed Winston—my dearest friend—had stopped seeing Penelope because he met me, and I knew I should find that reassuring. I tried to tell myself that our connection was so strong that he altered his plans and ended his relationship with Penelope so he could be with me.

And yet, the knowledge made me uneasy. The thought of Winston discarding Penelope so easily, much as he tossed her journal into the fire . . .

It left me feeling less sure of my relationship with him, not more.

CHAPTER 43

$\mathcal{A}$nna found me in the parlor, staring into the fireplace. "Miss Sheffield?" Her thin arms strained under the weight of a coal bucket. "Miss Sheffield, are you all right?"

I continued to watch the flames die, their task of consuming the journal complete.

She set the bucket on the hearth and glanced toward the empty foyer, then joined me in front of the fireplace. We stood in silence, watching the pitiful flames together, the room growing chill.

Anna cleared her throat. "I heard some of your conversation with Mr. Carmichael. I apologize. I did not mean to eavesdrop."

"It's all right, Anna."

I did not wish to speak with her now. I needed time with everything Winston had told me—his complicated relationship with his father, with Penelope—and how resolutely he had kept it all from me. I understood Winston better now, but that did not resolve my feelings around all he had withheld.

"I have not known the Carmichaels long," she admitted, blinking her pale lashes. "I have known you for even less time.

So perhaps it is not my place to speak. But please, Miss Sheffield, do be careful."

Mama had asked me before she passed to be careful with Hope. I thought of how careful meant not only cautious, but also full of care, which was exactly how I approached every decision with my sister.

"My mother passed away eight years ago," I said. "She died when my sister, Hope, was born. I promised her I would take care of Hope. When I made that promise, her face grew peaceful, as if the worry of Hope was what was hurting her more than anything. I made the promise and she looked happy again. Not twenty minutes later she passed away."

Suddenly I longed to be near Hope, to care for her in person. The wedding could not come quickly enough, if it brought us together again. And if learning to ignore Winston's portrait allowed me to care for Hope, then that was exactly what I would have to do.

"We go to great extremes for those we love, don't we, Miss Sheffield?"

CHAPTER 44

"*O*nly three more days until the wedding," Winston announced as I climbed into the carriage. He leaned toward me for a kiss and I complied. Ever since our discussion about Penelope, Winston and I were a bit unsure around each other, as if we feared the other were made of glass. I hoped the feeling would fade, and soon.

I forced a smile and held up the fur muff warming my hands. "I bundled up as best I could."

Winston frowned. "I hope you're wearing gloves beneath that. You will need your hands free."

"Where are we going?"

He shook his head. "I already told you, my dear, it is a surprise. I cleared my morning because I wanted to spend a little time with you before the stress of the wedding on Saturday."

But as we rolled closer to Hyde Park, my stomach dropped.

"We're checking on the progress of the exhibition," I said, trying to hide my disappointment. Our day of amusement was to center around Winston's obsession. Though Paxton had met multiple times with Chance Brothers, he was yet to make a final decision and Winston was doing his best to remain optimistic.

"No, the Crystal Palace is not our destination today. Here, open this."

He pulled a box from the floor. Inside I found a pair of ice skates, their leather a deep coffee brown.

"Ice skating." I tried to mask the disappointment in my voice.

"I know you refused to go when I last took Hope, but I promise to hold your hand the entire time. The ice is finally thick enough for skating. You will love it."

Winston was trying: trying to make up for our conversation in the conservatory and the parlor. Neither of us had mentioned it since—I was quite sure we would never discuss Penelope again—but he was doing his best to make things right. I forced a smile as I pulled the bladed boots from the box.

It was early and we were the first people on the Serpentine. My ankles wobbled in my new skates, and I was grateful Winston was the only witness to my clumsiness.

"There, you're getting it. Just keep pushing forward."

I pushed my left leg forward, then the right, but the act of shifting my weight caused my ankle to topple.

"Easy!" Winston caught my free arm before I could fall.

"Perhaps we should go back to your home," I suggested, grabbing onto him as if the ice were pulling at me. "Have a cup of tea in front of the fire?"

"Nonsense. You're doing wonderfully. That was at least five minutes without falling."

Despite my poor performance on the ice, the park was pleasant. The air was crisp with cold and inviting with the scent of pine. Plump clouds hung overhead and, with the trees in the distance all around us, one could almost pretend not to be in the middle of the city.

Winston held my arm so firmly, I forgot to be afraid of the ice beneath me for a moment. I gave him a small smile and freed one hand to adjust the scarf around his neck. Perhaps this outing was just what we needed after our difficult discussion. I reached my gloved hand hesitantly to his chin, and then to his cheek. I recalled when he proposed to me in the park, how he spun me around as if we were the only two people in the world.

"Look at that," he murmured, his eyes following something behind me. I turned to see nothing out of the ordinary. A group of children, lacing their skates. Behind them, two black carriages rolled along the dirt path.

"That second carriage. It's Paxton's."

It looked like any other black carriage. There was nothing remarkable about it. But Winston continued to follow it with squinted eyes.

"It has the Paxton family crest on it. Don't you see the two doves?"

Rather than looking at the doves I widened my eyes at Winston, probably with the expression of a pigeon, as James would say. I could not help myself. It constantly surprised me how obsessed Winston was with everything about the commission.

"Paxton is heading toward the construction site. I'm sure of it. I have been desperate for an update on his thoughts."

He added, as I knew he would, "Would you mind if I hurried over there?"

And what of your promise to stay by my side, I wanted to ask. But I knew the glass commission would be announced any day, and as I still wanted us to mend things, I bit back my disappointment.

"Of course I don't mind. Would you like to walk over there now?"

"I won't make you come. I can hurry over there quickly by myself and be back in fifteen minutes—if you are sure you don't mind?" he asked, his lips spreading into an uncertain smile.

"Go ahead. I will be fine here."

Winston kissed my numb nose then glided toward the edge of the pond.

"Don't fall without me!" he called.

"I promise not to move!"

He sat on the iron bench where we had left our shoes and made a quick change. Then he chased after a hansom cab rolling slowly down the dirt path. I wrapped my arms around myself and watched him until he climbed into the cab. It rolled past a cluster of trees and out of sight.

The crowd on the Serpentine grew—couples holding hands, children practicing figure eights. I held my ground and willed my ankles to stay straight.

"Miss Sheffield?" came a voice from behind me.

I knew its source before I turned my head.

There stood James at the edge of the ice. He wore a long brown coat, its wooden buttons fastened up to the plaid scarf around his neck. He pushed his shoulders back, as if he knew I were studying him, the artist suddenly the subject.

"I need to speak with you," he yelled. He beckoned me toward him. I looked down at the ice around me. I did not dare move.

"I'm not steady on skates!" I yelled over a group of children gliding around me. A girl in mousy brown braids sped past me and nearly knocked me over. My arms windmilled, my bladed feet jerking forward again and again until I regained my balance.

"Obviously," James called. "I'll come to you."

"No, I can manage. Just let me gather my courage."

"I don't want to be responsible for injuring you three days before your wedding. Stay there," he commanded.

The girl in the braids turned around and headed in my direction again. She pushed her way against the stream of skaters, gathering speed as she neared me. I hurried forward to give her space to pass behind me. She did, with room to spare, but my panic sent me diving too far forward and my left skate caught on my dress. My ankle bent in an impossible manner as I crashed onto the ice.

"Miss Sheffield, are you all right?"

I gulped a sharp breath of wintry air, unable to speak. Hot-white pain shot from my ankle and through my leg.

"Put your arms around my neck."

"I'm fine," I breathed, "I don't need—"

"For heaven's sake, Miss Sheffield, you're injured. Let me help you."

I pressed my lips together as James carried me to the iron bench where my shoes sat. I could think of nothing but the relentless throbbing inside my left skate. He set me on one end of the bench and lowered himself onto the other.

"May I see it?" he asked.

"I don't think I can lift it."

He gently lifted my legs onto the bench so my heavy skates lay in his lap.

"The blades. They'll rip your pants," I said between breaths.

"What a shame," he said drily. "I was hoping these pants would impress you." He lifted my skirt enough to expose my skates and a sharp chill hit my legs.

"I'm going to remove your left skate, if I have your permission."

Stop bothering with the politeness and make the pain stop, I wanted to scream.

He untied my skate with as much care as if he were unswaddling a sleeping infant. It made me think of how his mother had wished him to become a doctor. He loosened the laces gently and opened the boot as much as he could. When he began slowly pulling it off my foot, I groaned in pain.

"I'm sorry," he said with a frown. "I fear it's about to swell, though. You can squeeze my arm if you'd like. Perhaps inflicting pain on me would make you feel better."

"Quite likely," I muttered as I wrapped my hand around a rung of the bench.

Once he had my skate off, he took my socked foot in both his hands and bent it gently toward me. I gritted my teeth.

"Does this hurt as well?" he asked as he bent it away from me.

Further gritting.

"Side to side?"

I nodded, unable to form words. Best he had not become a doctor. He was only making the pain worse.

When James stopped moving my ankle, I felt a moment of relief. I looked down. His hands were still, his palms cupping either side of my foot. Our eyes met. He did not remove his hands. Our time in his studio threatened its way forward in my mind.

"Did you come here to skate?" I asked, pushing the memory back.

"I came to tell you that the painting is nearly complete. I should be able to finish the rest from my studio."

"Oh." A sliver of ice melted off my skates, dripping from the blade and becoming a dark circle above James's knee. "I suppose that means that we are—"

"Finished," he said. Another drip and the spot grew. "You will not need to endure my presence any longer."

The ice was busy with skaters now, men in black hats and women in fur-collared coats. The girl with the braids stood still in the middle of the pond, perhaps tired from so many close calls. We sat far enough away that the skaters' noise was a low hum, a neutral backdrop to our words. James's palms were warm over my stockings.

"Perhaps I shall see you when you come to borrow the portrait—to display it with the Academy in the spring."

"I don't think you will see me then either, Miss Sheffield," he said softly.

"Why not?" I knew why but wanted to hear his answer.

"I don't believe it would be wise."

Suddenly a voice boomed from behind.

"Iris!"

Winston ran toward us. James slipped his hands off my ankle. I tried to pull my foot toward me, but the pain was too much.

"What is wrong, darling?" Winston crouched in front of the bench, his eyes darting between James and me.

"It's my ankle," I said quickly. "I fear I've sprained it. I did not last five minutes without you before I fell."

He placed a hand on my cheek. "I'm so sorry, my dear. I never should have left you."

He glanced at James on the bench.

"James, what brings you here?"

"I stopped by your home and Anna said I would find you here." He rose from the bench. "I came to tell you that the portrait is nearly done and can be delivered as early as your wedding day."

"James helped me to the bench after I fell," I added.

"Thank you for your assistance," Winston said. "And for all your work on the portrait. You can have it sent to the house on Saturday, anytime after three o'clock. By then there should be someone at the house to receive it."

James nodded. "Would you like me to fetch a carriage for you and Miss Sheffield?"

"That would be much appreciated," Winston said. "Have the driver pull up as close as he can."

"Of course. Good day, Mr. Carmichael." James's eyes flicked toward me. "Miss Sheffield."

Winston took James's spot on the bench and reached for my foot. I did not allow myself to watch James cross the park toward the queue of cabs for hire. Instead, I studied Winston's sharp, aquiline nose and his dark eyes. The white tuft of hair poked from beneath his hat. He looked just as formal and serious as his portrait above the fireplace. This was the face I would see most frequently for the rest of my life.

"Winston," I said.

He looked up from my foot in his lap. "Yes, my dear?"

He is memorializing you in paint, James had said of my portrait. *Winston is making you his.* I would never have imagined how romantic a portrait could be, how much it could mean for the viewer, before James had explained it to me.

"Why did you want to have my portrait painted?"

His mouth pulled into a bemused line. "Why do you ask, darling?"

"Well, to begin with, it is a great undertaking. I suspect it is expensive."

The subtle point of your chin, James had said. *The twin peaks of your top lip.*

"My father had my mother's portrait painted, then his, and then mine. It is not unusual among London's high society. Does the portrait really bother you that much?"

It had in the beginning, but that was no longer the point.

"I just wondered why it was so important to you." After a beat, I added, "If it was something you wanted for yourself, or if it was merely a family tradition."

Winston nodded, as if he understood why I would ask, though I knew he did not understand in the slightest.

"It's just something we do in our family, my dear."

"Of course." And if I had not heard James's thoughts on portraits, I would have found Winston's explanation perfectly satisfactory.

"Does this hurt, Iris?" Winston asked as he bent my foot to the right.

I gave no answer. Instead, I glanced toward the row of carriages and searched for James, a distant figure with dark hair and a long brown coat. But I could not find him. He was already gone.

CHAPTER 45

$\mathcal{B}$y the time we returned to the mansion, my ankle had swollen like rising bread. Winston carried me to the turret guest room, where he insisted I rest for the remainder of the day. He ordered Anna to bring me dinner and told Stanley to search the house for the family Bible so I could study the penmanship inside the front cover.

"Do you think you'll be able to walk down the aisle?" Winston asked as he pulled a blanket over me. "We could have you ride in on a horse if you'd rather."

He smiled as he said it, though there was a tinge of fear in his voice.

"With a little rest, I have no doubt I'll be fine in a few days. I don't think it is broken."

"I'll send for the doctor just in case," he said.

"Miss Sheffield?" Stanley called from the doorway. He held a silver tray in his right hand.

"Come in, Stanley," Winston said. "Did you find the family Bible?"

"Not yet, but a letter arrived for Miss Sheffield with this morning's post."

I recognized Papa's boxy writing immediately. I slid my finger under the flap and ripped through the seal. Inside was a single page, indented with the pressure of Papa's hand. I read silently to myself.

My dearest Iris,

There is no easy way to write this letter. We cannot come to London for your wedding. It is my hope that this letter reaches you in time, so you are not surprised when we never arrive.

Please know how desperately we wish we could come. If it were only I who had to travel, I would make the voyage a hundred times to see you in your mother's dress, marrying the man you love. However, Hope's health has taken a poor turn again, and a trip of any significant distance, particularly overseas, is out of the question.

Hope and I share the same wish for you, that you can enjoy your wedding despite our absence. The only thing that would pain me more than missing your special day would be the knowledge that our absence prevented you from enjoying it.

No doubt you will be busy after the wedding, but I beg you to come as quickly as you can to see your sister. I hesitate to share this and further risk ruining your wedding day, but Hope has been asking for you, and a delayed visit may prove too late.

Despite her current condition, she and I remain eternally grateful to you and your husband-to-be for this last attempt at improving her health.

Papa's square signature turned blurry and his letter trembled in my hand.

He had not written the actual words. He did not have to. Hope was dying. A sob caught inside me, much sharper than the pain in my ankle had ever been. It caught in my chest and dug its nails into my heart.

Winston sat wordlessly beside me, waiting.

"Hope is not well," I finally said. I raised my hand to my nose and sniffed. "Papa says the voyage is out of the question, and we should come as soon as possible to see her."

Winston laid his hand on mine.

"We can change our honeymoon plans and visit France instead," he said quietly. "Dover is miserable this time of year anyway. I'll reach out to other physicians when we arrive there, too. We'll knock on every doctor's door in Nice until we find one who knows how to make her better."

Dear Winston, promising that which was not in his power to grant.

"It all means more expenses for you."

"Expense is of little consequence when it involves those you love."

I tried to steady my breath.

"I could go ahead myself," I offered. "I know you need to be close to the factory, particularly while the commission is about to be announced."

"And be apart from my new wife?" Winston shook his head. "I wouldn't think of it. That's why we are marrying so soon in the first place, so we can be together."

He hesitated. "Would you like to postpone the wedding until your family can be here?"

The thought had occurred to me as well, but I quickly pushed it aside.

"Hope will never be well enough to come back to London. And your mother has already arranged everything. It would be more complicated traveling to France if we weren't married. We should wed immediately so we could take on everything together."

Winston sighed. "I was hoping you would feel that way."

I leaned my head against the pillow behind me, exhausted by Papa's letter.

"I owe you an apology," Winston said quietly. He blinked quickly but the tears still pooled in his eyes. "I was awful when you asked me about Penelope. I have no excuse. The commission had me agitated, but that was no reason to take it out on you. You had every right to question me about the journal you found. I should never have kept Penelope from you. I was ashamed, and I wish I could erase that piece of my history. I nearly convinced myself I had. But I should have told you. I am so sorry, Iris." He looked at my hand in his and swallowed. "Might you ever forgive me?"

Something heavy within me lifted at his words and the desperation in his eyes. For a moment I even forgot to worry about Hope. I had never seen Winston afraid before, but there it was on his face: fear. It simultaneously hurt and reassured me that the potential of losing me had put it there.

"Of course," I promised him. "Please, don't mention it again."

He leaned over and kissed my forehead.

"Pardon the interruption, Miss Sheffield, Mr. Carmichael." Anna stood in the doorway. "I have food for Miss Sheffield and some ice for her ankle."

Winston released my hands and stood aside while Anna arranged my meal on the bedside table.

"I will check on you in an hour," Winston said. "I hope I will find you sleeping."

Winston excused himself as Anna placed a brick of ice wrapped in cloth against my ankle. When the shock of its freezing burn wore off, I had the familiar sense that Winston was watching me. I looked up to see him standing in the Hall of Mirrors, just past my doorway, observing Anna's care of me.

There were worse things, I decided as Winston and I exchanged a smile, than having someone who simply wanted to watch over you.

CHAPTER 46

$\mathcal{B}$etween my injury and Papa's letter, Winston refused to let me leave the mansion. I spent the night before my wedding alone in the turret guest room, my left ankle propped on a pillow. Mrs. Carmichael had arrived and slept down the hallway in her old bedroom. All night, I wondered if she was tossing and turning as I was, unable to sleep. And I could not help thinking of Penelope. How would she feel, knowing that I was sleeping in the room where she had hidden her journal, on the eve of marrying the man she loved?

The next morning, Anna awoke me before the sun peeked over the horizon. She lit the gas lamp on the vanity. I stood before the full-length mirror as she adjusted my corset and began to tie it.

Mrs. Carmichael appeared in the doorway. Based on the gray circles beneath her eyes, I knew she had slept no better than I had.

"Anna, please pack my things. I will leave tonight as soon as the festivities are over. I can help Iris with her dress."

Anna curtsied and left the room. I braced myself for Mrs. Carmichael to tug my corset laces tighter than was comfortable.

I was surprised when she stood behind me and pulled at them gently.

"Is that the dress?" she asked, nodding toward my gown sprawled upon the bed.

"Yes," I said, not quite meeting the reflection of her eyes in the mirror.

"It is lovely. I have no doubt it will be beautiful on you."

When I looked up, there was a softness to her gray eyes that I had never seen. She looked at me with something near to warmth.

"I know that I have not been particularly welcoming to you," she said. "When you have children of your own, you will understand how difficult it is to pass them on to the care of another. Winston is my only child, and I knew that I could never see him settle for anything but the best."

She paused in her work at my back. The creases at the corners of her mouth deepened.

"I know you will find this difficult to believe, but my husband was even harder to please than I am. And Winston was always so anxious to please his father. Merely the mention of Andrew's opinion could cause Winston to completely alter his course of action." She pressed her lips together for an instant, checking her emotions. "I suppose Winston told you about the night my husband died?"

I nodded. "He told me Mr. Carmichael's heart gave out. I'm so sorry."

Mrs. Carmichael turned her head away from the sympathy in my eyes. "Winston was always so sensitive to what his father thought of him, that for his father to die the way he did, right in front of Winston's portrait . . . "

My eyes locked on her.

"Mr. Carmichael died in front of Winston's portrait?" Winston had never admitted to Penelope's presence in the

225

EMILIA KELLY

portrait, and he certainly hadn't said his father died in front of it. "Winston never told me."

"That's because he doesn't know," Mrs. Carmichael said impatiently. "The shock of Mr. Carmichael's death was enough to blanch some of Winston's hair. If he knew his father died in front of the portrait it would absolutely devastate him. Which is my point, how sensitive Winston is to everything concerning his father."

"Of course." No wonder Mrs. Carmichael had not told Winston his father died in front of his portrait. Winston was already so broken by his father's death that I couldn't imagine how that knowledge would horrify him.

She pulled my corset ribbons snug and tied them before crossing to the bed. She picked up my mother's dress and held it before her.

"Andrew spent his entire life building his fortune and reputation," she said as she brought the dress to me. "He always told Winston that a fallen business may be rebuilt, but a broken reputation is irreparable. He tried for so long to keep Winston in line, to make sure he went to the right parties and kept company with the right people."

And discarded the wrong people, I wanted to add. I wondered, not for the first time, if perhaps Mrs. Carmichael had persuaded Winston to dismiss Penelope. Would he have ended things without his parents' judgment weighing upon him so heavily?

I stepped carefully into the dress and Mrs. Carmichael pulled it up around me. My hands slipped through its long, lace sleeves. I sensed that she did not want to hear from me. She only wanted to relieve herself of everything building up inside her as she prepared to pass her son on to someone else.

"I hope you understand the good fortune you have in marrying Winston. He lost his way for a time, but he turned his life around and has made tremendous personal sacrifices for the benefit of our family name and company. I never thought I would say this, but Winston works harder than his father. I still believe that no one will ever be good enough for my Winston," she said frankly. "But you support his career and do no damage to his reputation. Winston truly loves you, and I can tell you love him. For these reasons, I believe that Andrew would approve of you wholeheartedly, and by extension I do as well."

It was perhaps the worst wedding speech ever spoken. I wished for the hundredth time that my mother were here. If only she were helping me into my dress rather than Mrs. Carmichael. I could picture Hope standing by in a new dress of her own and a wreath of flowers on her head, Papa downstairs and waiting to walk me down the aisle.

"Who will walk me down the aisle?" I wondered aloud.

"I thought Stanley could," Mrs. Carmichael said.

I blinked in surprise. "Stanley? You would let the butler walk me down the aisle?" Such an act would surely fly in the face of her determination to protect the family's reputation.

Mrs. Carmichael's face was tight, but she attempted a casual shrug. "I know that you and Stanley share a bit of a bond. You're not very good at hiding it. Since your father can't be here today, I thought Stanley would be the next best choice."

In spite of myself, I embraced Mrs. Carmichael. Not because I was thrilled to have Stanley walk me down the aisle. He *was* the best choice given my circumstances, but he was nothing like a father to me, and no one could right the hole in my heart caused by my family's absence.

What moved me the most was Mrs. Carmichael's efforts for my benefit. Never would I have expected her to let down an inch of the stone wall that constantly surrounded her, but here she stood doing her best to lessen my loss, even if it meant letting a butler walk me down the aisle toward her son.

She remained stiff for a moment in my embrace, then finally bent her own arms and reluctantly patted my back.

"Very well then," she said, pulling from me and looking away. "I shall have Anna finish helping you dress. I must find Cleo. She has disappeared again. I believe this house spooks her as much as it does me."

"Thank you, Mrs. Carmichael."

She waved my gratitude away with her hand. "The carriage will take us to the church in forty-five minutes. I will see you in the foyer then and not a minute later. I, for one, will appreciate the change of scenery."

"I'm sorry you aren't comfortable in this house, Mrs. Carmichael."

"It's the smell of it," she said as turned away from me. "I am incredibly sensitive to smells."

And with that, she left me alone in the room, sniffing the air for the faintest trace of offense, but finding nothing.

CHAPTER 47

*I*t was a mercifully warm day for a December wedding.

I waited outside St. Pancras Old Church as the guests arrived. From my spot behind the bell tower, I stood as high as my beaded slippers would allow and peered through a leaded window. A sea of silk top hats and plumed bonnets bobbed along each side of the aisle. Most belonged to faces I did not recognize, though a few cousins from the country were in attendance, and I saw Margaret laughing with a man who looked twice her age. But most guests were from Winston's side, which came as no surprise. I had needed no one else in London after I met him.

I smoothed the front of my mother's wedding gown. Layers of lace scalloped the bodice. From a satin ribbon at my waist, the smooth skirt bloomed, full as a bell. I wondered how many brides before me had stood here, awaiting their cue. Stanley would appear soon, ready to walk me down the aisle, but for now I stood alone in the churchyard, which was as still as death.

The brown grass stretched beyond me in small, rolling mounds. Headstones clustered in a tight circle around a young tree, crowded after their relocation from the path of the new railway. The sight of them made me think of Hope, and my throat tightened. I was desperate to get out of the churchyard, desperate for the wedding to begin. Once the sun dipped into night and rose back into morning, Winston and I would begin our journey toward France, toward Hope. She was waiting. I could not marry Winston quickly enough.

My breath eased the instant I heard Stanley approaching. Dry leaves crumpled behind me, and I took a deep breath. The time to move forward had finally arrived.

"Hello, Stanley," I said without turning toward him. "I am ready."

The footsteps stopped and the silence returned, but the air changed around me, taut and uncertain. Even the birds in the towering tree stopped their chatter, as if they felt it too. The voice that finally broke the quiet was deep and soft. I knew it at once.

"Miss Sheffield."

I turned to see James. He wore his dark suit from the ball and his usual, serious expression. He kept a formal distance from me as we stood facing one another, my back to the bell tower, his to the churchyard. Neither of us moved.

"James," I said. "What are you doing here? Is there a problem with the portrait? Because I don't think Winston would—"

"I'm not here about the portrait. How is your ankle?" He glanced at the hem of my dress.

The memory of him on the park bench, warming my ankle in his palms, sent a rush of blood to my cheeks.

"It's fine," I said shortly. His concern angered me. I did not have time for it. "You should go. I'm about to walk down the aisle. If you still need payment from Winston you can discuss that with him later."

"He's paid me in full," James said irritably. "That's not why I'm here."

I narrowed my eyes. "Why *are* you here?"

He ran a thumb down the side of his nose. James was nervous. Why would James be nervous?

"Miss Sheffield," he began again, "there is something I have to tell you, even if you don't want to hear it."

I glanced toward the church—still no Stanley. A cloud drifted over the sun, dimming the churchyard and causing my skin to prickle.

"Be quick about it, James. Stanley will be here any moment."

James watched me with worried eyes, as if he were seeing something terrible unfold at the sight of me. "You're making a mistake, Miss Sheffield. Don't marry Mr. Carmichael."

I pressed my lips tightly together, my teeth digging into them. "Who are you to decide that I am making a mistake?"

"You don't love him. That's all the information I need."

"Just because my love for Winston does not match your idea of what love should be does not mean it isn't real."

James ran a hand through his hair, pulling it from his face. I glanced toward the church. Where in the world was Stanley?

"I know you find me arrogant and unfeeling." He dropped his hand. His hair fell toward his eyes again. "I am in a class beneath your standing. I know we must seem like an impossibility. I have known this from the beginning, but I tried to convince myself that I did not care."

He stepped toward me. The remains of autumn crunched beneath his feet. He came close enough that I could smell paint on him and could see the amber specks in his eyes.

"I have spent the last decade believing that I could build a wall around myself and disappear into my art, and that doing so would protect me from ever needing anyone. This approach worked remarkably well until I met you, Miss Sheffield. A warning went off inside my head the moment I saw you, but I told myself I was strong enough, calloused enough, to resist it. I simply wouldn't talk to you. But you made it so difficult. You refused to be ignored. And then in my studio I came up with my mad experiment for the benefit of the portrait. But if I am honest with myself, our moment in the studio was never about the portrait."

Suddenly most of my breath seemed to be outside of my body. "It wasn't?"

He answered so softly that I felt his words as much as I heard them.

"No, it wasn't. Not for me, anyway. Because I have fallen in love with you, Miss Sheffield."

The grass began to sway below me. I was losing hold of myself. This wasn't happening. It couldn't be happening. James's love was his art. He didn't have room in his heart for me.

"When I met you, Miss Sheffield, my first thought was, how am I going to match the shade of her eyes?"

He studied my irises.

"I spent weeks trying to find the right combination of brown, gold, and green. If I had not been so intent on seeing you again, I would have quit the portrait for the frustration of it."

His shoe skimmed the hem of my dress. I was moments away from marrying Winston and all I could think of was James's shoe against the hem of my dress.

"Your hair is something from a Botticelli painting," he murmured as he brushed a stray curl from my forehead.

"James, I—"

"I fear that Winston has grown used to you and has stopped seeing you." Each word he spoke made a soft breath on my lips, like a kiss. "But I promise you, Miss Sheffield, that no matter how often I might have the privilege of seeing you, if it were every day for the rest of my life . . . "

He had to stop talking, before he said more and I lost all my resolve. He was going to ruin everything—for Winston, for me, but mostly for Hope.

"I promise," he continued, "that I would never stop seeing you. If I painted you every day for a hundred years, I still would not stop seeing you. What is that phrase? *You are always new to me?* I used to think that was rubbish, but it's not. It's you."

"Stop." The word came out softly. Too softly.

"If you would let me, Miss Sheffield—"

"Stop," I repeated, louder and more forcefully this time. My heart flapped inside of me. My breaths were so shallow I had to force out my words between them. "Stop talking like you are a nice person, like I am someone you might court. Stop talking like we are a possibility because we aren't. We aren't, James. We never will be!"

He froze in front of me. I reached out my hand and grasped the corner of the bell tower. The cold of its stones seeped through my glove. I breathed deeply, willing the earth to stop spinning.

James studied me. "You want to marry him, then?"

I did not answer. It made no difference what I wanted.

He stepped away from me and his shoe left my hem. He clenched his fist and studied the church behind me. When his eyes fell on my face again, their softness had vanished. He looked as furious as I felt. A breeze swept through the church-yard and into my bones.

"I'm marrying Winston," I said, more to myself than James. "I love him."

He laughed once, short and cruel. "You don't love Winston."

"What do you know of love? What type of person believes his love is his art? As if art were something you could hold, something that could love you in return?"

"All right, then." James bared his teeth as he spoke, launching his words at me as hard as he could. "If you love Winston, then tell me this. Have you ever been jealous of Penelope?"

I opened my mouth but had no words. I was not following him.

"In all your digging into Winston's past," he continued, "I've seen you worried, frustrated, angry—all because Winston *kept* something from you. Because he was *hiding* someone from you. But never did I see you jealous at the idea that Winston had *loved* someone other than you. You read the journal entry. You saw the daguerreotype. You studied the portrait after she was painted out of it. I'm sure you imagined Winston and Penelope together. And yet none of that ever made you furiously jealous. What does that tell you?"

My mouth still hung open, but I said nothing. James was right. I had never envied Penelope—even in the smallest amount—when I had imagined her with Winston.

"Would you like to know what that tells me, Iris? That you don't really love Winston. If you did, you would hate—" He swallowed. "You would hate the idea of him giving his arm to another woman while they walked together, or him leading her from the room by the small of her back. And the thought of him kissing her, of him holding her . . . Even if he did it poorly, as Winston does, it would drive you mad, him loving someone who is not you. It would disturb your work and haunt your nights. Because that is what love does to you, Iris. It makes you crazy to think how that person should be with you." He looked at me with tired eyes, no longer talking about Winston and Penelope.

"Please go away, James," I begged. "You have to leave."

"Then say you don't love me. Say it, and I will leave you forever."

"Love you?" I cried. "Love you? I hate you, James! I hate how I can never guess what you're thinking when you look at me. I hate how you scowl even when you're perfectly happy, and how you claim to love your art more than people."

At the word *hate* his eyes flashed at me, a spark behind them.

"I hate how your hair falls over your eyes when you paint me and you don't even notice, as if you can't be bothered with a proper haircut. I hate how you can almost kiss me one moment and then stop talking to me the next, and that either action from you drives me completely mad. I *really* hate how you choose to say all of this now, when I am about to be married, as if you and I were a possibility, as if what I want makes the slightest difference in the choices I must make. But most of all, James, do you know what I hate? More than anything in the world? I hate how much I wish we were a possibility. I hate how much I wish I could say yes to you right now, and that that choice was mine to make."

The spark behind James's eyes erupted at my words. He was at me in two strides and pushed me against the bell tower. Then he kissed me like he was pulling all the breath from me. Each pull was more insistent than the last. I wrapped my arms around his neck to keep from falling. His hands slid down the length of my back, then up until his fingers were beneath the veil in my hair. All the while kissing me, as if he had been thirsty for it since we met.

CHAPTER 48

*W*hen James finally pulled away from our kiss, my cheeks were wet with tears. He lifted his hand to my face and wiped it with his rough thumb.

"Why don't you think this is your choice to make? I have money for us to travel to France together. We won't have much once we get there, but it will be enough." He slid his fingertips across my cheeks until he was holding my face in his hand. "You deserve the most compelling happiness. We both know you won't find that with Winston. If you would let me, Iris, I would do everything in my power to give you such a life."

He spoke the words quietly, like they were a secret between us. James was speaking softly to me and tracing my jawline because that was what he wanted. Not because I was his experiment or because he was proving his skills or being paid to paint me, but because he wanted to hold my face, perhaps as much as I wanted it.

I closed my eyes and let my world shrink down to nothing but his palm on my face, his fingertips grazing my cheekbone, his shoe at the hem of my dress. I saw a life with James, living in a tiny cottage in Barbizon. The inside of our house would be small, cluttered with brushes and canvases. I could see myself outside, in the garden, tending the lavender and sunflowers and tomatoes. James would come up the dirt path toward me, his day of painting men in the wheat fields at its end. I would stand to greet him, and he would not stop until our shoes were touching and he was holding my face, just as he was now. For a moment, when I closed my eyes, I could see it all.

The bell rang in the tower behind us: nine deafening booms that pealed through the silence of the churchyard and ripped me from my reverie. Church bells could mean a wedding, or they could mean a funeral. And occasionally, Hope had informed me on the day we moved to London, they were meant to chase away demons.

I opened my eyes.

I hadn't scared away Hope's demons the day we left Pembrooke, when I led her from the darkened bell tower. I had only kept my promise to Mama. That was all I ever wanted to do. I had nearly ruined things by moving Hope to the gray air of London but now, thanks to Winston, I had one last chance to redeem myself. It may not be enough to save Hope, but I owed it to Mama to do everything in my power to keep her child alive.

I owed it to Hope.

When I finally spoke, my eyes had dried, and my voice was calm. "I have an eight-year-old sister. Her name is Hope. I promised my mother I'd do all I could to take care of her, but then I moved Hope to London and it made her sick." I paused as the familiar pulse of guilt tightened my throat. "But now she has a doctor, and a flat by the sea. She has all those things because of Winston. I can't risk her losing any of it. They are her only chance."

James held very still. "What are you saying?"

"I don't have the luxury of choosing what I want. The choice is not mine to make."

"Did you ask Winston about his portrait?"

"I didn't have to. He discovered the journal and then told me more about Penelope. It's complicated. He ended things with her right after his father died, and—"

"Winston still doesn't know that *you* know Penelope was in his portrait?"

"No, but that doesn't—"

"And he never told you about the portrait himself, even after you showed him the journal?"

"Enough with the painting, James," I snapped. "It doesn't matter!"

James grabbed my arm and pulled me closer. "It does matter, Iris, you know it does. You can't erase someone from your life, but that is exactly what Winston has tried to do. He would have done it completely if you hadn't discovered Penelope. And now you're too afraid to make him tell you the complete truth."

His accusation rang through the churchyard. He glanced around, then bent toward me again and lowered his voice. "Anna told me about your conversation with him. I went to Winston's before I found you ice skating and she told me."

"She only heard a piece of that conversation."

"He *burnt* Penelope's journal, Iris."

"I promised my mother—"

"What did you promise her?" he cried. "What did you promise your mother? That you'd enslave yourself to a crazy man? Is that what your mother would have wanted?"

My nostrils flared. "He's not crazy. You don't know what he has been through. And you certainly have no idea what my mother would have wanted."

"She certainly wouldn't have wanted this!" He threw his hand toward the church. "Iris, you don't even know what happened to Penelope! What if she was in danger? What if you are putting yourself in danger?"

"He's not like that. Winston would never hurt anyone." I may have been surprised to learn about Penelope, but I had no doubt of Winston's love for me, and that he could be trusted to care for me. That was all he had ever wanted to do.

"I would venture to guess, Miss Sheffield," James said, his voice low, "that three months ago you would have sworn Winston would never hide a previous lover from you, either."

"There is no shame in having loved before." My voice was shaking, climbing high. I could not bring it down. "And weren't you the one who claimed we all have secrets in our past?"

James scowled at me. "Stop being stubborn, Iris."

I exhaled through my nose. "Your insults won't cause me to change my mind, James. I must do this for my sister, even if it's not what I want for myself. I'm not like you."

He narrowed his eyes. "What does that mean?"

"You left your family without ever looking back. I could never do that to Papa, and especially not to Hope."

"I had to pursue my training." The amber in his eyes blazed. "The opportunities in Boston could not compete with New York and Paris."

"Exactly. You *chose* your art over your family. And though your sister moved to Brighton, you've never bothered to see her! You assume she will always be there, so you never make time for her." I swallowed the memory of Mama on her bed, the last moment I had seen her. "When someone slips from your life forever it is rarely expected."

James spoke through tight lips. "You've made your choice then. I wish you and your husband every happiness. This is for you. A wedding gift."

He pulled something from his pocket and tossed it at my feet.

"Use it as you like. Or keep it as a memento. If you store it somewhere safe, perhaps Winston's next lover will find it once you are gone."

His words were biting, but I saw fear behind his anger. He believed he was speaking the truth.

"I'll be fine, James," I whispered.

He watched me for a moment as if he did not dare let me go. Then he turned and left, his arms hanging stiffly from his broad shoulders.

I bent to pick up the gift that lay among the brown blades of grass. It was an envelope with *Miss Sheffield* scrawled in confident, even letters across the front. It was the first time I had seen James's handwriting. I lifted the flap to find two vouchers inside. The first was for the London & Dover Railway. The second was for White Star Channels, which crossed from Dover to Calais. Five gold coins rattled in the bottom of the envelope. When I scooped them out I saw they were francs, each bearing the profile of Napoleon.

My throat grew tight. I dropped everything back into the envelope. James had paved the path to Barbizon and, without knowing it, to my sister. He had handed me everything I needed to reach her, down to the French coins for trains to the southern coast.

If only that were enough, I thought with a turn of my stomach. If only reaching her were all that Hope needed from me.

CHAPTER 49

I closed my eyes. Perhaps if I stood there long enough I could forget about James walking away, his offering in my hand, the crushed look I had put on his face.

But how dare he? I thought as I opened my eyes. What if Winston had seen us? Or his mother? They would have called off the wedding if they had witnessed our kiss.

Our kiss.

In truth, I had kissed James back, and perhaps I should feel guilty. But anger eclipsed any trace of guilt: anger at James for initiating the kiss. Anger at myself for wanting more.

"Miss Sheffield?"

Stanley. I glanced down at my wedding gown. It had no pockets, but the scallops of lace across the front were deep enough to serve the same purpose. I bent the envelope from James in half, then in half again, and slipped it inside the lace before Stanley appeared before me.

"Miss Sheffield, don't you look lovely. I apologize for the delay. Mrs. Carmichael decided she wanted her cat here for the ceremony, so I was called upon to fetch her. She must be hiding in the house somewhere, I couldn't find her. Anyway, they're ready for you now."

I dabbed at my lower lids for any lingering tears, then looked heavenward and blinked. I turned and forced a smile at Stanley, but he stopped at the sight of my face.

"Is it that bad?" I asked.

Stanley shook his head. He wore a silk top hat and had grown out a white mustache for the wedding. He looked like an aged Prince Albert.

"You look lovely, Miss Sheffield." He paused. "You remind me of my Agnes as a young bride. I wish she could have come today."

He lifted his hand, which held a tight bundle of white roses. The bouquet. My forced smile faded.

"Miss Sheffield, what is wrong?"

"Hearing you speak of Agnes . . . " I stared at the cluster of roses in his hand. "You've always expressed such love for her. I hope Winston and I will have a marriage like yours."

Stanley placed a hand on my shoulder.

"I have worked for the Carmichaels for four years, Miss Sheffield. Mr. Andrew Carmichael hired me when no one else would. I was new to London and had no references, only my good word. Their family took a chance on me, and they have proven to be the most loyal masters I ever had. I can't think of a better man than Winston to have on your side."

Loyal. The same word Mrs. Carmichael had used.

"Are you doubting your decision to marry Mr. Carmichael?" Stanley asked.

I shook my head firmly. "I have made my decision." Or perhaps the decision had been made for me. Regardless, I would marry Winston, and together we would reach Hope as quickly as we could. Maybe Winston was right: maybe there was a doctor somewhere in Nice who could cure her. If there was, Winston would find him.

Stanley breathed a sigh of relief, as if his livelihood depended upon him delivering me to the bridegroom.

"Miss Sheffield, may I ask what first drew you to Mr. Carmichael?"

"His eagerness," I said without hesitation. "In everything. Regarding me, or his work, or his mother, anything he deems important. My father loves his family dearly, but he couldn't quite . . . He was never fully . . . " I paused. "I always felt that Winston was someone upon whom I could rely. I know that does not sound particularly romantic, but it has always made me feel loved—probably because I have spent so much of my life having others rely on me."

Stanley studied me. "You've been a mother to Hope for half of your life, haven't you? That is a great responsibility from such a young age. I can understand why you might choose someone eager to care for you."

I reached for the bouquet. "I must admit," I said as I plucked off a wilted petal, "I was surprised Mrs. Carmichael would permit you to walk me down the aisle."

Stanley shrugged. "The Foxes once allowed a scullery maid to be a flower girl in their daughter's wedding. The public adored it and practically made Mr. Fox a saint out of it."

Ah, the mystery of Mrs. Carmichael's generosity solved.

"The Carmichaels aren't perfect, Miss Sheffield. But you will be in very good hands with Winston. I would do anything for this family—short of burying a body," he added with a chuckle. "They are loyal to their people, and I feel honored to be among that circle."

I nodded. Stanley was right. Winston took care of me. He took care of Hope. With that knowledge, I knew what I had to do. I always had.

I pulled my veil over my face. I took Stanley's arm, and together we skirted the bell tower. As we made our way toward the church, I ignored the temptation to look back. Only forward-facing now, I told myself. Each step would bring me closer to Hope.

We reached the portico. I saw Winston, standing tall in a dark suit at the end of the aisle. He caught my gaze and held it, unblinking.

It was time to move forward.

CHAPTER 50

"Welcome home, Iris."

I stood in the entry of the Carmichael mansion and looked around me. A fog was rolling in with the night, making the foyer dimmer than usual, but otherwise everything was the same. The steep staircase ahead of me, the library to my right and the parlor to my left . . . all were as they had been this morning, except now I shared them with Winston. As his wife.

Winston shut the front door behind us and kissed my cheek. He was my husband. This was our house, and tonight was our wedding night.

As his lips met my cheek I knew I could not stomach romance with Winston right now. Not with the memory of James's kiss still tapping at the back of my head. I would have to delay things.

"Long day." I forced a yawn.

"Agreed. That Margaret Darby friend of yours talked to me for nearly an hour. That woman is exhausting."

"Did you see your mother off?" I asked.

"Yes, she left right before we did. She hoped to depart before dark, but the guests kept cornering her."

"Did she ever find Cleo?"

Winston shook his head. "Anna promised to leave food out for her before she and Stanley take the weekend off. Mother will return for her as soon as she can."

We would leave for Dover in the morning, stay there for a night, then cross the channel to France and take a series of trains to Nice. It was not the honeymoon we had originally planned, but it would bring me to Hope quickly.

Winston busied himself with removing his jacket and cufflinks. I turned away.

"It's quiet as the dead in here," I murmured.

"I saw Stanley depart after the wedding, and Anna has surely left by now."

"Her bag is still here." I motioned toward the end of the foyer. There it sat, a faded gray lump at the top of the stairs leading to the servants' quarters.

"I'm sure she will see herself out," he said as he climbed the staircase. I stood at the bottom and watched him ascending until he called to me over his shoulder.

"Well, come along, Iris. I still need to finish packing for the trip. I forgot to ask Stanley to do it before the chaos of the wedding."

"I'll only be a moment," I called, my mind grasping for an excuse. "I . . . left my gardening shears behind the house. I don't want them to rust."

"Very well," Winston allowed, an amused smile on his lips. "I'll be waiting upstairs."

I let myself out the back door and into the small garden, draped in fog. There, beside a rosebush deep in winter sleep, sat my garden shears. I picked them up and turned them over in my hands. The blades were dull and speckled with auburn. I had left them in the garden months ago.

A creak sounded near me. It was the pull of the gate, stubborn at the hinges. I looked up in surprise at a hooded figure, its back to me as it pushed the gate shut again.

"Winston?"

But it was too short, too frail to be Winston, I thought as I watched it secure the gate. The hinges shrieked in resistance until it latched into place. The figure turned and I let out a small laugh of surprise.

"Anna."

She pulled the hood from her head. Even through the thickening fog I could see that something was different about her. She looked at me with an intensity unmatched in our previous encounters, her eyes flashing with determination.

"Winston and I thought you'd have gone home by now."

"I had to take care of something first."

Perhaps it was the harsh look in her eyes, or the thickening fog, which seemed to shut away the rest of the world. It may have been the silence in the small garden, or the way she had seemed to appear out of nowhere. Whatever the cause, for the first time, I found myself afraid to be alone with Anna.

"Why are you here?" I asked.

"There is something I have not told you about myself." She stood firm at the gate. "Something that you need to know." She paused, eyes pinning me. "About Penelope."

"Penelope." I blinked. "What of Penelope?"

"She is my sister."

Sister. My insides tightened. It could not be. But as I stared at Anna I saw that her fair complexion, with brows and lashes nearly transparent, had distracted me from the broad forehead and protruding eyes resembling a certain daguerreotype.

"Your sister," I repeated, my mind struggling to make sense of her confession.

"I planted her journal where you would find it."

The journal had lain beneath the mattress, out of sight but just within reach of one making the bed.

"I have been watching you, Iris—as you have accepted Winston's proposal and gone on carriage rides with him, and now married him and moved into his house. I have watched it all."

Her words were an accusation, icier than the fog between us.

"Watching me?" I asked. "Why?"

"Because you have won," she said, forehead raised. "You now have everything that Penelope ever wanted, everything she might have had, until you came along."

I shook my head, jaw set. "Winston never meant to marry her."

"We have no way of knowing, do we?" Anna approached me slowly. "Because you walked in and changed the outcome of her life."

"You think it's my fault, then." I hated to say the words, for I had thought them long before Anna's accusations, and had felt responsible for Penelope's fate. "You blame me for her heartbreak."

She did not answer but continued her slow advance toward me. My grip on the gardening shears tightened.

"So you have come here for revenge?"

"Revenge?" She stopped and stared at me, then erupted into soft laughter. I had never heard Anna laugh before. It was a bitter, unsettling sound. "Miss Sheffield. *Mrs. Carmichael*, rather. I'm not here for revenge."

She leaned closer to me, so close that her breath heated my skin.

"I am here to warn you."

My grip on the shears remained tight. "I don't understand. Where is Penelope now? Is she still in London?" Perhaps I could speak with her, settle all that had gnawed at me since I first learned of her.

Anna straightened, distancing herself from me again, and her eyes softened.

"Haven't you put it together yet, Mrs. Carmichael? Penelope is gone."

Gone.

"She never came home after Winston rejected her. The journal entry you found is the last record we have of her alive."

The chill of the fog sank into my skin, spread through my bones. "You believe that she is dead?"

"I believe that she was murdered."

Penelope, murdered. The suggestion hurt, a sharp stab to my temple. But somewhere lower, in my chest, I felt my insides shift at her words—as if I recognized them, as if I had suspected this all along.

And now Anna was trying to warn me.

"What are you suggesting, that Winston's mother killed Penelope?"

"Winston's mother?" She let out another harsh laugh. "The woman can't make herself a cup of tea, let alone do away with someone."

I swallowed, scared of my own next words. "You think it was Stanley, then."

It broke me to admit it made sense. Stanley, so indebted to Winston, so intent upon providing for his dear Agnes. Had he not admitted to me—only today—that he would do anything for the Carmichaels? Short of burying a body, he had said.

"Stanley?" Anna squinted at me. "The man must be a hundred years old. I could ward off Stanley, and I haven't half the grit that Penelope had. Don't be a fool, Iris. It's Winston. *Winston* needed Penelope to disappear. Winston is the one who did away with her."

Winston. My fingers loosened around the shears.

"He and Penelope met at the local public house. She was madly in love with him and almost convinced him to marry her. Then Mr. Carmichael died, and Winston was set to inherit the family business. He needed a suitable wife to match the image."

"No." Anna had heard Winston's confession after I asked him about Penelope, and now she was twisting his words. "I trust Winston. I have no reason to trust you."

Anna pinned me with her large eyes. She spoke slowly, as if a careful pace could convince me.

"Penelope ran away from home last March. She only wrote us one letter during that time, asking for money. But when I arrived at her return address, no one was living there. It was a small flat, practically empty, but there was a journal in it. And Winston was the only person she mentioned by name in the journal."

"Winston said Penelope returned home after he ended things."

"Of course he did. He needed a story to match her disappearance. Why do you think he burnt the journal you found? He has done his best to erase every last bit of her."

I could not take another moment of this—not from Anna, who had treated me coldly from the beginning, who never bothered to hide her dislike of me despite my kindness toward her.

"Leave." I took a step back, as if she were a flame. "Leave immediately, and never return."

Anna lifted her chin. "All right. But I left you something under the pillow on Winston's bed."

I turned my head away from her and stared through the shriveled rosebush. *Even breaths*, I ordered myself, not wanting her to see my fear. I could no longer look at her, could not stand her pointed stare.

She watched me in silence, as if she expected me to change my mind. When I did not, she pushed the garden gate open and did not bother to close it behind her. I listened as her footsteps faded into the fog. Only when they had disappeared could I truly breathe.

CHAPTER 51

*B*ehind me, the back door creaked open.

"Are you coming in, Iris?" Winston called from the doorway. "Or do I need to come fetch you?"

I tossed the scissors back onto the grass and followed Winston's voice into the house. I could not look at him, for fear he would read Anna's words on my face. It felt like a betrayal just to have listened to them.

Together we climbed the stairs and made our way down the Hall of Mirrors. He led me past the turret guest room and to the end of the hall, the last door on the right.

Winston's bedroom.

I hesitated in the doorway. I had never stepped inside it before. The room was vast, twice as large as the guest room. Dark-green velvet covered the bed and hung from the windows, and all the furniture was a deep, bleeding mahogany. The effect was masculine and heavy.

"We have to leave early in the morning to catch our seven o'clock train," Winston said as I hovered in the doorway. "With the servants off, I hired a knocker-upper to tap on the window at five-thirty. We should get to bed as soon as possible."

My wedding dress hung on the door of his wardrobe. Anna must have brought it back after I changed out of it for the wedding dinner. Winston eased the wardrobe open carefully and began selecting shirts from it. When he found one to his liking he laid it on the bed.

Our bed.

I did my best not to look at it.

"Don't just stand there." Winston laughed. "Come pack your things. I've almost finished already. Here's your trunk."

I forced myself into the room and pushed back the lid of my steamer trunk. On top of the stacks of clothing and blankets lay the landscape of our country home. When I held it up, Winston smiled.

"Pembrooke?"

"Yes, my mother painted it. She painted many versions, but this one is my favorite." I set it on the floor, carefully leaning it against the Mora clock in the corner.

"That reminds me, we forgot to look at the portrait. It should be downstairs."

"Perhaps we should wait until morning."

"Why?" Winston asked. "Aren't you curious to see it?"

I had no desire to see the portrait. As much as I wanted an excuse to distance myself from Winston and delay the inevitable, I did not wish for the reminder of James and our recent time together, which was surely our last.

"It's been a long day, and we have so much to do before our trip." I pulled a lace shawl—Mama's—from the trunk. I breathed deeply, searching for her scent, but it was not there. I folded the shawl into a neat square.

"We'll be even busier in the morning, and I refuse to wait that long. Come, Iris. Let's see you in all your painted glory."

He reached for my hand and pulled me along behind him, past the Hall of Mirrors again and down the stairs, until we reached the parlor. Stanley had left a small fire crackling in the fireplace. It bathed the room in dim, warm light.

In the corner stood James's easel, where it had always been during our sessions. It held a large rectangular package wrapped in brown paper. A card inscribed with *Mr. and Mrs. Carmichael* was propped against it, along with a bouquet of indigo flowers. The writing was in the confident, even penmanship I had first seen this morning.

"Perhaps we shouldn't," I said, staring at James's handwriting.

"Why not?"

"Suppose we don't like it. It would ruin our trip. I'd rather know after we return if it isn't any good."

"Don't be ridiculous, Iris. James already told us we would not be disappointed. You don't have to look, but I must see it."

I crossed to the window, the same window from which James had watched the man shoveling snow the night of the ball. Now, with the fog rolling through the night, one could hardly see the street, and the commons beyond had disappeared completely.

Winston opened the card and read aloud.

Mr. and Mrs. Carmichael,

Congratulations on what should be the happiest of days for the two of you.

After a great deal of last-minute labor, the portrait is finally complete. Please open it carefully, as some of the paint may still be drying.

It is always my artistic intention to convey a message with my paintings. I hope you will find that this portrait accomplishes its intended purpose.

The commission to paint Miss Sheffield—now Mrs. Carmichael—was simultaneously a challenge and an honor. I offer my greatest appreciation for the opportunity, and all my sincerest wishes for your happy future.

Your servant,

Thomas James

Winston took the bouquet of flowers from the easel. "I assume these are for the bride."

He tossed me the bouquet. I reached out my hands without thinking, and the scent of the petals swept over me before my fingers closed around them. Sweet, with a hint of citrus. And something more: the smell of memories.

"Those flowers almost look like those in the painting you just showed me—the one by your mother."

"Freesia," I whispered to myself. Yes, freesia, the scent of my childhood. That had been it all along, I remembered now. Mama had had a field of the flowers planted in front of the house, and she waited until they were in full bloom, a sea of deep blues, before she painted Pembrooke.

I could see her standing in the middle of a field of them, her belly bulging with the promise of Hope and her arms filled with stems of freesia. Freesia for the parlor, freesia for the bedrooms. Even jars of freesia in the kitchen for the servants to enjoy. The entire house had smelled of it. My mother had smelled of it. Her letters once smelled of it.

As Winston tore the brown paper from the portrait, I recalled the corners where Mama would tuck vases around the house. There was so little of my mother left. A dress, a necklace, a shawl. Her letters and her rocking chair. The painting of our home. The child she had passed on to me. A list of seven things that kept my mother alive. And now, with the discovery of her scent, James had brought the number to eight.

I was so consumed by this new piece of my mother that I did not notice when the sound of ripping paper ceased, or when Winston fell silent in front of the portrait. I do not know how long the room was still before I finally looked toward him.

The back of the canvas hid his expression from my sight.

"Well?" I asked, pulling myself reluctantly from my newfound memories. "How is it?"

Winston said nothing. I placed the bouquet of freesia on the windowsill and took a step toward him.

"You don't like it?"

"No." Winston's voice sounded far away. "No, it's not—It's not that."

"Well, then, what's wrong? What is it?"

Winston stepped away from the painting. His face was pale.

"This painting isn't of you."

I crossed the room. Winston watched me carefully. His body blocked the canvas from my sight and he took his time moving aside. When I saw the portrait, when I stood before James's easel and was face-to-face with it, I knew why.

Its background was nothing more than a few broad sweeps of gray, as if James could not be bothered with any details beyond the sitter's face, which was painted in thick, loose strokes, the marks of a rushing artist, intent to send his message in time.

The sitter stared just past me. Her eyes were reddish brown and narrow beneath long, flat lashes. Her lips curled slightly at one edge and her thick burgundy hair tumbled around her shoulders. I felt my insides flex at the painted sight of her.

Penelope was just as beautiful in color as I had imagined.

CHAPTER 52

$\mathcal{J}$ stared at Penelope's portrait. Her colored image brought her to life more than the black and white daguerreotype ever had. She seemed to be scrutinizing the room and, though her eyes did not quite meet mine, I felt her also scrutinizing me, the woman who had replaced her, who had gained everything she had hoped for.

Winston walked away from the portrait and toward the window. From outside came the sound of clacking hooves and creaking wheels as a carriage passed the mansion. I reluctantly pulled my eyes from the painting to see Winston, squinting through the fog.

"This is a mistake. James must have been working on two portraits simultaneously and accidentally brought us the wrong one."

His voice was smooth, the same voice he used to discuss business with Paxton. Winston, who had promised to keep no more secrets from me, who had confessed he never should have hid Penelope from me, now spoke with the voice he saved for deals and negotiations.

"Whoever that woman is," he continued with a subtle nod

toward the painting, "she probably has your portrait and is wondering who you are. We'll get it all sorted out after our trip. Heaven knows we're not going to worry about it on our wedding night."

Winston put a hand on my back and gently led me toward the stairs. He stayed at my heels as I climbed them. My heartbeat pounded in my ears.

Once we were alone in the bedroom again, he shut the door behind us. This time, though, he was the one who lingered by the door, his hand on the knob.

"Did James mention that he was painting any portraits besides yours?"

"Not to me." I had to force out the words. "He only painted me in the mornings, so I suppose he could have painted someone else in the afternoons."

Winston did not release his grip on the doorknob. "We'll sort it out after our trip, I suppose. It's too late to do anything about it now."

"Of course," I said, desperate to equal his feigned indifference.

He crossed the room to me and I held my breath. I knew what was coming. Our honeymoon would begin tomorrow, but Winston was my husband tonight. He reached me and began to kiss me: long, slow kisses that began on my cheek, then moved to my neck. I stood silent, and as still as a portrait.

His hands rested at my waist. As his kisses trailed down to my collarbone, his fingers began to ascend my ribs. I took a wide, deep breath.

But there was something mechanical about Winston's movements. His kisses were never smooth, as both Margaret and James had guessed, but he had always seemed intent on the act. Now I could feel that his mind was elsewhere.

His hands stopped and he raised his head to me. His eyes were glazed. He looked as distracted as I felt.

"Did you speak with James much? As he was painting your portrait?"

I forced myself to look Winston in the eyes. "He did not wish to speak to me," I said evenly. "He preferred to paint in silence."

Winston ran his tongue over his teeth, calculating. "We'll return it to him in the morning," he decided. "The two of us. Before we catch our train."

"The two of us?" My eyes widened. "But we don't know where he lives."

"I do. He gave me his address so I could send him payment."

"You said the knocker-upper is coming at five-thirty. We'll miss our seven o'clock train if we visit James first."

"We'll be quick about it." He pressed his lips together, his mind made up. "I'd like this portrait situation remedied immediately."

Dread pulled at me as I imagined what type of remedy he meant, and what he might say to James in the morning. If James were lucky, Winston would simply demand that he hand over the correct portrait. But he could also question James about Penelope and insist he explain the meaning behind such a pointed gesture. Either way, by sending Winston the painting of Penelope, James had sacrificed exhibiting my portrait with the Royal Academy. Winston would never allow it now.

"Stanley forgot to put out the fire. I'd best take care of that. Do you need . . . " He paused. "Do you need help undressing?"

I shook my head quickly.

"Wait here then. I'll only be a moment."

Winston disappeared into the hallway. With numb fingers, I slipped off my clothes and laid them over the back of a chair. My wedding dress hung on the wardrobe door, ghostly white in the dimming room. The envelope from James still lay beneath the folds of its lacy bodice. I would have to dispose of the vouchers and francs without Winston knowing. I would sort it out later. I could not think now, with Anna's warnings and Winston's lies a storm inside my brain.

Through the open doorway a faint stench wafted into the room, timid but acrid. It made me think of Mrs. Carmichael and her distaste for the house and its smell. Perhaps she was mad, I thought, and now that we shared the same name I was becoming mad as well.

There was no fireplace in the bedroom. My bones were cold, my teeth chattering. I reached into my steamer trunk and pulled out my warmest nightgown. Winston should have the fire out by now. What could be taking him so long? And what was that stench?

Winston's bed was firm when I sat upon it. Anna, presumably, had turned down the bed. I stared at the pillows as if there might be something poisonous beneath them. I lifted the pillow nearest me and found nothing. When I lifted the pillow beside it, I found a small piece of newspaper, folded neatly in half.

I stared at the paper for a moment, debating. Finally, I picked it up. My hands shook as I smoothed it open and read.

Local Woman Remains Missing
Moreton-in-Marsh Bulletin
30 August 1849

Nineteen-year-old Penelope Bromley remains missing since her disappearance on 15 March of this year, reports her father, Mr. Abraham Bromley. Miss Bromley has pale skin and long red hair. She may be in the company of a male, whom her father could neither identify nor describe. Anyone with knowledge regarding Miss Bromley's whereabouts should contact the Moreton-in-Marsh Police Department immediately.

I crumpled the paper and clenched it in my fist. Then I burrowed myself beneath the velvet spread and lay on my side, my back to the door. I could not stop shaking, and the smell—whatever it was—grew stronger.

Missing, the paper said. Just as Anna had claimed. Winston told me she had left London to be with her family after he turned her away. Yet her father had reported her still missing at the end of August.

By that time, Winston and I had met.

The stench heightened and the blood behind my eyes pounded. Could this be the same phantom smell that haunted Mrs. Carmichael so incessantly?

I imagined Winston downstairs in the parlor, standing in front of Penelope's portrait, the rich Axminster carpet below his feet, the damasked wallpaper and heavy curtains around him. All had been replaced when I first met him last August. He had been stripping his life and his home of something—something that tainted it. Something that threatened him. Whatever it was, it drove even his mother away. Stanley stayed, though. Sweet Stanley, so desperate to provide for his wife he would do anything.

I imagined Winston at the painting, glaring at Penelope with a mixture of resentment and desire, a shadow from his past that kept returning to torment him. I imagined him picking up the portrait and carrying it across the room until he stood in front of the large fireplace.

My eyes flew open. The stench was thick now: bitter, angry.

Burning.

As I lay shaking in Winston's bed, I knew what he was doing—standing in front of the fireplace, portrait in hand, the mantel so high a person could easily walk into it, could easily stumble into it. I could see him staring into the fire, hypnotized by the flames.

And I knew what Winston had done before, just as I knew what he was doing now— studying the flames as they destroyed his past, creating a stench that would require stripping the walls and the floors and expelling anyone suspicious, anyone not desperate enough to keep quiet.

Winston was watching Penelope as long as he could until there was nothing left of her. The portrait was going the way of her journal, crackling to life in the fire before succumbing to seeping black stains, and finally crumbling to ashes.

Exactly, I feared, like the last time he had taken care of her.

CHAPTER 53

J lay shivering in Winston's bed, the stench of burning oil paints and canvas staining my breaths.

I could continue to pretend I did not know what Penelope looked like, that I had not recognized her portrait, and its appearance in our house had nothing to do with me. If I remained silent, both in the morning when we visited James and every moment after, Winston would never question me. He wanted Penelope to disappear. He would be relieved if we both pretended her portrait had never appeared in the first place.

But if I did that, James would assume all responsibility for Penelope's portrait. Winston would know that James suspected him of causing her disappearance. Even if James were already in France, I feared what Winston might do to James's reputation to protect his own. He could use his connections to hit James hard, just as James was realizing his dream of Barbizon.

If I wanted to protect James from Winston's revenge, I had to let Winston know that I recognized Penelope and to make him think that her portrait had been *my* doing, *my* test for him to pass, not James's. And that, in failing my test, I no longer trusted Winston to care for me, or to care for Hope.

Thanks to James's gifts, nestled safely within the folds of my wedding dress, I could reach Hope without my husband.

Winston's steps sounded in the Hall of Mirrors. I closed my eyes to feign sleep and prayed he would not try to wake me. His steps grew louder until they were inside the room and approaching me. He lowered himself beside me and I felt the mattress give beneath his weight.

He reeked of burning.

He stretched out beside me without removing his shoes. I waited for him to speak, but he said nothing. After a while, his breaths grew slow and deep.

Only then did I dare turn toward him.

His tie hung loose around his neck and his hands rested on his dress coat, rising and falling with each tide of breath. When he began to snore softly, I sat up. I blinked at the shapes against the wall—the rounded back of the Louis XVI chair, the low rectangle of my steamer trunk, the mahogany wardrobe where my mother's wedding dress hung. When I had admired it in years past it seemed to glow, whiter than a lily. Now, in the night, it was the color of ashes.

I watched Winston's chest rise and fall twice more before I forced my legs over the side of the bed. Each movement I made twisted my stomach another half turn.

The wooden floors were creaky, with no rug to soften the sound. I brought my right foot to the ground as slowly as I could. The creak I pressed from the floor was nearly imperceptible. My left foot came down with just as much caution. I stretched my bare toes, anticipating the coolness of the oak panels. But before my foot found the ground, a commotion sounded outside our window, the sloppy voices of a pair of men in the commons. They hollered at one another, erupted into belting laughter, and then fell silent, all within a few moments, their noise gone as quickly as it had appeared.

Winston stirred. His snores ceased and he parted his eyelids.

The darkness swallowed his pupils and I could not tell where he was looking. Then his lids slipped shut and his cheek rolled back against his pillow.

I tried again. My movement pressed creaks out of the bed, but it was not enough to wake him. Holding my breath, eyes pinned to him, I stood and moved gingerly toward his side of the bed, toward the door, breath still held.

As I reached the wardrobe and my wedding dress—gray in the night—Winston mumbled a stream of indiscernible words. He rolled away from me, then grew still as death.

The sight of Winston's back to me sent a tide of courage through my veins. I lunged silently toward the bedroom door, twisted the knob, and slid into the hallway. I pulled the door behind me until it shut silently into place.

CHAPTER 54

From that moment, my slow, calculated movements ceased. I rushed past the Hall of Mirrors and flew down the stairs. On the last few steps, I tripped over my nightgown and fell to the bottom. I stumbled to my feet and just missed the large umbrella vase. Finally, the front door—I twisted its lock, then the knob. Mercifully, it yielded easily under my hand. I pushed myself outside, into the sea of fog, and ran as fast as my bare feet would go.

When I was convinced no one was following me, I paused to catch my breath. My nightgown had ripped when I tripped on the stairs. The fall had left a tender spot on my forehead, and my left ankle throbbed again.

I wrapped my arms around myself. I had to reach my townhouse. There was a spare key beneath the flowerpot, and clothes in my room. I would find a carriage to take me to Dover tonight. When Winston woke in the morning, I would already be crossing the channel. I would reach my family and find us a new flat immediately, perhaps in a nearby town. I could become a governess in exchange for our family's room and board. We would work it all out when I arrived. We would find a way.

James had been right. We could have managed, just as I must manage now. I said a prayer of gratitude for the gift from James. I would have no way of traveling to Nice without the vouchers and coins in the envelope.

The envelope.

My heart froze hard against my breastbone. I had fled the mansion so quickly, I had forgotten to grab it. Without that envelope, I had no hope of escaping London, no way of joining Papa and Hope. No means of adequately distancing myself from Winston.

The vouchers and francs still lay in the folds of my wedding dress, hanging on the armoire by the window.

Practically within arm's reach of my sleeping husband.

CHAPTER 55

*A*ll was quiet when I opened the door of the Carmichael mansion. The smell of the burning portrait lingered heavily in the foyer. My breaths shallow, I eased the door closed behind me and forced my bare feet across the Axminster rug to the bottom of the staircase.

The steps had been a blur when I rushed down them, but now as I braced myself to climb back to the room where Winston lay, they looked like they continued forever, unfurling before me like a tower, each step growing steeper and steeper until they ascended into darkness.

I forced myself up the first step, hoping my legs would not buckle beneath me. I tried to blind myself to what lie ahead, to think only about ascending, one weighted step after another, until there were more stairs behind me than in front of me. As I reached the top, a wave of dizziness swept over me. The stairs swam behind me, a tide that threatened to pull me backward. I stumbled into the Hall of Mirrors and my terrified reflection bounced infinitely around me.

Winston lay sleeping behind the fourth mirrored door on

the right. I counted the doors slowly as I passed them, ignoring my movements in each door's reflection.

One, the first door, the turret guest room. What would I be doing now if I had never spent the night there, had never found Penelope's journal beneath the bed? I slid my damp palms against my ripped nightgown.

Two. The second door was closed, another guest room. The hallway grew darker as I stepped farther into it. From Winston's bedroom, the clock ticked. The air felt thick and tainted, like smoky breath on my neck.

Three, past Mrs. Carmichael's empty bedroom. The clock was ticking more loudly than it had ever ticked before. Surely Winston could not sleep through that deafening ticking. Its only accompaniment in the sleeping house was my heartbeat, thudding inside my ears.

Four.

I peered through the doorway. There, hanging on the armoire, was my wedding dress. I would not take my eyes from it. I knew if I allowed myself a glance at the bed, at the dark heap of Winston asleep, I would never dare cross the room. With my gaze riveted on the dress, I tiptoed carefully around the bed and the dresser and chair, until I was at the dress and reaching into its folds and clutching the precious envelope. It went immediately into the breast pocket on my nightgown. I turned around silently and glided again past the chair, past the dresser, past the bed, where I still had not looked.

It was only when I walked through the door and back into the Hall of Mirrors that I realized the bedroom door had been opened upon my return. I was certain I had pulled it closed behind me when I first fled. But now it stood wide open. I peered over my shoulder, back into the room.

The bed was empty.

I whipped back in horror, coming face to face with my terrified image on the mirrored door before me. A familiar feeling twisted my stomach.

Winston was watching me. I could sense it.

My glaze slid to the left. I saw nothing.

I looked to the right.

There was Winston, reflected in the glass behind me.

CHAPTER 56

I flew through the hallway, down the stairs, Winston
at my heels. Pounding on the steps behind me.
Fingers reaching for me.

Suddenly he tripped and knocked into me. I fell hard onto
the steps. My head hit the wall. My left ankle rolled and stabbed
with pain.

Winston lost all footing and barreled past me. He tumbled
down the stairs until he reached the bottom. His head slammed
against the wrought-iron newel post.

It was a hard hit. It must have knocked him out. I prayed it
knocked him out. I could not waste time checking. I flew past
him and to the front door, my hand reaching for the knob,
fingers grasping. I gripped the knob and twisted it, but it would
not turn. I rattled it. I yanked it toward me.

Please, no. Please, no.

I heard rustling behind me. I shook the knob with both
hands. Panic vibrated inside my chest. My breath heaved,
shallow and desperate. I would not turn around. I rattled the
knob harder.

Please no please no.

A hand rested on my shoulder, its fingers long and cold. I felt breath on my neck.

"You have to push," Winston murmured into my ear, his words calm. "And then twist. Remember?"

He reached his other arm around me and pushed the knob, then twisted. It slid clockwise. He pulled the door toward us. Its moan filled the foyer.

"Let's go for a walk, shall we, Iris?"

He grabbed my arm and pulled me out into the fog. My vision reached only ten steps ahead of me. I walked blindly, but Winston's steps were sure, pulling me along as my ankle throbbed with each step.

Anna, I thought with a drop in my stomach. She was my single lifeline, and I had ordered her away.

I did not see the Vauxhall Bridge until we were nearly on it. *Closed to carriages*, a sign read. Winston yanked me around the barricade. In the haze the Thames was invisible below us, but I could smell its sour sewage and hear its groan, wide and slow. My head was starting to spin. I breathed deeply, as if the cold London night could revive me. But the air of London brought death, not life.

Winston waited until we were halfway across the bridge. Then he stopped, hand still tight on my arm, and watched me.

He smiled.

He ran a hand along my face, up to my temple.

"You hit your head," he said softly. His fingertips sent my head spinning. "When we fell down the stairs. A goose egg is already forming. You poor thing."

I cringed.

"I'll call on the doctor first thing in the morning." He stroked my wounded forehead. Each touch caused a stab of pain behind my eye. "I'll take care of you, Iris. I will always take care of you."

I tried to move, but he tightened his grip on my arm and pushed me back against the bridge wall.

"Stay here," he ordered, still smiling.

He looked behind him toward the bridge's entrance, but the fog hid everything around us.

"I often rode over this bridge with Penelope. You wanted me to tell you about her, didn't you? She liked a dress shop on the other side and, well." A laugh escaped him. "You know how I am about women and dresses."

Pain stabbed my left ankle. I could never run fast enough from him now, even if I could escape his grip.

"We'll get the doctor to inspect your head first thing in the morning. Then we'll go to Dover and on to France to see Hope. I'll take care of her too, just as I promised you."

He picked up my trembling hand and planted an icy kiss on each knuckle.

"When I met you, Iris, I was caught in a terrible whirlpool with Penelope and couldn't break free. I didn't know what to do, how to save my reputation from being tainted by her when I still craved companionship. And then I saw you, on that train to London."

He brushed the hair from my eyes. I said nothing, hoping his rambling might buy me time to think.

"You couldn't stop watching Hope as she slept on the train. I could read the worry on your face. You cared so deeply for her. Penelope was only ever concerned with herself."

My hair was well out of my face, but he continued to stroke it, his hands always on me.

"I knew you were the type of woman I wanted as my wife, as the mother of my children. My father would have adored you. Your beauty. Your lineage. I only wish he had witnessed our wedding."

Winston trailed his finger down my cheek. I feared I would be sick. He pulled his gaze from me toward the river, invisible in the fog.

"When I tried to end things with Penelope after I met you,

she went mad. She followed me to work. She haunted my doorstep. My friend at the *Times* said she had contacted a writer there and claimed she had a story about me. Surely she meant a story about *us*. The writer wasn't interested. The *Times* isn't a gossip column. But she didn't know that. She was intent on ruining my reputation. And I realized . . . "

He paused and his jaw twitched.

"Penelope would not stop until she was satisfied. The *Times* would only be the beginning. She was hitting me where she thought me the most vulnerable. Eventually she would think to seek out my father's clients. *My* clients." He swallowed. "Maybe even Paxton."

"I'm sorry, Winston," I said, my voice strained. I would tell him anything to clear the madness from his eyes, anything to buy me time.

"Penelope had to dig up problems. I had given her so much, but she was determined to leave me with nothing."

Winston turned from the river and his gaze, distant and clouded, landed on me.

"And you," he whispered. "You, to whom I offered everything. All I wanted was to love you and give you whatever you needed, but it wasn't enough. You forced Penelope back into my life. You insisted on digging up problems. Just like she did."

His fingers squeezed tighter around my arm. With his other hand, he dug into his pocket and pulled out a crumpled bit of newspaper—the article from Anna. He held the paper in front of my face.

"She wanted to ruin me. Just like you do."

"No, Winston."

He tossed the paper over the bridge into the river. His free hand crawled up my arm and found my neck.

"I'm nothing like Penelope. I love you, Winston. That's why I married you. That's why I am your wife."

"No, you did this for Hope. For you it was always about

Hope. And now I have to figure out what to do about it." He scowled toward the river. "With Penelope, I just had to keep quiet and the situation disappeared. She was nobody."

He spoke to himself, as if I weren't there, as if his fingertips weren't testing the skin at my throat.

"Stanley probably suspected something, but he never asked any questions. He is too indebted to me to say anything. The old portraitist who had painted me when Penelope was . . . in London, he was so senile he thought she was my sister."

Even now, with his mind unraveling, he still refused to tell me that Penelope had once been in his portrait. Why was he so intent on keeping that secret, even now as he admitted everything else he had done to her?

The smile dropped from his face as he remembered me again.

"But it's different in your case, Iris. We were just married in a crowded church. I could never deny knowing you. I shall have to play the mourning husband."

His gaze toward the river suddenly terrified me more than his fingers on my throat. He was imagining it as a resting place for me. If I fell from the bridge into the Thames I would never be missed. Winston had said as much himself.

"Winston," I pleaded. "Look at me."

His eyes, still hazy, slid to mine.

"Don't do this," I begged. My breath plumed before me in the icy fog. "I love you. I always have, since you sat by me on the train and asked where I bought my hat. Do you remember how my father fell asleep in the seat behind us? How he snored so loudly we started to laugh?"

Winston's eyes sharpened a fraction at the memory.

"And then you left me with your umbrella and I couldn't wait for you to call on me again."

He sniffed. "The rain ruined my new suit but I was too happy to care."

"And I returned your umbrella to you when we took our first walk through the park. Do you remember that big oak we sat under? By the Serpentine?"

His eyes were clearing. My insides unwound a fraction, enough that I could force a smile.

"You're my husband, Winston. We love each other. We'll go to France and walk by the sea together every day. When we return, you'll win the commission and watch the Crystal Palace be built with your windows."

At the word *commission* his eyes faded. He stopped seeing me again. I had taken a wrong step.

"We'll watch it all together," I added feebly. "As husband and wife."

Winston shook his head, clearing his sympathies. "Penelope would have ruined me if I had let her. You're no different."

Yes, I am, I meant to say, but suddenly he took my neck in both his hands and began to squeeze. I swung at him, but he only tightened his grip in response.

"My time with Penelope taught me something." He bent toward me, the fog a velvet wall behind him. "When my companion has neither friends nor family, she disappears easily. A little stumble into the fireplace, a fall into the Thames . . . It will be weeks before anyone realizes you are gone." He squeezed harder still and the edges of the world blackened. When I tried to cry out, he lowered his mouth to my ear. "It's no use, Iris."

He was right. There was no one to hear me. The bridge was silent, as if all of London had dissolved into the fog.

"I'll tell everyone tomorrow you went to France without me. By then, you'll be at the bottom of the Thames."

My sight was going, my ears ringing, my thoughts swimming. Mama in her bed. Papa kissing her hair. Hope a baby in my arms.

Hope. I had to see her once more, to care for her until she could no longer be cared for. If Winston would deny me that, if he would rob me of my final moments with my sister, I would make sure it cost him dearly.

"Did your mother . . . " I gasped, my air nearly spent. "Did she tell you . . . where your father died?"

At the word *father* Winston's grip eased a fraction on my neck.

"She told me. This morning."

He swallowed, a swift pulse of his Adam's apple. His hold lessened enough for me to continue.

"He saw your portrait. With Penelope," I breathed. "*That* was what killed him. The sight of her. In your painting."

The color drained from Winston's face.

"He died of a broken heart. Disappointed in you."

Winston stared at me as if he had seen a ghost. He could spend a lifetime trying to make his deceased father proud, but he could never live with the knowledge that his father died of disappointment in him. The horror on his face confirmed it.

That was where Winston was the most vulnerable.

A faint shuffling sounded in the distance. It grew louder, until footsteps were pounding on the bridge behind us and a figure appeared in the fog beyond Winston.

Anna.

Winston released my neck as he turned to face her. In one swift movement I kneed him as hard as I could. Anna swung something shiny at him. It met his head with a heavy thud.

The blow knocked him backwards and his hands fumbled for the slick bridge wall. I shoved him with all my strength. He tumbled over the wall and disappeared with a single moan, sharp and swift before a pull of silence.

Anna clutched the fireplace shovel in her hand and I gasped for air. For a moment, we stared into the thick fog and waited.

When a splash finally sounded in the invisible Thames, it was so quiet that, unless listening for it, one would have missed it completely.

* * *

Local Glass Magnate Missing
London Times
23 December 1850

MR. WINSTON CARMICHAEL, proprietor of Carmichael Glass Company, went missing from his London mansion on the twenty-second of December, the day after his marriage to Miss Iris Sheffield.

Carmichael's mother contacted Scotland Yard the day after her son's wedding, after stopping by his home in Kennington to retrieve her cat. There she found a note in Mr. Carmichael's hand explaining that, instead of taking his new bride to France as originally intended, he had sent her ahead to visit her family while he stayed in London to settle some business matters. His mother waited for Mr. Carmichael, but he never returned.

An anonymous source and close acquaintance of the family claims that Mr. Carmichael had been under a great deal of stress as he attempted to secure the commission to provide windows for the Crystal Palace. It was publicly announced on the day Mr. Carmichael went missing that Chance Brothers and Company had earned the commission instead.

CHAPTER 57

*A*n open market filled the street below. I watched it from the kitchen window of our third-story flat. Vendors and shoppers squeezed into the narrow strip of road, bartering over wicker baskets, lavender sachets, and spoons made of olive wood.

Hope and I had joined them the past three Saturday mornings since my arrival in Nice. I insisted on buying her something at every visit. The first week, she had picked out a dishcloth tied in the shape of a doll. The second week, it was a bouquet of dried hydrangeas, which I later found on my pillow. Last week it had been an old copy of a French Bible for Papa.

Today, I only saw the market from the window.

Beyond the crowd below, and past the roofs with sunset tiles, swung the lazy arc of the Promenade des Anglais. It was early, but the path was already crowded with families like ours seeking the living waters.

Until Sunday, we had walked to the sea every day. Hope had filled a sack with the shiniest shells and smoothest rocks that the shore could offer. We picked the largest boulder on the beach and spread out a picnic of cheese and baguettes, dates and oranges. We watched the sea ripple silver before us, slippery as a fine piece of silk. I did my best to memorize the warmth of Hope's fingers against my palm and the sight of the wind whipping her hair across her cheek. All three of us breathed deeply of the sea air, breathed deeply of the quiet time spent together.

A small girl watched me from the market below, her neck craned at an angle only a child can manage. I imagined how my situation must look to her: the top floor of a boxy building, smeared with lemon stucco, studded with mint-green shutters. How cheery it all looked from the outside.

I looked down at the glass of water in my hand. There was no time for daydreaming. There was no time left for anything. I turned from the window and hurried down the hallway, past Papa sleeping in his bedroom. He had been up with Hope all night. He had insisted.

She was a small mound in her bed. I picked the bloody handkerchiefs from her bedside table and shoved them into my apron pocket. I sat beside her and took her hand. Her fingers were twiggy as birds' feet.

Her eyes were closed, pale lids mapped with tiny veins. Already I had grown used to her blanched face, her protruding cheekbones. Her hair, too weak to support curls, hung straight and thin.

We go to great lengths for those we love, Anna had told me. But my lengths had not been great enough.

I pulled gently on her bottom lip and parted her dry mouth. I lifted the glass to it, but the water dribbled from her lips and ran down her chin.

"Shall I lie by you?" I whispered, though I knew she would not answer. I rested my head next to her and put an arm gently across her stomach. Her breaths were impossibly slow. My arm rose a millimeter, then fell a millimeter. Rose, fell, almost imperceptibly. I closed my eyes and, for just a moment, gave myself permission to leave. I left the foreign town outside the window, my exhausted father in the next room, and the small broken body beside me. I left, and I took Hope with me.

We were outside, in the shadow of a white stone house. Its shutters were once navy blue, but the sun had bleached them to the shade of a clear summer sky.

Hope was staring at her little finger, mesmerized by the creature resting upon it: a tiger swallowtail butterfly, its black and yellow wings pulsing apart, then together. Apart. Together. She held her breath—intent on not scaring her newfound pet—until I feared she would faint.

A strange look passed over her face, the prelude to a sneeze. Her nostrils flared and her eyes squinted. I silently cursed the poor timing of the sound that was about to escape her. It was a tiny sneeze, as restrained as she could manage, but it was enough to scare off her small winged friend.

The butterfly jumped from her finger and began its ascent, zigzagging around Hope, unsure of its wings. Its path soon grew more purposeful, and it went up and up, growing smaller and smaller, until it was sweeping over the roof and Hope was racing around the house to catch the last glimpse of it. She chased the butterfly and I chased Hope, fearing her reaction when the butterfly disappeared completely.

At the front of the house, next to the azalea bush, Hope watched as the butterfly shrank from a dot in the sky to nothing. Hope's curls fell down her back as she craned her head upward as only a child can manage.

But when she turned back to me she was smiling.

And there on the bed of a small flat in Nice, as Hope grew very still, I thought of our view from the ground, how that butterfly seemed to shrink down to nothingness the higher it climbed. But the butterfly itself must have felt larger and freer with each upward sweep as it ascended the sky toward far better things.

I opened my eyes. The tears spilled off my chin and onto

Hope's limp hair. I placed a palm upon her sharp cheekbone. But when I closed my eyes again I could see Hope as she had been before: round-cheeked, curly-haired. She was walking hand in chubby hand with Mama through a garden, its blooms dense and fragrant, and as blue as the sky.

CHAPTER 58

*D*earest Iris,

I have received your letter and find that no words can express my sorrow at the news of Hope's passing. My deepest condolences are yours. Please extend my sympathies to your father. I wish I were near you to express them in person.

I hope you will not fault me for sharing this newspaper article with you, and that I did not say too much in it. Sometimes my words get away from me and I cannot help myself.

You said you shall never return to London, but if you change your mind please let me know. I would gladly make the trip to meet you. The Great Exhibition opens in May, and I shall think of you the entire time I am there.

My apologies for the brevity of this letter. A new friend has just arrived to call on me. I will tell you all about him in my next letter.

With love,
Margaret

* * *

Body of Glass Magnate Found
London Times
29 January 1851

THE REMAINS of Mr. Winston Carmichael appeared along the banks of the Thames yesterday morning. Mr. Carmichael disappeared a month ago, following his wedding to Iris Sheffield. It is assumed that he jumped from the Vauxhall Bridge upon learning his glass company, Carmichael Glass, had failed to secure the Crystal Palace commission.

Carmichael's widow is thought to be in France, and his mother—who has been ailing since his disappearance—refused to comment. A close family friend, who wishes to remain anonymous, reported that "the situation is heartbreaking, but not surprising. From the beginning, Mr. Carmichael's family worried that this would be his course of action if he did not obtain the Crystal Palace commission."

CHAPTER 59

$\mathcal{T}$he crocuses were in bloom by the time I dared to find his cottage.

It sat at the end of the Rue de Calais, where trees lined the street and wisteria clung to the trees. The windows were open, with cornflower shutters yawning wide and ivy bearding the brick exterior.

The yard grew wild with grape hyacinths and misplaced daffodils just beginning to open their yellow faces. Not until I reached the sun-bleached door did I notice a woman beneath one of the windows, tending a patch of dirt. A gardener. I watched her, debating if I should speak. Before I could decide, she looked up.

"Bonjour," she said. "*Comment puis-je vous aider?*"

"Hello. I mean, *bonjour.*"

"Oh, thank heavens." Her voice was high and American. She stood and wiped her hands on her cotton dress. "I know how to offer help in French but can't understand the response."

I pushed a stray curl beneath my bonnet. "I'm looking for Thomas James. Someone at the café told me he lives here."

"He does. I'll be happy to fetch him for you. What's your name?"

"Iris Sheffield."

"Pleased to make your acquaintance, Miss Sheffield. I am Caroline James."

My tongue went sour. Caroline James. In only four months since seeing him.

I had not come expecting anything from him, and I had no right to be disappointed. I was only here to pay him the thanks I owed. But when I realized this was James's wife, tending to a piece of earth outside their Barbizon home, I wished to dig a hole in the ground myself, one large enough to crawl into.

"The pleasure is mine, Mrs. James," I lied.

She laughed, an easy, rolling sound. "*Miss* Caroline James. Thomas James is my brother. I'm planting his garden. He won't stop painting long enough to do it himself. James, you have a caller!" she shouted toward the open window. She picked her way out of the garden. "It was a pleasure to meet you, Miss Sheffield. Knock on the door if you need to. My brother gets lost in his work and blocks out the world."

I watched her walk away, waiting for the pit in my stomach to loosen, but it didn't. I approached the door, then stood motionless before it.

I had wanted to write a letter instead. I had tried several times, but it seemed so inadequate for what James had done for me.

When he did not come to the door, my insides knotted tighter. I knocked three times, short and loud raps. I heard a shuffling inside, a bit of mumbling, and then the door swung open and I found myself face to face with James.

A pencil was tucked behind his left ear. He wore a light-blue smock, its sleeves rolled up to his forearms. His presence sucked the breath from me. So often I had wondered where he was, what he was doing, and now he stood before me, so near that I could reach out my hand and touch the streak of white paint on his brow.

He stared blankly at me. If he was surprised by my presence he did not show it. His face revealed nothing.

"Hello, James."

"Miss Sheffield." My stomach fluttered at the sound of my name on his lips until he corrected himself. "Mrs. Carmichael, rather."

"I am sorry to bother you, but I hoped to speak with you."

He stared at me silently. I thought he might refuse me, but then he pulled the door open and gestured me inside. I glanced behind me, aware I should not enter the house with him alone. But no one was around to witness our indiscretion, and I had not waited this long, come this far, to let my manners get in the way.

It was a one-room home, smelling of earth and cedar under a strong current of oil. A porcelain sink and wood-burning stove stood in one corner. A worn table and two mismatched stools occupied the wall beside the front door. Along the remaining walls leaned finished paintings waiting to be framed. Easels were scattered around the room, holding canvases in various stages of completion: gleaners, stonecutters, peasant hands kneading dough.

James pulled a stool from the table and motioned for me to sit. As I sank into it he took the other stool for himself.

"You've gotten your wish, I see." I studied the painting nearest me: a young girl bent over a bush of lavender, her back a graceful arc. "They are beautiful."

"Yes, well, it's definitely not London," he said from his side of the scarred table.

"No. It's not." I tried to smile, but James's face held no trace of friendliness. "Your sister seems lovely. I did not know you were in touch with her."

"Yes, well." James rubbed his nose, a quick, rough motion. "I wrote her after I arrived in France. It turned out she was tired of Brighton so she moved to Fontainebleau. She lives with a family there, teaching their children English. She visits Barbizon a few times a month." He paused. "I did not realize how much I had missed her."

My gaze dropped to my lap.

"Are you in mourning?" He gestured at my black dress.

"My sister, Hope. She passed away two and a half months ago."

His face softened. He reached over and put his hand on mine.

"I am deeply sorry."

I clenched my jaw, silent until I could get through the sob within me. The sob never left, it only varied in how deep it stayed inside me, whether it decided to surface. In this moment, I was able to push it down.

"Were you able to be with her before . . . ?"

I nodded. The sympathy in his eyes threatened to push tears into mine.

"Yes. For a month, fortunately. Due to your generosity."

James frowned. "How so?"

"The voucher and francs you gave me—for the trains, and to cross the channel. They brought me to Hope. I came here to thank you for them."

His brows lowered in confusion. "You used the envelope to come to France?"

I looked at my gloved hands and nodded. "You brought me to my sister before she died. I had to thank you for that in person. I also came to thank you for your portrait of Penelope." A combination of grief and gratitude tugged at me whenever I thought of Penelope. "When you painted her portrait and left it for Winston to see, you saved my life."

"What do you mean?"

I took a breath. I had rehearsed this conversation so many

times, but with James across the table from me I forgot all I had planned.

"When Winston saw the portrait," I said carefully, "he pretended he did not know who the sitter was, for he did not know I would recognize Penelope. When he had the chance to be alone with the painting, he destroyed it. That was when I realized you were right, and I could not trust him. I fled that night. Thanks to your gift I was able to come to France, but I came alone."

James held very still. "Is Winston still in London?"

"Winston is dead." I said it with no emotion. Any grief I once had for the man I thought Winston to be had passed. I felt nothing for him now.

James stood and busied himself gathering jars of murky water, as if he were done with our conversation. He carried them to the sink and drained their contents.

"I owe you my life, James," I continued, intent on expressing my gratitude. "And the remainder of my sister's life that I spent with her. I don't know how to thank you."

"There is no need to thank me," he said, his back to me. "You did not need to come here."

"I feel that I owe you . . . *something*." He was done speaking to me, but I had to thank him properly before I left. "I could never repay you for what you have done for me, but I found someone who wants to buy *La Donna*. Do you remember my friend Margaret Darby? Her father collects art for his home. It is a private collection. No one would ever see it, so Isabella could never fault you."

"It is a thoughtful gesture," James said as he reached for more jars. His long fingers dipped into their mouths and pushed them together until he held four at a time in each hand. "But I am not interested in selling *La Donna*. If you came here set on me doing so, I am afraid you have wasted your time."

"Wouldn't you—" My bonnet ribbon tugged at my chin.

"Wouldn't you like to be rid of it, though? You said you never knew what to do with it."

"You needn't concern yourself with *La Donna*. I'm afraid I must return to my work now."

He placed the jars in the sink. Then he collected his brushes, keeping his back to me.

I studied the span of his shoulders, the sweep of his hair against his collar. I would never be this close to him again. I would walk through the door and then he would be nothing more than a memory for the rest of my life. I squeezed my eyes closed and took a breath, reaching deep inside myself before I spoke.

"I hate Isabella's portrait. I rarely hate anything, James, but from the moment you showed it to me, I absolutely despised it."

He turned to me, face twisted in irritation.

"Are you an art critic now, Miss Sheffield?"

"It's a beautiful painting, and it's awful that Isabella won't allow you to display it. But I can't stand the sight of it, because from the moment I saw it . . . "

My stomach rose to my heart.

"From the moment I even heard of it, I was jealous of her."

The irritation disappeared from James's face. He looked past me to the window, toward the Rue de Calais, not meeting my gaze.

"I was jealous when you said her portrait was your favorite of all your paintings, and when you told me you fell for her quickly and completely. I envy the time the two of you spent together while painting it, but mostly the time you spent together when you weren't painting it."

He would not look at me, but I pressed ahead.

"I hate that when you took me to your studio, it was to show me *her*, and that you have kept her portrait for the past decade hidden in your studio like a secret. I wanted you to sell it, because I could not stand the thought of Isabella's portrait being with you when I couldn't."

This was where I was the most vulnerable. I laid my soul as an offering before James. In return, he fixed his gaze on the window behind me. He would not even condescend to look at me. His indifference was my answer.

The air in the room was stifling, the quiet like cotton in my ears, and my head began to spin. I tugged at the ribbon of my bonnet, loosening its grip on my chin, and turned toward the door. I placed my hand on the knob, but as I turned it, James took hold of my other hand.

"Come here, Iris. I want to show you something."

He led me to an easel and pulled a stool in front of it, then gestured for me to sit.

I found myself facing a landscape of a wheat field. A boy napped in the foreground of the painting.

"Allow me to show you my new favorite painting."

He lifted the landscape to reveal another canvas behind it. A portrait.

My portrait.

There I sat in Winston's bergère, the white dress I had worn to the ball as soft as a cloud around me. My mother's ruby necklace hung around my neck, and a curtain of jade silk hung behind me. The canvas was smaller than I had remembered. The painted version of myself stared back at me with quiet yet sure eyes.

I swallowed, struggling to find my voice.

"I would not have expected you to bring this to France."

"The original is still in London. It is about to be exhibited with the Royal Academy."

"Mrs. Carmichael allowed that?"

"I never asked her permission. I borrowed money to reimburse Winston and wrote to him that I could not sell the portrait. I suppose Mrs. Carmichael received it on his behalf considering Winston's misfortunes, but she never responded to me."

Of course. Mrs. Carmichael would have no use for a portrait of me.

I gestured toward the painting. "This is not the original?"

"It is a copy. I painted it here."

I said nothing, not trusting the hope rising inside me.

"I've worked on it every day since I arrived in France. I only finished it last week."

The blank look in his eyes was gone and his stone expression had cracked. Breaking through was an intense stare, a determination. He took my hands and pulled me to my feet until my nose grazed his collar.

"I thought I would be through with you once it was finished. It was to be my farewell to you, Iris. And now you appear on my doorstep, ruining my plans."

I studied his stubbled jawline, his scarred lip, the tiny pinpoints of paint like stars across his cheek.

"I did not need the original when I painted this copy, Iris. Do you know how unheard of that is for me? But I have memorized you."

His fingertips brushed the hair across my forehead.

"You and your wild Botticelli hair," he murmured. His palm, warm and rough, slid onto my cheek.

"I'm surprised you thought the portrait worth replicating, what with the trouble I gave you." His thumb grazed my bottom lip and I struggled to form words. "Looking at you like a pigeon and all that."

"You never gave me any trouble."

"But you said the way I looked at you—"

"Your look unnerved me every day I painted you. It was like you were looking straight through me."

"Then why the lecture about how I wasn't giving you

anything to work with? When you took me to your studio to show me Isabella's expression?"

"I didn't take you there to show you Isabella's expression."

"Then why?"

James pressed his lips together. "For a moment, I did not want to be the artist painting you in your fiancé's house. But then I took you to my studio and you scared me, just as you are scaring me now. If I were smarter, I would have meant it when I told you goodbye."

With his free hand, he tugged gently on the black ribbon under my chin, slipping the bow undone.

"You broke my heart with your stubbornness, Iris. If I could, I would have broken your heart in return. I'm too much of a gentleman, I suppose. Which will prove terrible for my work. I've been distracted merely by your portrait. With you in here all the time? I'm never going to get anything done."

"Stop teasing, James," I said softly. "You're ruining it."

"What am I ruining?"

My cheeks burned. I did not dare say what I hoped was about to happen between us, that we would relive our moment in the studio, in the churchyard.

"Ah, I see." A smile played upon his lips. "Aren't you Miss Confidence. You think I'm about to kiss you."

He was so close, his mouth so near, I could hardly breathe.

He leaned his face half an inch closer. Just shy of my mouth, his lips parted into a grin, a satisfying combination of dimples and teeth.

"Do you think it's going to be good, Iris?"

I smiled. But before I could answer, his lips were on mine and his fingers were in my hair and my bonnet was on the floor. All before I could say yes. Yes, I knew it would be good. It would all be good. Sometimes, one simply knows.

EPILOGUE

*D*ear Miss Anna Bromley,

  I trust this parcel will find its way to you, and that you will then find someone to read this letter for you, as you always manage.

  The last time I saw you, you watched me imitate Winston's writing perfectly to compose an important letter to his mother. I wish to thank you for suggesting I write that letter. It allowed me start a new life, free from the shadows of my past. For this, and many other reasons, I am forever indebted to you.

  I once found a daguerreotype that was rightfully yours. Unfortunately, someone crumpled the image before realizing how precious it was, and how much its preservation would mean to the sitter's family.

  To apologize for his thoughtlessness, he has included the crumpled daguerreotype and an oil painting of the sitter as his gift to you. He and I both hope the painting will ensure that the sitter's beauty always remains vivid in your memory, as it will in ours, for a similar portrait once changed the outcome of his life and mine.

  Sincerely,

  Mrs. Iris James

* * *

Royal Academy of Art Exhibition Review
Thomas James
Woman with a Lavender Sash
1851, oil on canvas

THOMAS JAMES'S most esteemed high-society portrait is also, he alleges, his last. The sitter—Miss Iris Sheffield—lounges in an upholstered bergère with a reserved yet knowing look. The painting is rich with details typical of Mr. James's work: the drape of silk in the background; the sparkling ruby around the sitter's neck; the splash of lavender fabric at her waist.

At the time of the painting the sitter was engaged to Mr. Winston Carmichael of Carmichael Glass. Immediately following the portrait's completion and the couple's marriage, Mr. Carmichael jumped from the Vauxhall Bridge, presumably distraught by business matters. The sitter is no longer in contact with her late husband's family and is thought to be living abroad.

Mr. James originally painted the portrait as a commission but later purchased the work back from the Carmichael estate. He currently lives in France, where he is a member of the Barbizon School and is receiving praise for his genre paintings, particularly of gleaners.

Having submitted entries to the Academy for years, Mr. James sends his apologies for missing the exhibition. "If I could bring myself to leave France for any reason," he writes, "it would be for this exhibition. Participation in it was once my greatest ambition. But I now find myself unable to leave my new home, even for the shortest amount of time, for here I have found the most compelling happiness beyond my greatest expectations."

THE END.

AUTHOR'S NOTE

Though *The Portrait* is a work of fiction, I drew from my favorite art and architecture to help me form the characters and plot.

For Iris's portrait, I had in mind *Lady Agnew of Locknaw*, painted by John Singer Sargent and hanging in the Scottish National Gallery in Edinburgh. I have only viewed this portrait in person once, but when I did its beauty stopped me immediately.

Inspiration for *La Donna* came from *Portrait of Madame X*, also by Sargent. The painting was originally received with a great deal of criticism and viewed as scandalous, thus devastating its female subject. It now hangs in the Metropolitan Museum of Art in New York City.

A Maid Asleep by Johannes Vermeer also hangs in the Metropolitan. It is, as James described, a painting of a woman sleeping at a table with a door partially opened behind her. X-rays have revealed that a man originally stood in the doorway, but Vermeer ultimately painted him out of the scene. This history always intrigued me, and led me to write about a subject's mysterious removal from a painting.

Joseph Paxton designed the Crystal Palace for London's Great Exhibition of 1851. Chance Brothers and Company provided its glass. A fire destroyed the palace in 1936.

For further reading on Victorian London:

Flanders, Judith. *Inside the Victorian Home: A Portrait of Domestic Life in Victorian England* (London: W.W. Norton, 2003).

Flanders, Judith. *The Victorian City: Everyday Life in Dickens' London* (New York: Thomas Dunne Books, 2012).

Picard, Liza. *Victorian London: The Life of a City, 1840-1870* (New York: St. Martin's Press, 2006).

ACKNOWLEDGMENTS

Writing this novel has been a marathon, and I am grateful to the many people who helped me cross the finish line. Thanks to my agent, Kimberly Whalen, whose enthusiasm for this story gave me much-needed courage. To my editor, Laurie Chittenden, who magically knew all the right questions to ask and which threads to pull. To Cathy Carmode Lim, for her impeccable attention to detail. And to Sarah Whittaker, for a cover so beautiful I hope the inside does it justice.

To the writers who have shared their knowledge, experience, and love of story with me throughout the years, including Emily Inouye Huey, Katy Glemser, and Kim Harris Thacker.

To my willing and wise readers, who soldiered through numerous drafts, many of which were terrible. Kate, Tom, Kathy, Camile, Jill, Rachel, Ryan, Paige, Matt, Jessica, Paul, Dave, Kiersten, Madalyn, Kimberly, Alexandra, Emily I., Carli, Katy, Eileen, Kim, Brittany, Hilary, Kristi, Michelle, Jennie, Lindsy, Sarah, Stacy, Emily L., Sara, and Melissa: thank you for the thoughtful feedback and encouragement. This book is better because of it.

To my art history professors, particularly the Marks, Marian, Martha, and Heather, who introduced me to much of the art and architecture that inspired my plot. And to Lee, curator and mentor extraordinaire, who helped me keep in touch with the world of art history during a hectic time in my life.

I am grateful to my children, who enhance all my artistic

pursuits. And to my husband, who always supports me in everything important to me.

Thanks to my mother, who taught me to love books long before the other Kathleen Kelly came along. And to my dad, who told me I should try writing a novel. Thank you for giving me the permission I needed. I only wish I had finished it sooner.

ABOUT THE AUTHOR

Emilia Kelly holds an MA in Art History from Brigham Young University. She loves reading with her children, taking walks with her husband, and visiting small towns in New England. *The Portrait* is her first novel.

emiliakelly.com
Facebook.com/emiliakellyauthor
Instagram: @emiliakellyauthor

Printed in Great Britain
by Amazon

36738101R00173